MATTERS OF THE

The Hart Series

book three

M.E. CARTER

MATTERS OF THE
Hart

The Hart Series
book three

#metoo

ONE

Jaxon

"**B**lue 52! Blue 52!" the QB shouts.

My ears perk up. That's me. The play has changed. I move my foot slightly to the left, shifting my weight, knowing I have to run wide this time. That's not what we set up for, but apparently the defense has figured out our play.

"Hut, hut, hut, HUT!"

I push off from the line, trucking it down the field as fast as my legs will carry me. Making a wide turn to the left, I'm barely out of the reach of their defender, who grasps at a piece of my jersey but not enough to take me down. Just as I cross the forty-yard line, I look over my shoulder and see the ball flying through the air, arching toward me. I reach out my arms, and it lands in my finger-tips, then I secure it up against my chest, cradling it like a baby, and keep running.

"Oof!"

I don't get far before my ass is knocked to the ground.

That's going to hurt like a bitch.

When we finally come to a stop, Heath Germaine—my teammate, roommate, and best friend—pops up off me, reaching his hand down to help hoist me off the grass.

"Nice play, Hart," he says as he smacks the top of my helmet, his mouthguard dangling down by his chin. "Too bad you're not as quick as me. You were *this close* to making it into the end zone," he jabs, holding his forefinger and thumb centimeters apart.

"That's only because I'm tired from the extra workout I got with your mom last night," I shoot back. He pushes me while calling me a highly inappropriate name, which makes me laugh. Getting back to business, I grab him by the facemask and pull him toward me. "You may be faster than me, but you've got bigger problems than Troy Hunter gunning for you. Don't get cocky."

He scoffs. "Hunter is a fucking puss. He may think he's faster, but he hasn't gone up against me yet this season. I'm not worried."

The rivalry between those two runs long and deep. For three years, they've chased each other down on the field, while chasing either other's stats on the leader board. Why they hate each other is still a mystery to me, but I know how bad Germaine wants to one-up him. What he doesn't understand is he's got bigger problems this year.

"You misunderstand me, my man. They have a new cornerback. Abel Anders. Just transferred in from some small school in Minnesota and is running circles around Hunter."

His grin immediately falls. "Shit. How'd I miss that?"

"Transfer just happened last week. He isn't just gunning for Top Ten Cornerbacks this year. From what I hear, he's got a shot at being number one."

Germaine goes straight into work mode as he realizes

the seriousness of the situation. He has to decide if he's doing the draft this year or next, which is already a huge amount of pressure. But if he gets knocked out of the Top Ten, there won't even be a decision to make. In his mind, that's not an option.

"Get back on the line and let's go again," he finally says. I nod and head across the field to get ready for another play.

For most people, being on the practice team of Southwest San Antonio University's football team would bother them, but not me. I kind of like it. I get all the fun of playing the game I love, but I don't have the pressure of having to be the best. Yes, my dad is the great Jason Hart. Yes, he will probably be inducted into the Football Hall of Fame as the best defensive lineman in the history of the game. But I haven't had that dream since I was nine years old, so it's not a disappointment to me that college will be the end of my football career.

That, and without having all the travel, I have time to focus on my other loves—math and science. I love all that shit. Math is like doing puzzles. The rules never change, there is only one right answer. Science, on the other hand, changes all the time and the puzzles are never ending. Add on my weird ability to remember all kinds of statistical data, and it makes me really valuable to the team. I can make predictions most people don't see coming, which comes in handy for people like Germaine.

Plus, I always win a shit ton of money in fantasy football.

As Germaine and I jog back into our respective positions on the line, ready to go over the play again, I shake my hands out and put my toe on the white paint. Crouching down, ensuring I'll shoot off the line quickly, I listen for my cues.

"Blue 71," the QB yells and my mind zones out. It's the same play as before, only this time, someone else has to adjust at the last second. My only goal is to do it better.

"Blue 71," he yells again. "Hut, hut, HUT!"

Using my full power, I explode off the line, this time running straight through the pack of bodies that are too busy trying to sack the quarterback than to notice me. It works, but just for a split second. As soon as I twist to see the ball coming my direction, something catches my peripheral vision. I'm only going to have enough time to snag it out of the air and haul it in before I'm mowed over again.

"Ooof!"

As we slide across the turf and come to a stop, all I can say is "Now that's what I mean by some speed!"

Germaine laughs as he pulls me to my feet. "Hell yeah. No way I'm letting that new kid catch me this year. He's probably a dick."

I smack him on the ass in support, and we jog back to get into position again.

This is what we do for the next hour…run play after play after play. Perfecting our techniques, our speed, and our moves. I probably won't ever get a chance to use these skills on the field during an actual game, but I don't care. I'm here for the exercise, the comradery, and the fun. Besides, I was bumped up to third string this year. That means I have an actual shot of suiting up during a game. If Rudy could bring a crowd to its feet in just one game, who's to say I can't either? And if not, I still get to see the game from the best seats in the house.

Finally, after dozens of hits and even more yards, practice ends and we're headed back into the locker rooms. By the time I make it back and strip off my sweaty pads, half my teammates are already talking about the plans for a night out.

Grabbing my phone, I check to see if my boss has texted with any changes to tonight's schedule. Nothing from him, but there is a text from my dad.

Dinner at 7 at DeLuca's. You in?

With a groan, I toss my phone back in my locker and rub my hand down my face.

"What's up, Hart?" Germaine saunters over with a towel wrapped around his waist. I swear he showers faster than anyone I've ever met in my life. "You coming out with us tonight or is your baby ass gonna go have a happy nappy?"

My teammates used to invite me to go out with them all the time. But, after blowing them off time and time again, they finally accepted it wasn't going to happen. It's not that I don't want the bonding time or whatever. I just physically can't. One of the long-term side effects of chemo as a kid is I tire a lot easier than other people. It doesn't keep me from functioning through everyday life, but football practices aren't normal exertion levels. They're extreme, so I always have to rest afterward, before I can do anything else.

I peel off my socks and throw them at him, making him squeal like a little bitch. "Neither. I gotta go to dinner with my old man."

He lets out a hearty laugh before grabbing me by the arms. "Here, I'll give you a warm-up on the inquisition." Looking me over, he says, "You're getting too skinny. Are you eating enough? Your skin tone is looking a bit pale. Let me see your pupils. Are they dilated?"

"Get the fuck away from me." I bat his hand away when he tries to peel open my eyelid. "That's fucking annoying."

Germaine is still chuckling as he swipes on some deodorant. "Don't get me wrong, your dad is a cool guy, but he is so far up your ass, it's a wonder he doesn't smell like shit."

"Tell me about it," I say with a shake of my head. "There's a reason I went to school six hours away from home."

My parents really are awesome, but Germaine isn't wrong when he says my dad is too overprotective. Especially when it comes to my health. I never noticed it when I lived at home, I guess because he saw me every day. But now that I only see them every few months, he's much more intrusive.

I get it. He was in that hospital room when I almost died all those years ago. I'm sure he still has some weird form of PTSD. But for the love of all that is holy, if he doesn't get his shit together, I may have to move to Europe.

"What brings the senior Hart into town today anyway? Any special reason or just to get all up in your business?" he jokes.

I shrug and run my fingers through my sweaty hair, moving it out of my face. "I think he had some meeting for the foundation or maybe a speaking engagement at a corporation. He's hard to keep up with. I was really hoping he'd be too busy to meet up. I'm running out of undergrad classes to talk about."

He raises his eyebrows. "Wait. You haven't told him you changed your major yet?"

I avoid making eye contact, which confirms my guilt.

Germaine lets out another hearty laugh. I shoot him a glare, not thrilled that my family life is entertaining to him. "You are in so much troubllllllllllllllle," he singsongs.

He's not wrong. "At least I'll get something better than cafeteria food out of it," I grumble.

Germaine chuckles. "You better bring me a doggie bag. I know you only eat the best when you're with him."

"And let you have the benefit of a good meal without having to suffer through wearing a tie at some hoity-toity restaurant? Fuck you. No way."

"Your dad and those fancy meals." He shakes his head in amusement, knowing it's the same thing every time Dad's in town. The once-over. A suit and tie. Questions about my grades. I'm already exhausted just thinking about it.

"Wanna go out with us after you're done? Some beer and pussy will do you some good."

I chuckle at his cure-all to anything that ails you.

Feeling stressed? Get some beer and pussy.

Parents making you crazy? Gets some beer and pussy.

Got the flu? Beer and pussy.

"Maybe next time," I say, even though we both know it's not going to happen. "I have to work tonight anyway."

He puts his fist to his lips. "A double whammy night! Daddy Dearest and work until all hours. You're going to be fucking useless tomorrow in practice."

I wish I could say he was wrong. Unfortunately, the statistics are on his side this time.

TWO

Annika

"When are you coming home for the weekend? Haven't you run out of clean clothes yet?"

I laugh lightly into the phone. "It's the weirdest thing, Dad. There are these things called washing machines in the basement of my building, and they washed all my clothes for me last week."

He sighs heavily, ignoring my sarcasm. "I know. It just gets lonely without you guys here."

My poor dad. Ever since my brother and I went off to college, he's an empty nester with too much time on his hands. Never mind how much he used to bitch about the cost of feeding two teenagers when we were in high school. As soon as we were gone, his tune changed.

I'm a sophomore at Southwest San Antonio University. It's only a couple of hours away from home, but it has everything I need: a great football team, a pre-physical therapy program, and a training course where I can actually get on the field and hone my skills with the players.

It also has my best friend, Lauren, who is pretty much the exact opposite of me, but is also the best roommate I could ask for. I lucked out when I got her in the roommate lottery.

"Well maybe you should put yourself out there a little more." I'm picking the last of the pink nail polish off my fingernails. I hate it when there's color on my nails. I should have known better than to let Lauren talk me into that manicure last week. What a waste of money. "Maybe you'll finally meet a lucky lady."

He scoffs. "You know there will never be another lady as lucky as your mother."

I laugh again, louder this time. "You're right, Dad. You're such a catch, I don't think any woman could handle you."

He's been alone since my mother died when I was a baby. Not that he's worried about dating, per se. I'm sure he's been out a few times over the years, but more out of boredom than anything else. He always said he found love as a young man, and he has memories of the best years of his life to tide him over.

Personally, I think he's more afraid of pissing off me or my brother, Damien, than anything. But after nineteen years, you'd think he'd finally realize we'll get over it.

"I'll be coming back for Thanksgiving, Dad. You can wait a couple more months to see me. It'll give you some time to really home in on your fantasy football skills."

He grumbles. "I'm going to beat you this year."

I just laugh. "Dad, I don't think you could beat me any year at fantasy football. You'd have to get used to that fancy computer thingy."

"Har. Har," he deadpans. "What are you up to tonight? Getting that laundry done?"

"Kiersten's visiting, and Lauren wants to go out. I'm

sitting on my bed right now, waiting for Lauren to come badger me about getting into whatever trouble they're working on."

I can practically hear my dad go on alert. "You be careful when you go out."

"Yes, Dad." It's the same song and dance I've heard for years. As his only daughter, he is a bit hypervigilant about my safety. He used to make me practice "being attacked" by Damien. I have no idea if I can replicate the moves in the real world, but it was fun learning how to kick my brother's ass.

"What do you do if a guy gets handsy?"

"Lean in, knee to the groin," I respond absentmindedly, flicking away the final bit of polish.

"Good girl. What if he grabs you from behind and puts you in a choke hold?"

"Step to the side, fist to the groin, elbow to the face."

"Excellent," he praises. "What about if he grabs your neck from the front?"

"Tuck my chin, grab his elbows, pull him to me, knee to the face."

"Good. I think you're protected."

I chuckle and flop back on my bed. "We've only been going over this since I was like twelve. I think I'll be okay."

"You were then. And I know you will," he says gently. "I just worry about you."

"I know you do, Dad. I promise I'll be okay. Anyway, how is Damien doing? Finally getting some direction?"

My dad starts chattering about my older brother's new girlfriend and how he still hasn't declared a major even though he's a year ahead of me. The door to my room opens and Lauren walks in, tossing her backpack on her bed.

Hands on her hips, I know what's coming, but before

she can lay into me I point to my phone and mouth "my dad."

Her eyes light up, and she yells, "Hi Mr. Leander!"

Lauren and my Dad have only met a handful of times during parent weekends and moving days. But they click. Like *really* click. He thinks of her almost like a second daughter, and just hearing her voice makes him stop his babbling and say, "Is that Lauren in the background? You give her a big hug for me. And teach her how to get out of a choke hold!"

A laugh bursts out of me. "I will. I wouldn't want anything to happen to her. I know she's your favorite."

"No, honey, you're always my favorite."

I can't help but feel warm by his words. My dad is the best, and I really miss him sometimes. "I know. Hey listen, since Lauren just got in, I'm going to talk to her for a while."

"Okay, baby. Love you."

"Love you too, Dad." We hang up, and I toss my phone on the bed next to me. Lauren glares at me now that she finally has my attention.

I pretend I have no idea what she's up to, even though it's basically the same song and dance every weekend. "What?" I finally ask.

She throws her arms up in exasperation. "Come on, Annika! You can't just sit there all night long!"

My petite, blond, gymnast of a roommate scowls at me. How she has this much energy, I'll never understand. I'm always exhausted after a full day of class. She has school and at least a couple hours of practice, but she's still raring to go. And she wants to dance.

"It'll be good for you to get off your butt and shake it around for a little bit."

I roll my eyes and lean back onto the headboard of my

bed. "I don't shake my butt," I retort with a smirk. "That's your thing Lauren, not mine."

"Yeah, but you can't miss out with Kiersten being here." She plumps out her bottom lip and bats her thick eyelashes at me. It's a guilt tactic, but it always works.

Actually, it's not the guilt tactic that works. It's that she's going to hound me until I finally cave; really, there's no point in fighting anyway. I could be stronger, I suppose. But I usually end up having fun when Lauren drags me out, and we both know it.

Usually.

Plus, I really do like Kiersten. The first time Lauren's high school best friend came to visit, I assumed she'd be as crazy and bubbly as my roommate, but Kiersten surprised me. Yes, she's a social butterfly, but on a much smaller scale. Plus, she's really sweet and always has a kind word for everyone. At first glance, they seem like an unlikely pair.

Lauren is a tiny bundle of energy, who trains in the gym for up to six hours a day. Kiersten, on the other hand, is tall and willowy and has maintained her high school dance figure even through those dreaded Freshman Fifteen months. From what they tell me, it was strictly chance that led to their friendship. Being that Kiersten was in the studio as much as Lauren was in the gym, their paths should have never crossed. But randomly, they ended up sitting next to each other at a high school football game one night, and they've been besties ever since. Probably after bonding over their love of hard work and clubbing. Now when Kiersten visits, I'm always guilted into going with them, rounding out the threesome as the awkward, lanky girl with no coordination.

Come to think of it, I hope I'm not getting a pity invite. I'm sure being right next to me while we all dance makes them look good. Shrugging to myself, I push those thoughts aside. Lauren and I have fun all the time, whether we're going out or staying in.

Huffing, Lauren continues to glare at me, waiting for me to finally give in. She knows clubbing isn't my thing. My thing is tailgating, football games, and beer—not at all your typical college girl. I'd rather be sitting in a parking lot at ten o'clock in the morning waiting for kick off, than rolling out of bed at that time because I was getting my groove on the night before.

I finally breathe out a deep resolved sigh, and Lauren's face immediately changes. She knows she's won.

"Fiiiiiiine," I say, dragging the word out as long as possible. "I'll go."

She immediately begins bouncing up and down, clapping her hands together with a big smile on her face. I narrow my eyes at the fact that coercion makes her happy.

"But you have to do my hair and makeup," I add, sitting straight up. "And you're not allowed to make me look like a slut like last time!"

She scoffs. "You did not look like a slut last time. You were totally glam."

I quirk an eyebrow at her lie. She rolls her eyes in response.

"Someday, I'll teach you how to have a sense of style. Tonight, you'll just have to trust me to make you totally hot." I throw myself on the bed and slap a pillow over my face, trying unsuccessfully to hide from the myriad of brushes and glosses and glittery shit that she's going to use on me. "But first, let me go take a shower, because you know it's going to take me way longer to get ready than you anyway."

Removing the pillow so I can breathe, I watch her walk away. She's right. She goes all out when she gets dressed up.

Me, I could just do some mascara and lip gloss and be done with the whole thing. I was raised by my dad and older brother when my mom died while giving birth to me, so I was never taught anything about makeup and hair. I learned different things, like how to shoot a gun, how to make brisket in the back of a truck, and how to break a man's thumb if he gets too handsy– real-life skills.

But tonight, I will allow Lauren to use me as her personal styling doll in hopes it keeps her off my back for at least another couple weeks. My best friend is, by far, the most tenacious person I know. I love her for it, even when it annoys me.

As she grabs her shower supplies and trots down the hall to the communal bathroom, I stand inside our closet, staring at the clothes. We made a small portion of our room a giant walk-in closet when our third roommate ditched at the last minute for lack of funds after a public intoxication arrest or something. I never got the real story. All I know is it was too late for the housing office to assign another person to our room. Now our giant make-shift closet is the envy of every girl on this floor.

I don't appreciate fashion and even I can understand how cool it is.

Rifling through all my clothes, I long to put on some jeans and a nice top, but there is only one outfit I own that Lauren will deem "club worthy." A short black dress. It hits several inches above my knee but has a bit of flare to the skirt. It hugs me just enough that I don't need to worry if a gust of wind will catch it and flash everyone around me, but is loose enough that it has a pocket for phone and credit card so I don't have to keep track of a purse in the club. The plunging rounded neckline keeps me constantly checking to make sure it hasn't dropped too low, exposing the girls. The back is scooped low, too, making it impossible to wear a bra. Fortunately, the long sleeves help me not feel as exposed, and the large cut outs down the tops of the arms give it a little more sex appeal than your ordinary little black dress.

Lauren loves this outfit. I personally think it teeters the edge of being a little too slutty, but since she convinced me to drop a pretty-penny on it in a weak moment, I may as well use it. Besides, I'm not going out tonight to impress anyone. I'm just going to be with my friends. And with as much makeup and hair spray as I'm about to have on me, it's not like I'll be recognizable to anyone I care about.

And because, I suppose, at nineteen years old, I should be enjoying the "college experience," as Lauren calls it. According to her, going to college football games doesn't count if that's the only experience you have.

"Ugh!" I finally say, giving up and yanking the offending dress off the hanger and over my head, staring at myself in the mirror.

I guess it could be worse. I have the body for it, even if I don't put any effort into my physique. And it's not really as low cut as I think it is. I should probably make a habit of looking in the mirror instead of looking down to see if I'm flashing anyone. The angles are totally different.

Kiersten comes walking in the room, a towel wrapped around her head and a pink bathrobe wrapped around her body.

"Ooh! I like that outfit on you," she says, turning me this way and that, getting the full effect. "It really makes your cleavage look nice."

Oh good. That's what I was hoping. For my boobs to stick out tonight.

Sensing my apprehension, she changes her phrasing. "No, not in a gratuitous, 'Look here are the girls' kind of way. In a 'You know there's got to be a killer rack under there, but she's too classy to flash it' kind of way."

"Oh, well that makes me feel better," I deadpan.

She laughs, knowing it didn't and bends over to rub her hair with the towel, beginning the tedious process of getting ready for the night.

I'm still not thrilled about the prospect of clubbing, but I know I'll end up having fun with these two, no matter what. And by the time Lauren gets me all gussied up, I won't recognize myself anyway.

Maybe I should use a fake name for the night.

No. I'll just go with Annika. No one ever believes it's my real name. I've heard more times than I can count about how it's such an exotic name for such a bland girl. Okay, no one ever calls me bland, but what else would the opposite of exotic be?

That's okay. I don't mind not being the flashy one. That's what Lauren is here for. She can have the spotlight all she wants. I'll just cheer her on from the sidelines.

THREE
Jaxon

I tug on my tie as I wait for my dad at the restaurant. It's really constricting; I feel like it's strangling me, which is an interesting metaphor considering how constricting my life has been the last few years, but I try not to focus on that. I try to concentrate on the fact that my dad insists on having a fancy dinner with me whenever he's in town, which is the reason why I haven't completely given up on our relationship yet. Besides, who am I to argue when there is free food involved? So, I suffer through and wear the damn tie.

I don't know when our relationship changed. Somewhere around the time my little brother Matty became a superstar on the football field, I suppose. Up until that point, my dad was my hero. He was everything I always wanted to be—big, strong, kind, and funny. And he looked at me like I was his whole world.

Then something shifted. It wasn't a big moment that caused the tension in our relationship. It was gradual.

Slowly but surely, my teammates were bigger and faster than I was. Slowly but surely, Matty was bigger and faster than everyone on *his* team. That's when Dad stopped looking at me like I was his buddy, and started looking at me like I was tagging along for the ride. It hurt. A lot. But I tried to make it right. Holy fuck, I tried.

I made sure to walk-on the football team here at school, even though I knew it wasn't going to lead to anything except lots of time and exercise. I signed up to major in business, with the idea that eventually I would manage a couple of athletes and work at the foundation my dad set up all those years ago. I did my part, and I still do, hoping something will change and I'll stop feeling like his "extra" kid, and he'll be proud of me again. But I also have to live for me.

It's a weird contradiction and one that makes my head spin sometimes—do what makes Dad proud or be myself. These days, it feels like those are two very different things.

Staring at the lobsters in the lobby, I concentrate on memories of my childhood. When I was a kid, my dad used to set me free at fancy places like this, knowing I would never run away as long as there was a tankful of lobsters to mesmerize me.

I would stand and look at the tank and wonder how the lobsters felt. Were they aware of their pending death? Were they oblivious to their fate? It seemed weird to me that people would watch them walk around, living their little lives, and then eat them. Until I had my first taste. Now, I'm the one observing them because I'm trying to decide which one I'm going to pick for my meal. The meal I'm having with my dad when I drop the bomb about choosing the major *I* want, not the one he wants me to have.

I still think it's morbid, picking out your dinner while it's still alive, but I justify it by assuming that having a quick death in a pot of boiling water is better than spending your days running from your fellow lobster as he tries to snap your face off with his claw. Yes, these are the random thoughts I have the hungrier I get, which is a hell of a lot better than plummeting into my pity party while I wait.

Suddenly the door opens and a massive figure walks in—my dad, larger than life. He smiles at the couple leaving and holds the door open for them to pass. They have to scoot around him because he's so big, he takes up the entire doorway. Even in his forties, my dad still forgets he's a giant compared to the majority of the rest of the world.

Once they pass, he turns and catches my eye. If it's possible, his smile gets even brighter. "There's my boy!" Two steps later he's got me wrapped in a huge bear hug.

My dad has always been a hugger. I may be an adult now, but that doesn't stop him from showing his affection, publicly or not. I humor him because it has been a couple months since we've seen each other, and as much as he can be overbearing to the point of annoyance at times, he's still my dad.

He finally pulls away to give me the once-over, and I find myself bracing for what's next.

"You're looking tired. Are you feeling okay? Are you practicing too hard? Getting enough sleep?"

"I'm fine, Dad," I say with a roll of my eyes. "I just had a long practice today."

His eyebrows furrow with concern. "Are you pushing yourself too hard?" he continues to question. "Do you need to cut back? Maybe you shouldn't be working at night—"

"Dad," I interrupt. "I'm fine. They drew my labs a couple months ago when I did my annual physical. Everything came back perfectly normal. There's nothing wrong with me. I'm just tired."

"Okay," he says, but I know he's not fully convinced.

Not that he'll ever be fully convinced. It doesn't matter that I've got the highly coveted "cured" label that came after five years in remission. It doesn't matter that I've been considered cured for more than ten years now. He doesn't hesitate with the questions whenever we meet up. I've learned how to deflect.

"Come on, Dad, don't you have an eight o'clock reservation? I don't want to be late."

He flashes me a knowing grin. "You've been eyeing those lobsters, I see."

"Damn straight. I'm a growing boy. You need to feed me."

We walk up to the hostess stand. "Name?" the very blond, very buxom hostess asks in an equally very bitchy tone.

"Hart," I reply. "*Again.*" She cocks an eyebrow at me and scowls, still treating me like gum on her shoe, just like she did when I first got here, and she wouldn't seat me because I was by myself.

Of course, when she turns to my dad, she has a flirty smile. "I see your entire party has finally arrived, Mr. Hart. I'll be happy to seat you now."

I roll my eyes and huff as she grabs two menus and leads us into the seating area.

My dad leans into me as we walk. "What did you do to piss her off?" he asks quietly. It irritates me that he assumes I did something.

"Oh, you know—I didn't bring your wallet with me," I snark.

"What?"

"A girl in my statistics class works here. She says they're very good at pinpointing who the one with the money is. That's the person they're nice to because that's the person who tips them. The rest of us are an inconvenience and are in the way."

Dad chuckles. "That doesn't happen."

I shake my head. No matter how many times I try to explain that people treat him differently because of who he is, he never gets it. "Ask Mom about it again. She'll tell you."

He just laughs as we sit down, probably still not believing me.

As we settle in, the hostess leans closer to my dad, and puts a hand on his arm. "If you need anything, Mr. Hart, anything at all, just ask. My name is Mindy, and I'll be right there at the front."

"Okay." A strange look crosses his face as he finally realizes my assessment of her behavior was probably right. It still shocks him when people treat him special because of who he is, no matter how many times the rest of us complain about it. My dad has never met a stranger. Unfortunately, I've met many.

As she walks away, a waiter takes her place. Thankfully, he's a guy. In my experience, they're easier to deal with in situations like these.

"Good evening, gentlemen," he begins, placing small white napkins on the table in front of us. "My name is Luke, and I'll be your server this evening. May I start you with a beverage? Perhaps something from the bar?"

"I'll take two fingers of Johnny Walker Black," my dad says, surprising me. "Jax, do you want something?"

I shake my head. "No, I have to work tonight. I'm going to stick with water."

Dad flashes me that concerned look again, but he's distracted quickly by Luke. "Very good, sirs. Feel free to browse the menu. I'll be back with your drinks and to answer any questions you may have."

He walks off, and I look over at my dad. "Since when

do you drink whiskey?"

"Since Henry Davidson introduced me to it."

"Henry *who*?"

He looks at me like I've lost my mind. "Henry Davidson? Only the best tight end in the history of the NFL."

I stare at him blankly.

"Seriously, Jaxon? With all of that football trivia in your brain, you don't remember Henry Davidson?"

I continue to stare at him before finally asking, "When did he play?"

Dad peruses the menu absentmindedly as he answers me. "He played for the Browns all throughout the 80s."

A laugh bursts out of me. "He played for the worst team in the league like twenty years before I was born, and you think I'm going to remember him?"

His jaw drops open and he looks like I kicked his puppy. I actually have to stifle a laugh because of how disappointed he looks. Only this time, I know it's light-hearted, which gives me a boost.

"What part of best tight end in the history of football are you not hearing, son?"

"The part about his glory days being over before I was even born, Dad."

"You're such a little punk," he says playfully and looks down at his menu. "Anyway, he's working for the foundation now, and we were having a dinner meeting not too long ago when he introduced me to it. Turns out, I'm a whiskey man."

Again, I have to try not to laugh. "What you're saying is you have a man crush."

"All right, smart ass. You're not even looking at the menu. What do you want for dinner anyway?"

I look at him and wait for him to answer his own question. Finally, he looks up.

"You and that lobster," he says when it hits him. "You're going to eat me out of house and home."

"Hey, it was your idea to eat fancy. I could have gone for a pizza."

"Yeah, yeah."

I lean back in my chair, relaxing into the conversation. So far, I feel like it's going well. He's in a good mood and looks happy to be hanging out with me. This is good. It's really good.

"How is everyone doing?" I ask as he puts his menu down. "How's Matty? Mom says you've been going to his middle school football games."

Dad's eyes light up at the mention of my younger brother and his natural talent on the football field. Yet, they dim just as quickly as he sensors himself. The relaxed feeling I had fades as his demeanor changes.

"Good. He's doing good. They moved him up to the eighth grade team. He and Trace are playing together." He pretends to look at his menu again when we both know he's really avoiding eye contact.

This is the reason I went to school so far away from home. When Matty started playing on the pee-wee league, it was fun for all of us. Watching those little bitty kids play was funny, especially when they'd get nailed in their over-sized helmets with the football and fall over.

But as Matty got older, and it became obvious how much talent he has, my dad got more and more tight-lipped. At first, I thought it was because he didn't want to put pressure on my little brother. Then one day, I walked in on him talking about Matty's game with my mom. He was animated and excited, waving his hands around with a big smile on his face.

Until he saw me. His face dropped, and he stopped talking. I tried to re-engage the conversation, even throwing in a little extra excitement into my own voice, but he just downplayed everything. Knowing my dad as well as I do, I knew then and there he was trying to protect me from feeling like a disappointment to him. Which only made me realize *exactly* how much of a disappointment I was to him. And it hurt.

And yet, I still try to engage him in talk about Matty. Partially because I'm interested. Partially because it's turned into this weird twisted game for me as I struggle to keep my sanity with this situation. When will my dad realize that not everyone is going to be a football icon, and some of us are fine with that?

"But he's in the sixth grade." Watching him closely, I try to see any flicker of excitement from him. Any at all. But he continues to be stoic.

"Well, he's pretty big compared to the other kids."

I lean my elbows on the table, frustrated with this shit. I'm practically challenging him to show me some sort of real emotion about this. "Really? That's not how mom explains it. She says he's the biggest kid out there. He barrels over everyone else, and he's really good. He's on track to accomplish some great things on the field."

"Maybe. He's still young, you know. And everyone's path is different."

And there it is. The obligatory "everyone's path is different" bullshit he spouts whenever he wants to shut down a conversation. Once again, he reminds me what an utter failure I am because I'm not going down the same path he did. This conversation is about to get worse once I drop the college bomb on him tonight.

"Why can't you just tell me how excited you are?" I ask quietly, surprising even myself. He finally tears his eyes away from his menu to give me a surprised look. "Mom tells me how funny it is that you pace up and down the field during every game. That you can't hardly watch because you're just as nervous as the players."

"She told you that?"

"Of course she did. She says it's hilarious to see everyone's reaction to the big guy barreling up and down the field, trying to keep his cool and not stalk onto the field and get in the ref's face if he doesn't agree with a play."

"It's not that. It's…um…my back hurts from sitting on the benches for a long time."

He's lying to me. I know he's lying. Yes, a career ending back injury forced him into early retirement. And yes, it hurts sometimes. But we both know he's once again trying to cover up his own excitement.

"Whatever," I grumble and snap open my menu, pretending I don't already know what I want.

"What does that mean—?"

Fortunately, Luke shows up at that exact moment, interrupting what could have easily turned into a really nasty fight. I'm so frustrated I want to pull my hair out or scream or maybe both. Something—anything—to get him to see me, really see me for the first time in years. Instead, we take a moment to cool off as Luke places my water and Dad's whiskey on the table.

Before he can leave, we place our order. Lobster, double the seasoned vegetables, hold the rice for me. Filet mignon, double the seasoned vegetables, hold the potatoes for him.

Same meal, same downplayed conversation. Nothing ever changes with my dad. Not even his workout schedule. In spite of his retirement, he still meets up with Deuce, his longtime friend and teammate, several times a week for a couple hours. And now that they're old enough, Matty and Deuce's son, Trace, go with them. I'm sure that's information I'm not supposed to know in case it "hurts my sensitive little feelings." I'm curious to know how it's going, but I'll save those questions for Matty. He's much more open with me. Plus, the hurt I'm feeling is quickly morphing into anger. It's best not to push it. There are other important issues we have to discuss tonight.

Eventually, Luke leaves to put our order in, and I venture into more neutral topics of conversation.

"What are you doing in town anyway?"

"You know that project we've been working on?" I nod. "We need to acquire some land for it, but the land owner actually lives down here. I came to do some schmoozing to see if they're in the market to sell and if I can take some acres off their hands."

Once football was no longer an option, Dad threw all his energy into Hart to Heart, the foundation he established after I was diagnosed with leukemia as a kid. The mission of the foundation is to raise awareness about bone marrow donations and building the national registry. Hart to Heart's growth coincided with Dad's retirement and allowed him to focus his passion and energy away from playing the game to growing the organization.

The success of Hart to Heart has been amazing, and over the last ten years, the number of lives saved as a result has been tremendous. We've always loved hearing from the families who have benefited from the work my dad and his foundation have done. I think it helps him feel like he's accomplished something much more important than what he did on the football field.

Since its inception, the foundation has expanded to include several other umbrellas to help with research and medical bills. Now, they're looking to expand again to an even bigger project—opening a resort.

It's been niggling in the back of my dad's brain for a few years. One of the things he noticed and said for years was there were lots of pediatric oncology camps for the kids to go to, but there was nowhere for the parents to decompress. Even when their kids were away, the bills kept rolling in, the phone kept ringing, there were still jobs and responsibilities pulling them in every direction. He felt like the parents needed a place where they could go to recharge as well.

Now, the Hart to Heart board is in the process of acquiring some land to open up a spa/resort for parents of pediatric oncology patients. The concept is for parents to stay at a five-star resort for free while their children are only about ten miles away at their own camp. The spa would allow the parents to decompress, indulge in some pampering, and meet and spend time with other parents who are going through the same experience. The concept itself has a lot of merit and donors have been really interested. But, regardless of how interested the donors are, the process is slow. I think my dad first mentioned the resort about three years ago.

"That's really cool dad. How did the meeting go?"

"I think we've got a shot," he says excitedly, finally expressing a real emotion in front of me. "There are a couple of other areas we're considering, but this is our favorite at this point. It's only five miles from the kid's camp, which is great. And there are already several buildings that will only require renovations. Plus there is a large building that would be perfect for events and conferences, which is a great alternative for renting the facility for corporate retreats. And, if all goes as planned, we may be up and running in the next couple of years."

"That's awesome. This is going to really go over well with the parents."

His eyes soften as the memories come back to him. It's been ten years since my last hospital stay, but he'll never forget how close I came to death. None of us will. If it weren't for my brother being born early and the hospital getting medical clearance to transplant his cord blood into me, I probably wouldn't be here today.

"Yeah. Your mom and I could've used a place like this. We were lucky to have a huge support system, but most parents don't have that. It'll be nice to give parents some rest and pampering to help them through the hardest time of their lives. Plus," his smile perks up, "in a couple years you'll be joining the board, just in time for us to open."

I stiffen as I prepare myself for the next part of this conversation. I hoped to avoid it until after I'd at least eaten my hand-picked lobster. It doesn't look like that's going to work out.

Sucking it up, I finally confess. "Well, Dad, I wanted to talk to you about that."

"What's up, son?"

"See, um," I clear my throat to buy myself a second to calm my nerves. "I changed my major."

He gets a stunned look on his face. "What do you mean? You don't want to major in business anymore? I thought you wanted to work for the foundation and manage a couple athletes on the side?"

I tilt my head to the side and back. "I never really wanted to manage anyone, Dad. It was an idea I threw out there once, but I never really latched on to that."

He continues to look shocked, like this is coming out of left field. Which I guess to him it is. "But you're good with all that statistical data and crunching the numbers. The football trivia. We've talked about this for years."

"No, *you've* talked about it for years," I disagree. "I've kind of gone along with it because anytime we talk about football, you clam up and pretend to not be disappointed by my lack of skills."

I shake my head, angry with myself for going there. I'm not trying to pick a fight, but I think I just did. Sure enough, when I look up, his eyes are wide. "What are you talking about? I'm not disappointed in your lack of skills."

"We're gonna have to agree to disagree on that one," I say with a sigh. "My point is, I'm not getting a business degree anymore. I don't want to work for the foundation. I changed to pre-med."

He shakes his head in confusion. "Okay, we're going to get back to your last comment about me being disappointed in you—"

"No, we're not."

He shoots me a glare for interrupting him. "We are. But first, what do you mean you don't want to work for the foundation? It's *our* foundation."

"No, it's *your* foundation, Dad." I huff in frustration. "Do you even look at the posters hanging up anymore? The ones of you and me? I'm not nine years old anymore. I'm almost twenty-one; I have hair. I'm cured. I don't want to be the poster boy for Hart to Heart anymore."

"So we'll change the posters," he says like that fixes everything.

"Dad. Listen to me. I don't want to work for the foundation."

He looks at me like I've lost my damn mind. "Okay, if that's what you want. I don't understand what brought on this change. I've never once heard you mention medicine. I'm trying to figure out what's happening here."

"It's something I've been thinking about for a while. You know I'm really good at math and science, and I can remember just about anything related to it." He nods. "I was thinking how much Dr. Bates helped me and how my ability might work to my advantage if I were ever to be a doctor. The idea sort of grew."

He sits back, getting more comfortable. "Wow. That's a really lofty goal."

"You don't think I can do it?"

"I didn't say that. It's just a big commitment."

"That's why I didn't tell you before. I wanted to make sure I could hack it before I ditched the business degree. But I took a couple upper level science classes over the summer to try it out."

"And?"

"Straight A's," I answer.

He smiles at me. I have no idea why he's smiling. I hope that means I have his approval, but at this point, I don't really need it. It's already a done deal. "That random statistical stuff really came in handy, huh?"

"Sure did," I say, running my finger around the rim of my water glass to keep my hands busy. "I'm going for it. I'll be in school for an extra year, which means I'll need to work a little more, maybe a few more hours. I'll probably have to get student loans to get through med school…"

"Whoa, whoa, whoa, Jax, stop." He raises his hands up, palms out. "If med school is what you want to do, don't worry about the cost. We can cover it."

"Yeah, I know, but Matty and Lucy are going to need it too."

"Matty's probably going to get a full ride. Don't even worry about that." As soon as the words are out of his mouth, I see it on his face. He thinks he threw my brother's accomplishments in my face, so he clams up again.

I look to the ceiling and clench my fists in anger. He doesn't get it. I'm allowed to be proud of him too. He's my brother for fuck's sake.

"You have got to stop doing that shit," I practically growl at him.

"What are you talking about, Jax?"

"I know Matty is a fucking super star," I practically yell, slamming my fist on the table. He sits back, bewilderment crossing his face. Lowering my voice, I lean forward to speak again. "Matty has always been good at football. And why wouldn't he be? He's your son. It's a fucking given. But I'm *Austin's* son," I spout, surprising myself as much as the words obviously just shocked him. "I'm good at math and science and am interested in learning more about medicine. I come from a football family, but I'm not destined to be a football great. Never have been, and I'm okay with that. I wish you were okay with it too." Suddenly, I need to get away from him. I can't be a letdown to him anymore. "You know what? Forget it."

I push away from the table and stand up, throwing my napkin down. He stands up right along with me.

"Where are you going?"

"I'm leaving. I have to work tonight. Thanks for the… water," I say, realizing our food hasn't even come yet.

Turning away from him, I storm out the door. I may have the Hart last name, but I have the Bryant genes. And if he can't accept and appreciate that part of me, fuck him.

FOUR

Annika

The room is crowded. The music is loud. And if I look too closely at the strobe lights, I'm likely to have a Pokémon seizure. It's everything I don't care to be a part of on a Thursday night.

Sweaty bodies grind into each other all over the dance floor, making me grimace. I'm not a germaphobe, but I don't know how people rub all over each without knowing where that sweat came from. It grosses me out. But at least Lauren and Kiersten are having a good time. I can't begrudge them that, even if I can only hope they paid attention to my incessant badgering on the way here about being safe, staying together, and never going home with a stranger.

They both rolled their eyes at me and told me I was going to miss out on a really good one-night stand someday with an attitude like that. What they forget is I have an older brother who enlightened me to the guy's way of thinking about a one-night stand. *"If I'm never going to see her again, it doesn't matter if I'm a good lay or not."* I don't think I'll be missing anything by not going home with a stranger tonight.

Waving my credit card at the bartender, I continue waiting to catch his attention. It's hot in here, and I desperately need something to drink. For the first time, I'm grateful Lauren got me a fake ID. If I'm going to make it through tonight, I probably need a beverage of the mixed variety.

Just as I'm yanking my skirt down—the skirt that looks good in the mirror but likes to ride up when doing anything except standing—Lauren comes dancing up.

"What are you doing sitting over here, you party pooper?"

"Trying to get the bartender's attention," I yell over the music. "He doesn't seem very interested in me."

"That's because you keep pulling your skirt down. Why do you keep doing that?"

I bat her hands away as she tries to get me to let go of the offending garment. "Because I remember now why I hate this dress. It keeps riding up, and I don't need to flash the whole room."

She purses her lips, getting ready to make a point, no doubt. "Well no wonder you can't get any service. You're not using what God gave you." She jumps up on the counter and crosses her legs, leaning on her hand to flash some barely-there cleavage. The bartender immediately raises his eyebrows in recognition.

"I'm not sure why she gets to wear skinny jeans and I had to wear this stupid dress," I grumble to myself. But I suppose it has to do with the fact that her shirt dips low enough to give him a peek at those non-existent gymnast boobs.

Soon enough, he swaggers over with a smile on his face, looking her right in the eyes as he gets her order. Oh yeah. He's working for some serious tips.

"What do you want to drink, Annika?" she yells over to me, as she clings to his shoulder.

"I'd like a strawberry mojito, but I hate when the mint gets stuck in my straw."

He nods in understanding, noticing me for the first time. "I'll take care of that for ya."

I give him a thumb's up and slip my card back in my pocket as she whispers something in his ear. Oh geez. I don't know how she can even think about flirting with the bartender. Does she not realize he's making eyes with everyone else too?

I want to yell at her to have a little self-respect, but truthfully, she probably has more self-respect that most people I know. She's a big flirt by nature.

After paying for our drinks, Lauren shimmies off the counter. "Are you having a good time?" she asks as she continues swaying to the beat.

"Yeah," I respond, trying to sound brighter than I feel. "It's fun watching you and Kiersten dance. She's amazing out there," I say, gesturing toward the dance floor.

We look over and sure enough Kiersten is taking advantage of all those moves she worked hard to perfect for all those years. She's all tall and willowy and graceful. Pretty much every man on the dance floor has his eyes on her. Some guy is standing in front of her, gyrating to the music, when another comes up behind her, spins her around, and whisks her away. She doesn't stick with one partner for too long, enjoying working the crowd instead.

It's fun watching her dance. I never have that much rhythm.

Our drinks finally plop down in front of us, and Lauren blows a kiss to the bartender who winks back at her before moving to the next customer.

I grab my mojito, and just like I asked, the mint is mixed in, but he left it all on top to avoid any straw incidents. Now that's the way to get a big tip from me.

Taking a sip, I get a renewed boost for the night.

"Come on." Lauren grabs my hand. "Kiersten can't be the only one who has all the fun."

She pulls me into the crowd then grabs Kiersten, and before I know it, the three of us are dancing together. Judging by the looks on the guy's faces around us, I'm not doing as bad as I thought. Or they're all wearing beer goggles.

Neither way makes a difference to me. I begin swaying to the beat, really listening to the music, slowly shutting out the world around me. We're just three women, out on the town, enjoying our time together. No pressure to find a man. Just time well spent.

I close my eyes and enjoy the bass, raising my arms in the air, careful not to spill my drink. Allowing the loose waves Lauren put in my hair to brush against my face, I feel free. I feel sexy. I don't feel like the bland girl that's the exact opposite of her exotic name. Dare I say I'm actually having fun?

And then, inevitably, I feel it. Sticky booze sliding down my leg and into my shoe after some drunk guy bumps into me and spills his drink on me.

"Oh shit. Sorry about that," he says before dancing away, probably not even noticing the mess he left behind.

I grimace. There's nothing like the feel of sticky booze in your high heel. I tap Lauren on the shoulder and gesture over mine, pointing to the bar where I'm going to clean myself up. She nods and turns back to Kiersten.

"Make good choices!" I yell, not that she heard me over the music.

Shrugging at her lack of response, I make my way through the crowd, trying not to let anything else spill. As soon as I'm free of the mob, I luck out and find an empty stool. I sidle right up to it, plopping my drink on the counter and leaning over to grab some napkins from behind the bar.

Yanking my skirt down—again—I try not to flash everyone as I bend over and wipe all the way down to my foot. This dress is pissing me off even more, now that my mood is souring. I barely register the guy who moves into the stool next to mine as I take off my shoe and clean the inside.

"Hey," he initiates as I finally get the inside dry enough to be able to put it back on without making a squishing sound when I walk. Not that I want to wear it anymore. It's still sticky, but I'd much rather that than walk barefoot on this nasty floor. "What happened?" He leans into me so I can hear him. Or maybe it's to get close to me. I'm not sure which one it is, and I don't really care. Still, there's no reason for me to be rude.

"The normal club story. Dancing, drunk guy spills booze all over someone else. This time I'm the lucky recipient."

He laughs. "Oh, that just sucks."

I shrug and grab my drink back off the counter, taking a large sip through the straw, hoping the alcohol will help put me in a better mood again. "It happens."

"I'm Ron, by the way." He reaches his hand out for me to shake. This is why I don't frequent places like this. I'm not looking for a hookup, but judging from the look on his face, he thinks he stands a chance. Part of me wants to blow him off, but we're in the middle of a room full of people, and he hasn't really said anything inappropriate. So I take his hand and shake it.

"Annika. Nice to meet you." Grabbing the strawberry slice out of my drink, I take a bite and turn away, hoping he'll get the hint. He doesn't.

"Annika." He smiles at me, and I put my guard up, waiting for it. "That's a pretty name for a pretty girl.

And there it is. The cheesy line I was waiting for.

"Thanks." More drinking so I don't have to talk to him.

"So Annika, did you come with your boyfriend or are you here by yourself?"

Giving up on ignoring him, I finish off my mojito and try a new tactic. "Nope. With my friends. They're out there on the dance floor. We're having a girls' night. We're keeping it all girls. No boys. No one-night stands. Just girls," I ramble as I point to my friends.

He doesn't seem to notice my babbling. "They look like they're having a good time."

"Yeah," I say, suddenly feeling nauseous. I should have eaten before we left. Drinking on an empty stomach was dumb of me.

Putting my drink down, I yank my dress down one more time then put my hand to my forehead. All of the sudden I'm feeling clammy. Maybe I need some air. That must be it. Too much booze. Not enough food.

"Well, Ron, it was nice to meet you," I say and begin to walk away.

"Where are you going?" he asks, following me.

"Oh, just over here." I don't know this guy, don't know that I feel comfortable with him, but all I can think of how is much I really need to get out of here for a minute. How much did I have to drink?

Suddenly, my head seems like it's floating away from my body. I look over to Lauren and Kiersten, but they don't see me. They're too busy dancing.

As I begin stumbling my way toward the door, an arm wraps around my waist. "Hey, are you okay?" Ron asks, and I think I hear concern in his voice. I must be worse than I thought.

"I don't know," I answer. "I don't feel very well. I think I might throw up."

"You need some air," he says.

Oh, thank goodness, I think, but all I can do is nod before things go fuzzy around me.

"Come on. There's a side door right there. It's quicker to get you outside this way."

I nod again. And then everything goes black.

FIVE
Jaxon

'm glad to be out of that restaurant and that fucking tie. I don't care for my work clothes either, since they prefer our shirts to be snug, but I'll take it over that noose around my neck any day. Not sure which noose I'm referring to—the actual tie or the figurative one my dad keeps trying to put around me.

Pulling into the parking lot of Ambrosia, the club I barback at, I notice the place is packed tonight, which further irritates me. It's Thursday. I should have expected it. Ladies night always draws a big crowd.

Going through the back door, I head to the office to clock in. My boss, Paul, is sitting at his desk, probably doing inventory or counting money—something official that's back here, away from all the noise and lights and headaches.

Paul has worked here for over ten years, starting in the same position I'm in now. He prides himself on having worked every single job at this club, so he knows how to fill in anywhere he's needed. And he knows how exhausting every position can be. It makes him empathetic when your back hurts from carrying too many cases of beer around. Or your feet are aching from how much you've been running back and forth behind the bar. Or you're feeling sticky and gross from all the booze that's splattered onto your hands.

"Hey, we're running short on some of the liquor behind Macey's station. Go ahead and get her stocked up before you do anything else." He tosses the keys to the liquor closet my way.

Catching them, I answer with, "Sounds good," before heading out into the lights and commotion.

When I applied for this job, I didn't try for anything more than just a bar-back. I'm not lazy, I just don't have goals of the bartending variety, so I don't mind what I do. Not only does it feel like I'm getting a little extra training because I'm constantly lifting gallons of liquid, and booze is *heavy*, but I can also let my mind drift. I don't have to talk to people. I don't have to make nice. I don't have to be fake because I rely on the tips. I have seen way too much fakeness over the years and have fallen for it too many times, only to find out later that my new "friend" wanted to meet my dad. This way, I can focus, do my job, and get paid. It works for me.

"Hey Macey," I call out as I make my way behind the bar where she's at. She tilts her head up in a gesture of recognition and turns back to her customer. I've worked with her enough to know that's as much greeting as I'm going to get when she's slammed like this. Her bar is already three-deep with patrons, and it's just after ten. I don't take her lack of response personally. Instead, I grab the empty bottles she threw to the side to I can get them out of her way and make room for fresh supplies. Since she works next to Colin, I take a quick glance at what he's going to need as well. Might as well make only one trip if I can help it.

Looking down the bar, I see some girl wiping off the back of her leg and yanking at her skirt. Yep, the drunkards are out in full force if people are already getting spilled on. She looks as irritated as I feel. I can already tell it's going to be a long night, so I better pace myself. If things get out of control, the bouncers are going to need some help.

Gathering the empty liquor bottles and dropping them in the recycling container next to Paul's office, I head back into the liquor closet. It's more like a huge room stocked with all our supplies. There's liquor everywhere—every kind you can imagine. I load up the crate we use to easily carry bottles with everything I'm going to need and head back to the bar.

I start by restocking Macey's supply and finish up with Colin's side. As I place the crate under the counter, Macey turns to talk to me. Before the words are even out of her mouth, I already know by the look on her face she's about to ask about the dreaded chore.

"Jax. Hey. Do you mind taking this trash out to the dumpster? It's really getting in the way."

I cringe. This is the job none of us want to do. The trash can get really gross around here. It's all booze, people's dirty napkins, used straws. I always feel like I need to go through a decontamination room when I'm done.

Macey laughs under her breath at my reaction. I don't say anything as I gather all the trash from behind the bar. It's my job, so there isn't much I can do about it except get it over quickly.

Moving out the side door, I head to the dumpster and toss it all in. Hearing what sounds like a thump, one of the bags falls right back out.

"Shit," I mumble under my breath and haul it right back in. The last thing I want to do is pick the bag up off the nasty ground too.

As I turn to walk away, I hear the thump again. That's weird, I think to myself. *It sounds like it's coming from behind the dumpster this time.*

Then I hear what sounds like a low moan.

My body runs cold, and my feet are frozen in place. Something in my gut tells me I need to go see what's going on. It could be something as simple as a feral cat. It could be a homeless guy taking a dump. It could also be someone coming down off a bad high. Still, my feet inch forward, and as I peak around the corner, my entire stomach drops.

It's a man about my age on top of a woman, and it's clear she's unconscious. Her skirt is wrapped up around her hips, and her head is at an unnatural angle.

The anger I'm already feeling increases exponentially at what I'm seeing. I have a sister. I have friends who are women. Seeing this girl, this woman, being violated like this has me seeing red. Without even thinking, I yell, "Hey!"

His head whips up and he looks at me, a startled expression on his face. Then he scrambles to his feet and takes off running. My reaction is instantaneous, and I take off after him, sprinting faster than I ever have on the field. It takes only a couple seconds for me to reach him and tackle him to the ground. We immediately begin scuffling, throwing punches here and there, with him shrieking, "Get off me!" and me knowing instinctively that I can't.

"You goddamned motherfucker!" I scream as I continue to scramble to pin him down. "You think it's okay to treat someone like they're less than nothing?" I land a punch to his nose and blood squirts everywhere, but he doesn't stop flailing, and I don't stop fighting back. "You can't get laid any other way? You have to wait until someone is too drunk to say no, you piece of shit?"

I finally have him immobilized, but I can't stop screaming at him. "What kind of fucking coward takes advantage of someone like that, huh? Answer me, asshole!" I scream and pick him up by the back of the shirt, only to slam his head back into the ground.

As I open my mouth to shout at him again, I hear a moan and look over, only to see the girl rolling on the dirty concrete. She looks almost dead. Her top is torn, exposing one of her breasts. Her skirt is up around her waist, her panties ripped to shreds. And there's some sort of thick liquid coming out from underneath her. It's not coming from her head, but I can't tell if it's blood or vomit or…I can't even fathom the possibilities.

All I know is my anger dissolves into something else. Fear.

Oh god. Oh god. I hope she's not bleeding out everywhere. Oh god.

In a split second I have to decide: Do I hold this guy down and wait for the cops to get here? Or do I help her? It's both the easiest and hardest decision I've ever had to make.

Jumping off him, I race back over to the girl, knowing he's taking off as soon as I let him go. But I don't care. Right now, her life is the most important thing.

As soon as I get to her, she moans again.

"Are you okay?" I ask, not really expecting a response. Instead, I check to make sure she has a pulse and she's breathing. I don't know what the liquid underneath her is, but I know it's not blood. That's one good sign anyway. Still, she needs help, and she needs it fast.

"I need help over here!" I scream as loud as I can, praying that someone will hear me but knowing it's a long shot.

Turning my attention back to the girl, I say calmly, "It's okay. He's gone. You're going to be okay now."

Her eyes flutter open for a split second, and I swear she looks right up at my face. I breathe a sigh of relief. "It's okay. You're okay. I'm right here."

She sighs deeply and closes her eyes again.

"Help! I need help!" I yell into the alley again.

"Jaxon?" Thankfully, I recognize that voice.

"Paul! I'm over here, behind the dumpster."

He comes around the side, eyes widening as he takes in the scene. "What the fuck?"

"I don't know man," I try to explain, my words coming back in a rush. "I came back here to take the trash out and some guy was on top of her, doing…that fucking piece of shit was fucking raping her! Oh, god."

"Oh god," Paul repeats, squatting down next to me, taking in the scene but not trying to touch her. "Have you called the cops?"

"No man. I just got over to her. I don't think she's bleeding." Suddenly, I feel the overwhelming need to protect her. And not just from harm. But from prying eyes. "Dude, give me your shirt."

"What?"

"Give me your shirt. Don't look at her!"

Quickly, he realizes what I'm getting at and pulls his shirt over his head, leaving him only in the white Henley he was wearing underneath. I grab it from his hands and position the shirt over her to cover her private areas. There's no reason for anyone to see her this way.

I see red again, as Paul pulls out his phone. How could someone do this to another person? How can someone call themselves a man while fucking by force, not by choice?

Keeping my voice as calm as possible, I keep talking to her, hoping she knows she's not alone. "You're okay,"

I chant over and over. It may be more of a wish than any-thing else.

I barely register the sound of the sirens in the distance. I'm too busy looking at the girl. Who is she? Where did she come from? And how did no one see what was happen-ing before it got to this point?

She whimpers and starts to move, so I do what comes naturally. Very gently, I scoop her up into my arms so she's not lying on the filthy ground anymore. Her body stiffens, and her eyes open again.

Gently, I talk to her again. "It's okay. You're safe now. I won't let him hurt you anymore."

I feel her body relax and watch as her eyes close again.

Paul is still talking to the person on the phone, the si-rens getting louder now.

It takes hours, or maybe seconds, until the EMTs ar-rive. One approaches us cautiously before squatting down next to me.

"Sir, what happened?"

"I don't know. I came out here to throw the trash out and some guy was on top of her and he was…he was…" I can't get the words out, and I realize I have to blink back the tears burning my eyes. I keep going back and forth from angry to concerned. The emotion of it all is over-whelming. I can't believe this is happening to me. I can't believe this is happening to her.

"We're going to have to check her out, sir."

"Be careful," I demand, the overprotectiveness kicking in again. "I don't know if she's bleeding anywhere, but she has a pulse, and she's breathing." As they begin to move the shirt to get a better look at her injuries, I look over at my boss, who is watching the scene unfold. "Paul, don't look at her."

"What?"

"I said don't look at her," I growl. "She's already had too many people see her like this."

He nods in understanding and holds my gaze as they work on her. I can see some of it in my peripheral vision, but I refuse to look directly, out of respect for her privacy. She has very little right now. Several minutes go by before the EMT finally says, "It's okay, sir. She's covered again."

That's when Paul breaks eye contact with me, and we look back down at her. It's clear she took the time to get all dressed up to come here, and now she's lying in a back alley, behind a dumpster because some guy treated her like trash.

My stomach rolls at the thought of her getting ready for a night out with her friends, only to end up like this. I swallow back the bile. I will not let myself lose control until I know she's being taken care of.

"She's ready to be transported now," the EMT says, but I don't move. I can't. He puts his hand on my arm and continues. "You've done a really good job, young man."

I nod, but I'm not really hearing his words. Suddenly a gurney is rolled next to us, and before I know it, they're strapping her on to take her away. I refuse to leave her side, though. Not until she's safely on that ambulance.

As we come around the side of the dumpster through the back of the alley, I'm glad to see a police officer has already taped off the entrance, keeping people from taking any pictures. I know I don't want to end up on social media for this. I'm sure she doesn't either.

I walk to the back of the ambulance and as the medics load the gurney, I turn to them. "Where are you taking her?"

"To Memorial Hospital. It's the closest one. I'm sure the officers will give you more information since you're a witness to the crime."

"Sir?" A woman is suddenly standing next to me. I didn't hear her come up, but my mind kind of feels like it's in a fog now that I don't have adrenaline coursing through me. "Sir, we really need to check you out."

I look at her feeling confused. Why would she need to check me out? I'm not the one who was attacked.

"Sir, your hands."

I look down, and that's when the pain finally registers in my knuckles. They're red and raw and streaked with blood, the skin broken open.

"Oh yeah," I say, "I forgot. I caught the guy."

"You did?" Suddenly, she seems very interested in what I have to say, and just as fast, I seem to have lost my ability to put together coherent sentences easily.

"Yeah, um, he tried to run, and I tackled him to the ground, and I guess we threw a few punches. I think I broke his nose."

"Is he still here? Do you know who he is?"

"No. She…the girl…she was moaning, and I thought she was bleeding out, and I was afraid she was going to die. I got up to help her, and he ran away."

She pats my arm and flashes me an empathetic grin. "You did the right thing. You may have saved her life."

I nod, but I'm still feeling stunned, my thoughts swirling a hundred miles an hour though I'm only halfway comprehending anything.

She guides me over to the back of another ambulance, and as she's disinfecting my hands, an officer comes up and asks me questions about what I've seen. In the course of the conversation, he convinces me to give him my blood-stained shirt. Something about it being evidence. Paul must see what's going on because before I know it, he's handing me a clean logoed shirt.

"Jax," he says, "take the rest of the night off. Don't

come in tomorrow or the rest of the weekend."

"But, you'll be short-staffed."

"Don't worry about that," he says. "You know I can fill in anywhere. You've had a rough night. You need a break."

"Yeah," I say absentmindedly. "I guess call me when you put out the new schedule for next week."

"I will, man. And thanks for what you did tonight. You're a real hero in my eyes."

Hero. I don't feel like a hero. I feel like a real ass for letting that motherfucker go.

A picture of the girl flashes through my brain again, taking me by surprise, and I have to squeeze my eyes shut to get rid of the image, so I don't clench my fist and make it harder for the lady next to me to clean my hands. But she looked small and fragile and vulnerable. Is she someone's sister? Is she someone's girlfriend? Is her boyfriend somewhere in the club, looking for her right now? Are her friends? Who is looking out for her?

Once I'm deemed medically sound, I hop out of the ambulance, patting my pockets to make sure my keys are still in there. Crossing the parking lot quickly, I keep my eyes down, avoiding any questions I don't want to answer. Instead, I jump in my car and drive. There's only one place I want to be.

SIX
Annika

The light is bright and my eyes aren't open yet. Is it really that late in the day? Did Lauren forget to close the curtains? Or am I really, really hung over?

"Are you awake? Can you hear me? Do you know where you are?"

What? Why would Lauren ask me if I know where I am? Am I somewhere I'm not supposed to be?

"Can you tell me your name?"

Why would Lauren be asking my name?

I try to open my eyes, but the light is just too bright, so I close them again. Maybe if I get a little more sleep, my brain will stop hurting.

"You're okay. You're not going to die."

That's nice, is the last thing I think before I drift off again.

. . .

The light is still so bright. How much did I drink last night?

"My name is Stacy, and you're at the hospital. Can you tell me your name?"

Stacy? Who is Stacy? Where's Lauren? Why am I at the hospital?

I try desperately to pry open my eyes, so I can figure out what the hell is going on, but they aren't cooperating. It's making me anxious, as anxious as I can be while still groggy, but I keep trying.

"Can you hear me? You're going to be just fine."

Well that's good do know. I didn't think I wasn't going to be fine until now. But I'm still confused as to why I'm at the hospital, and who the hell is Stacy?

"Can you tell me your name?"

"Annika," I croak out, turning my head to the sound of the voice. "My name is Annika."

I can't figure out what's going on, but I know my throat feels dry.

"Annika, my name is Stacy, and I'm your nurse. Do you hurt anywhere?"

Do I? I don't know the answer to that. But as soon as she asks, I take a mental assessment of my body.

"My head." I reach up and touch my forehead. My arm feels kind of floaty as it reaches my aching head.

"Good. That's to be expected. Anywhere else you can feel?"

"Um…my arm," I realize. "My arm really hurts."

"This arm right here?" I feel a poke.

"Ow. Yeah."

"You have a really nasty gash over there, but we've already taken care of it, and it's already on the mend. Is there anywhere else?"

I think on it but don't feel anything. "No. Just my head. My arm." My eyes slowly peel open, and sure enough, that's not Lauren. I assume it's the woman who keeps calling herself Stacy. She has curly blond hair and a nice smile. I immediately want to like her, but I'm still confused.

"There you are," she says. "Nice to see you awake. I'm going to try sitting you up a bit to help the groggy feeling."

"Okay." The bed moves slowly, making me queasy. I push the feeling aside because I want some answers. "What happened?"

I think I say that out loud. In fact, I'm pretty sure I say it out loud, but she doesn't answer me. Maybe she's ignoring me. Or maybe it's because the door opens, and a doctor comes walking in.

"Hey, she's awake!" he exclaims.

Why is everyone happy I'm awake? Was I not supposed to be? Have I been in a coma, or something?

"My name is Dr. Thompson. I'm going to take a quick look at you, but Stacy is going to stay right here with us." The doctor comes over and puts his fingers on my wrist to take my pulse. When he reaches over to put the stethoscope on my chest, I flinch. My heart beat picks up, and my breathing gets more labored.

That was weird. Why did I react like that?

"It's okay," Stacy reassures me gently. "I'm standing right here. He's just listening to your lungs to make sure they're clear."

Dr. Thompson encourages me to lean forward, listening to the back of my chest as well. Then he pulls out a penlight and flashes it in my eyes, making me look this way and that.

"You're looking pretty good. Once we started flushing your system, you woke up quickly. It's only been a couple hours."

A couple hours? What in the hell happened?

The door opens again before I can ask the question and

another woman walks in. It's like everyone in this hospital was put on alert the second I opened my eyes. But this woman isn't wearing scrubs like everyone else. She's wearing jeans and carrying a clipboard. A loose bun is at the nape of her neck.

"What time is it?" I ask.

"It's about 2:30 in the morning," someone says, but I'm not sure who.

This whole situation feels weird.

"What happened anyway?" This time I make sure to ask out loud.

Dr. Thompson leans up against a counter across the room while Stacy keeps pushing buttons on machines and typing stuff into a computer. The woman with the clipboard pulls up a chair next to me and begins speaking. Maybe I'll finally get some answers now.

"My name is Pippa, and I'm a social worker at the hospital."

I just look at her. Why is a social working talking to me?

"We had a hard time figuring out who you were because you didn't have any identification on you."

I think for a second, wondering where my credit card and phone went. The fuzziness is fading away a little, but there are still so many unanswered questions. "My name's Annika. Annika Leander."

"Okay, Annika. Do you remember why you're here?"

I try to think back, but everything is really unclear. All I remember is feeling sick while sitting at the bar.

"No, I don't. I don't remember. Was I in a car accident? I wasn't drinking and driving, was I? I never do that."

She pats my arm. "No, you weren't drinking and driving. You don't have to worry. You're not in any trouble."

She's trying to reassure me, but something about the

entire situation feels wrong. From the way no one will look me in the eye, to the number of times I've asked questions without getting an answer. It dawns on me, I never asked about Lauren. Suddenly, I'm feeling panicked.

"What about Lauren? Is Lauren okay?" I try to lean forward, but Pippa puts her arm back on me, encouraging me to lie back down.

"We haven't seen Lauren. But we haven't had any other women your age come in, so I'm assuming she's fine."

"Oh. Okay, good." I relax a little knowing my roommate is okay. But that still doesn't answer the big question. "What happened?" I ask for at least the third time.

Dr. Thompson crosses his arms and legs. "Annika, when you were brought in you were unconscious. We ran a battery of tests, including blood tests to see what you ingested. Your blood alcohol content was only .002. That's well below the legal limits."

I shrug. "Well yeah. I think I only had one drink. And I didn't even drink it all."

"That's kind of what we figured," he continues. "What we did find, though, is high levels of GHB."

GHB. My mind scrambles. Why does that sound familiar. I know I've heard it before.

Suddenly, it hits me, and I feel my breathing pick up again.

"The date rape drug?"

Dr. Thompson clears his throat. "Typically, that's what it's known as, yes. Do you have any idea how it may gotten in your system?"

"I…no…I…" My heart is pounding as I scan through my memories. What can't I remember? Why can't I remember?

"It's okay." Pippa pats my arm. "We'll get there. Let's start from the beginning. Who were you with last night?"

"I went to a club. My roommate Lauren likes to go dancing, and I didn't want to go but she finally convinced me. I went because her friend Kiersten is in town. The three of us went to this place that they like—Ambrosia. Just us girls." I know I'm babbling, but all my thoughts are spinning.

"Did you meet anyone there? Or maybe become friends with anyone?"

"No. I didn't really talk to anyone. I sat at the bar. Well, there was this one guy…" It hits me and I stop. I never leave my drink unattended. Ever. I have been warned about that my entire life. I preach it to Lauren all the time. You can't trust anyone.

But I did put my drink down last night. I was standing right next to it, and I thought I had my eye on it. But I didn't. I turned my back when I bent over to wipe my leg off. I only took my eyes off it for a second, but a second was all it took.

My eyes widen, and I look at Stacy and Pippa, and I try to look at Dr. Thompson, but I can't hold his gaze for some odd reason. It feels safer to focus on Pippa.

"There was this guy," I whisper.

Pippa leans closer. "Do you remember anything about him?"

"Someone spilled a drink down the back of my leg. I went to the bar to clean it off. He started talking to me."

"Did he say his name?"

"Yeah, he said his name was Ron. I didn't really pay that much attention to him. I wasn't interested. That's when I began feeling sick."

Pippa starts writing frantically on her clipboard.

"Do you know what time this was?" Dr. Thompson asks.

I shake my head. "I wasn't paying attention to the

clock. We got there about 9:30. Maybe an hour after that."

Pippa nods her head. "Okay, do you remember anything else about what happened when you were talking to Ron?"

"Not really. It wasn't much of a conversation. Just me saying I was there with my girlfriends and wasn't looking for a hookup. But then my head started hurting, and I felt like I was going to be sick. I tried to get outside for some air."

"And then what happened?"

"I don't know. I guess Ron saw me getting sick and offered to help me. I don't remember anything else."

I blink several times, looking at Pippa with horror on my face. *Oh god, what happened to me? What happened to me?*

It takes a few seconds before I'm brave enough, but I finally voice it.

"What happened to me?"

Pippa takes a deep breath and puts her clipboard down, folding her hands and placing them on the bed next to me.

"An employee of the club was taking the trash out to the alley when he found you behind the dumpster."

"Behind the dumpster?"

"There was a man on top of you, and he was assaulting you."

Stacy grabs my hand when my breathing gets heavy. I keep hanging on to her hand for dear life. I've never met her before, but I'm grateful she lets me squeeze as hard as I can without saying a word.

"Okay," I finally say when I feel more under control. "And then what?"

"The employee chased the man off and called the police. That's how you ended up here."

All of a sudden a memory hits me. It's fuzzy, but it's

of a man holding me saying "It's okay. You're safe now."

"Oh god," I say out loud, "Ohgodohgodohgod."

My throat feels like it's closing up, the walls caving in. Stacy immediately puts an oxygen mask over my face when I can't seem to control my breathing, and Pippa keeps talking to me quietly.

"It's okay. You don't have to remember everything. We don't know many more details than that. But the police have already interviewed the witness and have gotten some DNA evidence from the man who helped you."

I barely register what she's saying. All I can hear is some of the words Stacy said to me when I was waking up. "Do you hurt anywhere else? Do you feel any pain anywhere else?" Those words are taking on a whole new meaning, and I begin assessing my body again. My head, still hurting. My arm, still hurting. Nothing else seems to really hurt.

Until I shift my body to get more comfortable. That's when I feel it.

There's a pain, a soreness between my legs. I don't remember how it got there.

And that's when I begin to cry.

SEVEN
Jaxon

I've been sitting here for hours in this waiting room. Just hoping to find out any information.

I know I'm not actually privy to anything about the girl, but I can't seem to leave her here on her own. No one has come in frantically looking for someone who meets her description. And that pisses me off. Does anyone know she's missing? Where are her friends? Where is her boyfriend? Where is her family?

Why has no one come for her?

I can't leave. Even if she doesn't know I'm here, I can't leave her by herself. I won't.

Waiting, though, means lots of time to think. And the thoughts running through my brain are not one I'd wish on anyone.

Self-doubt tries to take over. *Why didn't I do more? Why didn't I get there a few seconds earlier? Why didn't I notice something was happening? Could I have stopped it?*

I am a logical person. Logically, I know there is nothing I could have done differently. Logically, I know there was no way I could have anticipated what I was going to stumble across tonight. But when it comes to something like this, logic is blown out the window, and all I know is how it feels. And I feel guilty. I feel angry. I feel like I failed her. I feel like I should have done something different.

So now I wait. Wait for news that she's okay. Wait for news that someone is here for her. Wait for someone to protect her.

"Mr. Hart?"

I blink the fogginess out of my eyes and look at the officer next to me.

"Uh, yeah, that's me. Jaxon."

"I'm Officer Aguilar." He's short and stocky, dark hair and eyes. He's standing with his hands on his utility belt in the typical police officer stance. I tower over him when I rise to shake his hand, and I'm not what you would consider tall. "I just wanted to let you know the girl is awake, and it looks like she's going to be fine."

My eyes widen. "She's awake?" For the first time tonight, a niggle of excitement runs through me. "She's okay?"

"Well," he pauses briefly. "I wouldn't necessarily say she's okay. But she's awake, and her injuries don't appear to be life threatening. She's got a long haul, but physically she's going to be fine."

Physically. There is so much implication in that one word, and I understand his meaning. Physically, she'll be fine. Mentally and emotionally—that is all still to be determined.

"I can't give you any more information than that," he says almost apologetically, "But I wanted to find out if you remembered anything else. Maybe what the guy looked like or even what he was wearing."

I try to think back again, but the memories are still fuzzy.

Shaking my head, I'm pissed at myself for not knowing more. "I told the other officer everything I could remember."

"Well, sometimes memories hit us out of nowhere, and since you've been sitting here I thought I'd ask. Just to make sure we didn't miss anything before you head home."

"Yeah, I get it. Really, just like I told the detective, it was dark out and happened fast. All I remember is that asshole had kind of longish hair on the top. I think it was blond, but I'm just not sure. Now I wish I would have ripped some of it out of his head."

Officer Aguilar nods as he listens, but I can see him assessing my mental state.

"Sorry." I look at the floor. "I have a sister. Shit like this makes me rage."

"More men should feel that way about women being assaulted. It'd be nice to be out of a job." He adjusts his stance before saying, "Well, if you have any other memories, make sure to let us know. These things take time, and sometimes once the brain isn't pumped full of adrenaline, things come to you."

I nod again like I understand it's only a matter of time. Part of me hopes he's right—that maybe I can give them another lead. And part of me hopes I never remember this night again.

Just as Office Aguilar opens his mouth to continue the conversation, the automatic sliding doors open and a familiar face comes racing through. Almost immediately, he sees me.

"Jax!" my dad yells and jogs to me, pulling me into his

arms and holding me tight. "Jax, are you okay?"

"Yeah, Dad. I'm okay," I whisper, my whole body relaxing. It doesn't matter that we got into a fight earlier. We'll deal with that later. For now, having him here means I don't have to do this by myself. "I'm okay. But it was bad. It was so bad."

"I know, son. I know."

He keeps holding me and suddenly, emotions I didn't know were there take over.

"Dad, I tried to stop him," I sob. "But I let him get away."

"No, Jax. No. You helped save her. You did what was necessary, and I'm proud of you."

He holds me for a few more minutes while I collect myself. Then he backs away and looks me over. I know he's giving me the once-over, making sure I'm not too exhausted. I want to be angry at him for it, but there's other things to be angry about now, so I ignore him.

"Mr. Hart, I presume?" Officer Aguilar asks.

My dad is obviously surprised when he realizes someone is standing with us. "Yeah, sorry." He rubs his hand down his face. "I'm Jaxon's dad. Jason. Nice to meet you."

The officer gets a strange look on his face. "Jason. Jason Hart," he repeats absentmindedly. Then his features change as a lightbulb moment goes off in his head, and he snaps his fingers. "Hart to Heart Foundation."

My dad immediately switches into PR mode, a big grin crossing his face. I take a step back and let him do his thing while I wipe my eyes and rub my face. "Yeah, that's what I'm in town for. I'm glad to hear you know of us."

Office Aguilar resumes his stance with his hands on his belt. "You guys are the reason I ended up on the bone marrow registry."

This piques both our interests. I don't want to work for

the foundation, but it's been a huge part of my life since its inception, and I have a vested interest in whether or not it succeeds, whether I like it or not. Plus, it's nice to focus on something besides the trauma of tonight, however briefly it might be.

"I went and signed up ten years ago when you guys did the special event at the stadium," the officer continues. "It was really cool that you did that."

Dad looks at me and grins, his eyes crinkling. "I'm glad to see that hard work was effective."

"Oh, it definitely was. Turns out I was a match."

Now, this is where I could lose my dad's attention for hours. He loves hearing these stories—how someone who signed up through Hart to Heart ended up being a donor. There are pictures tacked all over his office of lives that have been saved due to those outreach programs. It keeps him motivated.

"Really?" he inquires. "Did you end up donating?"

"Sure did." The officer's chest puffs out slightly with pride, and I swear he seems ten feet tall now. "Twenty-eight-year-old mother of two. Non-Hodgkin's lymphoma. Did the transplant last year, and she got a clean bill of health a few months ago."

"That's awesome man," my dad exclaims. "I can't even thank you enough for doing that. What a gift!"

"We have plans to meet up in the next couple of months," he continues. "I can't wait to meet her. Saving her life was the most important thing I've ever done."

"I need to shake your hand," Dad says, reaching his own out. "And please, if you think about it, take some pictures when you guys meet up and email them over to Hart to Heart. We love keeping track of when we're doing good work. It helps keep up with our funding and really encourages us to keep doing our jobs."

"I will," he says with a nod. "I'll make it a point to email. But anyway, your boy did a great job tonight. He was a real hero."

My dad puts his giant paw on my shoulder and tugs me close to him again. "That's my Jaxon. He's been my hero for a long time."

I'm not sure where that statement comes from since I've never heard him say that before, but I choose not to react. Instead, I watch as the officer nods and begins to walk away but thinks better of it and turns back. "Don't forget, Jaxon. If you remember anything, please don't hesitate to give us a call."

"I will. Thank you, Officer."

As he walks away, my dad turns and hauls me into a hug again, breathing a sigh of relief. "God, Jaxon, when you said you were going to the hospital, my heart dropped."

And the irritation is back. I understand what he's getting at, and I understand why, but this is not the time for him to be overbearing. I can't carry the responsibility of reassuring him I'm healthy when my mind is spinning in all different directions right now. I have no hesitations telling him so as I pull away.

"It's not about me tonight, Dad. It's about this girl."

"I know," he says almost apologetically. "And I don't mean to downplay anything she went through. Are her parents here? Do you know?"

I shrug and sit down on the chair, him sitting next to me, leaning forward on his elbows.

"I don't know. I haven't seen anyone coming in looking for a girl. I'm not leaving until someone comes for her. I won't leave her by herself."

"I get it, son." He puts his arm around my shoulder. I stiffen briefly, but when he says, "I get it. And we can stay here as long as you want," I relax into him. We have a lot to discuss, a lot to sort out, but I refuse to do it now. Tonight, we're going to sit here and watch a rerun of some random comedy from the 70s. *What the hell is this show anyway?*

The volume is muted so we can't hear anything, which makes it seem kind of pointless to have a TV in here, and it makes it impossible to keep me engaged.

Looking around the room, I notice what my dad's wearing and realization hits.

"Wait, Dad, I called you at like 10:30. What took you so long to get here? You don't even have any real clothes on." I poke fun at the plaid pajama pants and white T-shirt he's wearing in public. If it weren't for the fact that he has Nike's on his feet, I'd think he'd just woken up when I called and rolled out of bed to get here.

He purses his lips before fessing up. "I wasn't exactly in town when you called."

My eyebrows lift just slightly. "What? Where were you? I thought you left tomorrow."

"I'd started the drive home last night. I didn't have anything to do, so I figured I'd head out early. I was about halfway there when I stopped for the night."

"What? Dad! You didn't need to turn around and come back! It's not me in the hospital," I protest.

"Yeah, I know, I know. I called your mom as soon as you called me, and she agreed that I needed to come back for you. Jaxon, you may not have been the one who was assaulted tonight, but you got a big dose of the ugly side of life. I don't care about our fight earlier." I bristle at the reminder. "None of that is important. You're important, and you need to know that I'm here for whatever you need."

Despite wanting to still be angry at him, I resign myself to being thankful that he's here. I'm still mad and hurt about so many things, but right here, right now, I'm glad he's putting everything aside to support me. "Thanks. But just know, I'm not talking about anything else with you right now. I'm here until someone shows up for the girl."

He puts his hand on my knee in support. "I know, son. And we'll stay here as long as you want."

Leaning back in my chair, I stretch my legs out to get as comfortable as I can and turn my attentions back to the polyester suits and afros on the screen in front of me.

EIGHT
Annika

Pippa. It's such a strange name for a woman in the United States to have. Especially a woman in her late twenties or early thirties.

I find myself wondering, where did her parents come up with the name Pippa? Does she have a sister named Catherine who lives in Buckingham Palace?

I stifle back a giggle. Not really a giggle. More like a hysterical laugh. I'm trying hard to keep my mind off the *click, click, click* of the camera between my legs.

I'm thinking about anything and everything to keep from hearing the murmurs of Dr. Thompson as he spouts off medical things that Stacy needs to document in my file. I'm trying desperately not to remember everything that has happened tonight, because I will be damned if I'm going to cry in front of these people again.

There is not one square inch of my body they haven't seen naked.

There is not one part of my nude body that hasn't been

photographed.

They have swabbed the inside of my cheek.

They have gathered skin cells from underneath my fingernails.

They have scraped my cervix.

And now I lie here with a camera between my naked, spread legs as they take pictures of my most private areas—parts of me I don't share with just anyone—looking for potential damage that was done by the assault.

An assault I don't remember. But I sure as hell will remember this.

Yes, I have consented to everything that is happening to me right now. But that doesn't mean I want to go through it. That doesn't mean the reason for my consent isn't for the sole purpose of taking this guy down someday. Because in the forefront of my mind, while I'm feeling shame and humiliation and degradation, I'm also feeling anger. And I can't help but pray that someday God will allow this Ron guy to feel the same kind of humiliation I'm feeling now. That someday he'll be forced to have an anal cavity search. That someday he'll be in prison and be made someone else's bitch and be raped over and over while dozens of people he's never met stare at his naked body.

I can't help the way I feel, and I won't apologize for it.

Instead, I'll think about the name Pippa.

Does she have a sister named Catherine somewhere? Maybe she's married to a prince.

Were her parent's hippies and they were trying to name her after Pippy Longstocking and got the name spelled wrong?

Where did a name like Pippa even come from in the first place?

"Two-centimeter laceration on the left side inner labia."

Dr. Thompson's words jerk me out of my own thoughts.

A two-centimeter laceration of my labia. Not the outer labia. The inner labia. Which means something was inside me.

"What does that mean happened?" I croak out, praying I can refocus my thoughts on the name Pippa again, but knowing it's a losing battle at this point.

Stacy has been good to me. She's been sitting here the whole time holding my hand when I've needed it. She's talked me gently through some of the procedures. She's been kind. I'm glad she's here. And I hope I never, ever see her again. Especially when she humors me and answers my question.

"It could mean a whole lot of things. It could be as simple as nicking yourself with your fingernail while wiping."

I look down at my fingernails. My fingernails that they had a hard time scraping because they're so short. Fingernails that I keep super short because I don't like the way they feel when they get too long. I hate that feeling so much, I religiously clip them at least once a week.

I know there is no way I cut myself wiping. She knows there's no way I cut myself. Everyone in this room knows there is no way I cut myself. Which means the only way it happened was because this Ron guy was inside me.

Was it his penis? Was it his finger? Was it an object?

I don't have any way of knowing.

Do they have any way of knowing? I have no idea. I don't even know if I care. All I know is that another wave of disgust flows through me as the realization hits that he was *inside. me.*

Pippa. Pippa. Pippa. Maybe her parents were drunk.

Pippa. Pippa. Pippa. Maybe she was an old British nanny Pippa's mom had years ago.

Pippa. Pippa. Pippa.

"Okay, you can sit up now. We're done."

Stacy quickly covers my lower half with a sheet as Dr. Thompson moves the camera out of the way.

They've promised me that these pictures go straight into an evidence locker and no one will ever see them unless absolutely necessary, but I know how that goes. Any detective who works on this case, and detectives rotate frequently, will have access to my records. They'll have access to naked pictures of me. Sure, they'll be looking at them as evidence, but will they? Will they always? Will some weird, depraved power-hungry cop be the one to take over my case? Will he look at the naked pictures of my body just for fun? Will I ever know if someone who has been on this case is walking down the street, sees me, recognizes me, and knows what I look like underneath my clothes? Will a jury see them? Hundreds of people may see these pictures of me. But they try to reassure me by saying it's "evidence" that's going to be "safely stored" in a locker.

I don't believe it for a second. I pray that somehow, some way, these pictures are treated with respect. That *I'm* treated with respect, because I won't ever know every single person who will see these pictures. I can never know. And that fuels my anger even more.

"Can I please use the bathroom now?" I ask, not sure who exactly I'm asking while I wait for them to finally be done inflicting this nightmare on me.

"Absolutely," Stacy answers and moves closer to my side.

"I put some clean scrubs on the counter in the bathroom," Pippa interjects. "You're welcome to use them. And if you'd like to shower, you can."

I nod, but there is no way I'm showering in this strange

place. No way I am taking my clothes off with these people in this room again. Never.

Stacy tucks the paper sheet around my hips and helps me climb off the bed. I'm still a little weak and groggy from the drug so it takes a second. But then I plod off to the bathroom, determined to do it by myself. And maybe even more determined to be alone for a few minutes.

Once the door is closed behind me, I get my first good look in the mirror and see my face.

Damn. I look like I had a really, really rough night. My eye makeup is smeared like I've been ugly crying, and my hair looks like I stuck it in a blender. My body is dirty.

I try to use my fingers to comb through my hair to put it into a messy bun, but I get caught on… *what is that? Is that a stick? In my hair?*

I start pulling random bits of debris out of my knotted locks. I have no idea what this stuff is or where it even came from. It's disgusting. I can't wait to get back to the dorm to clean this filth off of me.

Finally, my hair is on top of my head and out of my face. Maybe instead of washing it, I'll just head to a salon and get it cut or colored. Maybe I'll get a blond pixie cut. Something that's totally different. Something that makes me unrecognizable to the people who are going to see my naked pictures.

I pull the hospital gown off me so I can get dressed and take a quick assessment of my body. My hips and chest look okay. My breasts look okay, my stomach…

I run my hand through the curls of my public hair and… *Oh god. What is that? Is that liquid? What the hell?*

Some kind of sticky fluid is stuck on my fingers, and I'm revolted, I just want to throw up. But I won't do it here. I refuse to do it here.

Instead, I use the baby wipes that are on the counter to

clean away as much filth as possible until I can get home and take a nice hot shower. I use at least a dozen on my genital area alone to get the nasty, sticky fluid off my curls and my hand before quickly throwing the clean clothes on. The last thing I want is to wear part of the hospital home with me as a reminder of this night, but it's not like I have any choice.

Again.

My body, my choice seems to be a giant lie all the way around tonight.

And then I move away from the mirror. I can't look at myself anymore. I disgust myself. I revolt myself. I need that pixie cut so I don't recognize myself.

Shuffling back into the bedroom, I see Dr. Thompson is gone. The only ones here are Stacy and Pippa. They both smile at me when I come out of the bathroom, like there's anything to smile about.

"You look better," Pippa remarks. "Feeling a little better now?"

"Well, I'm not naked, and no one is taking pictures of my vagina," I snap back.

Their faces both fall, and I sigh.

"I'm sorry." I know my anger is misplaced as much as they do. "This is not your fault."

"Never be sorry for the way you feel," Pippa demands. "Therapy 101. You've been through an extremely traumatic event. You have a right to lash out at us. And it's okay that you never want to see us again."

That makes me almost laugh out loud, like she can read my thoughts. But I guess she's heard it all before.

"Um, I was thinking about something. The guy who found me." Pippa nods. "Who is he?"

"Are you sure you want to know all this?"

I think for a second and then nod. I know I'm not going

to like everything I hear, but I want to face this head-on. I don't hide from my problems. I prefer to power through them.

"Okay." She moves closer to the bed as I get settled on the fresh sheets they must have put on while I was changing. "He's a college student at the university like you. He works at the bar and was taking the trash out when he found you. He tackled the guy to the ground, and they threw a few punches, which actually works to our advantage because the police were able to collect some blood evidence from him. That gives us an eye witness to the crime, not just DNA evidence."

My eyes widen. "He fought him?"

"He did," Pippa nods.

"Is he okay?"

"Yeah. He probably has a little bit of survivor's guilt. But that's to be expected. I'm referring him to a counselor at the university, just like I'm referring you."

I furrow my brow at the pointed look she's giving me. I didn't realize she was going to be sending me to therapy. I suppose it's a normal part of her job, but I don't know that I want to go.

Suddenly, I feel like a truck has run over me. Dr. Thompson wasn't kidding when he said the drugs were going to make me tired for a while.

"Will I get to meet him?" I ask with a yawn. "I'd really like to thank him."

Pippa gets a strange look on her face, as Stacy looks at her, eyebrows raised.

"I wasn't sure how you'd feel about this, but since you said it," she sighs, "he's in the waiting room."

I sit straight up, the groggy feeling completely forgotten. "What do you mean he's in the waiting room? Has he been here all night?"

"He has." Pippa nods. "We've tried to get him to leave several times to rest, but he keeps saying until he knows someone is here to take care of you, he's not going anywhere."

I think about that for a minute and realize he's right. No one has come looking for me yet. Not Lauren. Not Kiersten. Not my parents. No one realizes I'm gone.

And yet, this boy stayed. This boy I never met. This boy who may have saved my life. He stayed.

A strange feeling of warmth runs through me.

"If it's okay with the police," I say, my mind made up, "I'd really like to meet him."

Pippa pauses but then nods. "I can go get him."

"Yeah," I say again, "I'd really like to meet him."

Just knowing he's coming makes my whole body relax, like having him close by makes me safe.

NINE

Despite this being a waiting room, these chairs are not meant for waiting. They're hard plastic and uncomfortable. My butt is aching from sitting here for hours.

My dad gave up a long time ago and began pacing. I'm not sure if it was nerves, adrenaline, or because that old back injury was hurting. Either way he's leaning up against the wall on the other side of the room while we wait.

We've been here for hours, but I'll wait as long as I have to. The thoughts are still swirling in my brain. The things I saw tonight. The things I did. The things I should have done. I bang my fist lightly against my forehead trying to get the memories to stop, but they just keep coming.

"Mr. Hart?"

I vaguely register someone talking to my dad, too wrapped up in my own thoughts again. Even a young, less plastic version of John Travolta on the screen isn't helping anymore.

"Jax." My dad's voice breaks me of the revelry in my head. "She's talking to you."

I look over and see a dark-haired woman holding a clipboard next to me.

I stand up to greet her. "Sorry. I'm used to people calling my dad Mr. Hart, not me."

She smiles kindly like my lack of response was to be expected. I notice that she's wearing jeans but has some sort of fancy bun in her hair. The combination seems contradictory, which is a really odd thought for me to have right now. But it also keeps my mind on something other than the girl. And I guess with the lack of sleep there's no telling where my thoughts are going to go. I must be getting delirious.

"My name is Pippa. I'm a social worker here at the hospital. Can you follow me?"

My dad comes over, and we follow Pippa into a small room labeled "family waiting." The lighting is terrible and the carpet is worn, but it's private. I assume that means this is a conversation she doesn't want overheard.

"Thank you for everything you've done tonight, Jaxon," she begins as soon as she shuts the door behind us.

I look at my dad and then back at Pippa. "I didn't really do much. In fact, I'm kind of pissed I didn't do more."

"It's normal to feel that way." She sports an empathetic smile. "But trust me when I say this…things could have been much worse. You quite literally may have saved her life."

I'm not sure I want to know this, but being the glutton for punishment that I am, I engage. "I did?"

She takes a deep breathe. "This isn't the first case like this that I've worked on. Annika is extremely lucky."

"Annika?"

"Oh yes, sorry. Her name is Annika. She's a student at the university just like you."

Oh god, I think. *She's my age.* I don't know why that makes it feel worse to me. I don't know why if she was older I would feel better about this. But maybe I wouldn't and her age just hits too close to home. She could be someone in one of my classes. She could be someone I've gone to parties with. She could be any woman I know.

"Physically she's okay?"

Pippa shifts the clipboard in her grasp. "Well, she has a few minor injuries. She had to have some stitches in her arm, and she has some scrapes. But for the most part, physically, she's doing just fine. That's not to negate the emotional and mental issues. Those are going to take much longer to deal with. But without having to push through serious physical issues, it's going to make the process a lot easier."

"How so?" my dad asks. "I wouldn't think the two really had much to do with each other."

"Put yourself in the victim's shoes," Pippa says. "Right now, she's likely feeling a lot of shame. A lot of humiliation. A lot of disgust. A lot of regret. But she'll walk out of here, and her clothes will cover any remnants of what's happened to her. She'll be able to continue on without every nosy person on campus asking her what happened because she has a busted lip or black eye. Victims who are beaten up have a rough go of it, because many times they either feel like they need to stay contained to their homes until makeup covers the bruising. Or they have to face all the stares and answer all the questions. And every time someone asks a question, they have to relive their nightmare all over again."

"Oh god." My dad runs his hand through his graying hair. "I never thought about that."

Pippa shrugs. "Most people don't. That's why I make it a habit never to ask anyone with a bruise on their face why they have it unless they volunteer the information first."

"I can understand that," my dad says, squeezing my shoulder.

"Anyway, I wanted to let you know, Jaxon, with your permission of course, I'm making a call to the counseling center on campus. I'd like to make a referral for you."

I furrow my brows. "Wait, what? Me? Why?"

"Jaxon, you've still gone through a horrible event just like Annika has. You may not have been the one assaulted, but you've been traumatized too."

My dad nods like everything she says is making sense.

"Jaxon," she says gently, "you've been sitting in the hospital for hours waiting for someone you don't even know, or to get information you are likely to never have gotten because of privacy laws. That's not normal behavior. It sounds a lot like survivor's guilt."

I wince. "No one came looking for her." I feel myself getting angry again as I try to explain myself, but I can't even wrap my own brain around why I need to be here so badly.

"I know. And I'm not judging you for it," she reassures. "I'm saying there is a lot for you to process, and it already seems like you're having a hard time. It wouldn't hurt to get some counseling to push through what you're feeling and what you've seen."

My dad squeezes my shoulder again, and I shrug him off, not wanting to hear that he agrees. "She's right, Jaxon. I really think you need to do this. Even if you don't do it for yourself, your mom and I worry about you."

I bite my lip and look at the floor. I don't like the idea of going to counseling. Nothing happened to me. But, dammit, I can also see their point.

"Can I think about it?" I ask.

"Of course," Pippa says. "I'll give them your name and number. You don't have to answer their call, but at least you'll know it's coming while you think about it."

"Okay."

"One more thing."

I look up at her. She has a strange look on her face that I don't understand, but it makes me question what's about to happen.

"Annika wants to meet you."

My eyebrows raise just slightly, masking how much surprise I actually feel. "She does?"

"She does. But only if it's okay with you."

"No. I mean yeah. I mean…" I close my eyes and let my overly tired brain pull itself back together. "I'd love to meet her. I think I'd feel a lot better if I could see that she's okay and not remember her the way I do…"

Every time my eyes close. But I don't tell them that part. They're already pushing this counseling thing without knowing the images that keep flashing through my mind.

When they both nod, though, I'm pretty sure they already know.

"Okay," Pippa says. "Well then, if you'll follow me, I'll take you back there. Mr. Hart, you'll need to wait out here for Jaxon. We're only allowing him to come back right now, and it's kind of an unusual situation to even allow that."

"Of course," he agrees.

"Actually, Dad, why don't you go find a hotel. Once I'm done here I'm going to head back to the dorm. There's no reason for you to stay when you have such a long drive ahead of you."

He narrows his eyes for a second, and I can tell he's thinking. "I do need to head home."

"It's 4:30 in the morning," I remind him.

"I know. But I'm wide awake. I might as well take advantage of it. If I make decent time, I can be home before the kids get out of school. Maybe even swing by the office."

"Or, you could go home early and surprise Mom by helping her clean the house."

His lips quirk up in a smile. "Or I could go home early and take a nap. But seriously, Jax, are you going to be okay here by yourself?"

"Yeah, Dad, I'll be fine." I wave him off, finding myself getting irritated again at his concern. Man, my emotions are going back and forth tonight. Maybe I'm just tired. "I'll let you know if something happens."

I turn to give him a hug, and as I'm holding him I say, "Thanks for coming."

"You're my son," he responds quietly in my ear. "Of course, I came when you needed me."

That right there is what I've been missing…knowing he loves me the same as he does Matty and Lucy. I don't know where that connection went, or if it's part of growing up, but I miss knowing without a doubt that I can lean on my dad for anything. That I'm everything he hoped I would be. I don't know how to get it back or if I'm even supposed to.

Pippa stands a respectful distance away as we say our goodbyes, my dad patting my cheek before walking his pajama-clad self through the sliding glass doors. Then I turn the opposite direction and follow her through a set of steel double doors down a long hallway.

"Just remember," she reminds me as we walk, "Annika may be a little skittish around you still. She's had a traumatic event, so I wouldn't try to touch her or hug her. You're really going to need to follow her lead. And don't be offended, but I will probably be in the room with you during your visit."

"Understood," I say, because I do understand. I understand why she wouldn't want to be in the same room with a strange man right now, and I have no problem being respectful of that.

Pippa stops in front of a gray door with a small window cut out. Looking through, we can't see into the room because of a curtain in the way. She knocks, opens the door, and sticks her head inside.

"Annika, Jaxon is with me. May we come in?"

I don't hear the response, but by the way she pushes the door open and enters, I assume the answer was yes. As we round the curtain, I see the girl. Only this time she's awake and sitting in a chair. She doesn't look half-dead, and I immediately breathe a sigh of relief.

"Annika, this is Jaxon," Pippa introduces us. "He's the man from the bar who found you. Jaxon, this is Annika."

If I had just walked into the room and didn't know the situation, I might have assumed Annika was one of the staff members here, being that she's wearing scrubs and doesn't appear fearful at all. The lack of shoes, however, is the dead giveaway.

"It's nice to meet you, Jaxon. Do you want to sit down?"

I'm surprised by the invitation to get close, so I slowly walk toward the chair she's gestured to, careful not to touch her. I wait for her to say something, but I don't expect what she says next.

"Pippa, it's okay. You don't have to stick around."

Pippa startles, looks at me, and then looks back at Annika. "Are you…are you sure? You don't want me to stay in the room?"

Annika lets out a humorless laugh. "This is the man who saved my life. He's probably the safest person for me to be with right now."

Wow. What a statement of trust on her part. I was hoping to see her looking better. I wasn't expecting to see the feisty side of her.

Pippa looks stunned for a minute but takes that as her cue. "Okay. I'll be outside while you two talk. Just let me know if you need anything." Then she turns to leave.

Once the door closes behind her, Annika turns and looks at me. "I'm tired of them babying me. It's really obnoxious."

Her words make me smile. She has no idea how much I can relate. I also can't help but admire her resilience. But just as quickly, her face turns stoic again.

"Jaxon, I don't know how to thank you."

I don't say anything for a moment as I try to figure out how to respond.

"I don't think there's really a reason to thank me," I finally get out. "I was doing what anybody would have done. But I have to say, you look much better than the last time I saw you."

She grimaces. "Yeah. I'm sure. I just got a glimpse of myself in the mirror, and it wasn't pretty."

"No, it's not that. You're beautiful." My eyes widen as I realize what I've said. It's not untrue. The timing is just terrible. "Oh god. I don't mean…I don't mean it like that. I just mean you just look….alive."

Tears well up in her eyes. "Like I said, I have you to thank for that."

We sit in silence for a few more minutes. It's not weird quiet though. It feels almost comfortable. I can tell she's still a little groggy, and I'm tired from lack of sleep. Still, I feel like we need to make conversation and not waste the time we have before Pippa and her overbearing ways come crashing in the room.

"So, uh, Pippa says you go to the university with me?"

Annika seems to snap back awake, clearing her throat before answering. "Yeah. I'm a sophomore. You?"

"Junior."

I open my mouth to ask another question when we hear the door open. We both glance up and see a nurse walking in the door. At least I assume she's a nurse. She's wearing the same outfit as Annika except she's wearing shoes and carrying paperwork.

"Guess who's almost ready for discharge?" the nurse sing-songs, and Annika flashes a quick, polite grin in her direction. "I know you don't have your purse on you, but do you happen to know what medical insurance you have? It shouldn't be hard to file with them."

Annika's eyes widen, and she almost looks fearful. "No!" she yells, realizing quickly how loud she was. Lowering her voice, she continues. "No insurance."

The nurse looks at her with question written all over her face. "You have insurance though, don't you?"

"Yes, but I don't want to file with it. I'd rather pay out of pocket."

"Annika, you do realize that's what insurance is for. So, it doesn't cost you thousands of dollars."

"No." Her voice is more forceful this time. "No. Insurance."

The nurse takes a deep breath and nods once. "Okay. No insurance. And you're sure you don't want me to call anyone for you?"

Annika shakes her head and the nurse presses her lips together, obviously not happy with Annika's answer. "Well then let me go grab my other forms and your discharge paperwork, and then we'll get you out of here. Sound good?"

Annika nods. "Thank you."

As she walks out, I ask the question I'm sure both the

nurse and I are wondering. "Why don't you want to file with your insurance? It's not my business, I'm just curious."

She bites her lip and resituates herself on the chair, her feet underneath her. "If I file, my dad will get the bill."

With those words, I have clarity.

"If your dad gets the bill, he starts asking questions about why you're in the hospital."

She nods. "And if it's an itemized bill, it'll give away why I'm here."

"You don't want him to know?"

She shakes her head. "Are you kidding? My dad would go ape shit. I'm the girl who took down Jimmy Fantoli with a knee to the groin in the tenth grade when he grabbed my ass in PE. I'm better than this."

"You were unconscious, Annika. You couldn't fight back."

Her whole body seems to deflate in front of me. "I know. But it'll break his heart. I can't do that to him."

I get it. I do. Earlier tonight, I tried to get my dad to understand I'm not the guy he thought I was, and watching his disappointment. I didn't want to explain that to him any more than she wants to explain this to her dad.

"I understand. But promise me when that bill comes in, if you need any help, you'll let me know. I have *a lot* of resources."

For the first time since walking in, I think I see a real smile on her face.

"Thanks. I really appreciate that. But I do have a different favor to ask you."

"Sure. Hit me."

"Like Stacy, that nurse, said, I left my purse in my roommate's car. I don't have my credit card or any cash. I hate to ask since you've done so much already, but if you're already going that way, can you possibly give me a ride?"

She looks almost embarrassed to have asked. Rubbing the back of my neck, I say, "You sure you want to get in the car with me? We'll be alone."

Her lips quirk to the side. "Right now, I feel safer with you than anyone else in this entire world."

Those words hit me like a punch to the gut. I like this girl. She's been through something horrible, but she's strong. She's stubborn. And I can already tell nothing is going to keep her down.

"Sure," I finally say. "As soon as they discharge you, your chariot awaits."

TEN

Annika

I wanted to walk to the exit, but apparently some stupid hospital policy says I must be pushed in a wheelchair upon discharge. It's hard to stay inconspicuous when you're being wheeled around like a patient, even if all your bruises and stitches are covered up. Still, I don't want to run the risk of someone I know seeing me like this.

Fortunately, Jaxon timed it just right, and by the time Stacy wheels me through the sliding glass doors, he drives up in a cherry red Toyota Corolla.

"Wow," I joke when he gets out of the car to open the passenger door. "You weren't kidding when you said my chariot would await. I always imagined it would be red."

He laughs, a rumbly chuckle that comes from deep within his chest. I like the sound. For whatever reason, it makes me feel like he's strong, and tough, and can protect me, which makes me feel more confident about my decision to get in this car.

Stacy helps me up and into the passenger seat. We say

our goodbyes and before I know it, Jaxon is climbing in on the driver's side.

"Buckle up," he instructs. "It'd be a shame for you to get through last night only to get seriously injured in a car accident."

I can't help but notice the grimace on his face as soon as the words are out of his mouth.

"Jaxon…"

"Yeah, sorry," he apologizes. "It's probably too soon to say stuff like that."

"No, Jaxon. That was actually kind of funny. Don't filter yourself around me. If something hurts my feelings or offends me, I'll tell you. But otherwise, just be you. I don't want anyone walking on eggshells."

I swear a look of admiration crosses his face when he glances over at me, but it's gone so fast I can't be sure.

"What dorm are we headed to anyway?"

"Anderson Hall, please," I respond as my seatbelt clicks together.

Settling into my seat, I realize my body is feeling groggy again. Dr. Thompson said it would take a few days for the effects of the drug to wear off. Now that the adrenaline of the last few hours is fading away, I really feel like I need a nap.

My chauffeur seems to notice when he remarks, "It's okay if you close your eyes. It's a twenty-minute drive, and you need the sleep."

"From what I hear, you need sleep too," I argue.

"Yeah, but if I sleep, we crash."

I laugh. "Good point."

Taking his advice, I lean my head against the window, watching the world whiz by. It all looks the same as it did yesterday. Nothing has changed. It's almost offensive; as if the entire world is disregarding my own personal hell.

Despite my life being turned upside down, everything else has kept on going like nothing is different. But for me, nothing will ever be the same.

Before I know it, Jaxon is calling my name.

"Annika. Wake up, Annika, we're here."

I blink my eyes open and realize I'd fallen asleep without even noticing.

"That drive was quicker than I thought it would be."

He chuckles and climbs out of the car, walking around the front. Before I can even get my door open, he's already helping me out.

"Thanks, but you don't have to walk me to my door. I'm perfectly capable…" I stop and groan.

"What?"

"I don't have a dorm key."

"Huh." He puts his hands on his hips as we look at each other trying to figure out what to do.

Sighing, I pitch the only answer I can come up with. "Can I borrow your phone, so I can call my roommate? Maybe we'll get lucky and she'll answer."

He hands over his device without a second thought. Lauren, however, obviously thinks about it before answering, since it takes me calling three times before she finally picks up with a groggy "Hello?"

"Lauren. Hey. Can you come let me in? My purse is in your car."

"Yeah, okay. Hold on."

She hangs up, and I'm praying she doesn't go right back to sleep. But sure enough, as Jaxon and I walk the few steps to get to the door, it swings open. As soon as Lauren sees Jaxon standing next to me, she goes from sleepy to wide awake.

"Hmm," she practically purrs. "I see someone had a good night."

I roll my eyes when she turns to walk back through the lobby, swaying her tiny little gymnast hips in her tiny little pajama shorts. There's not an ounce of cellulite on her. But I suppose that's what happens when you're a competitive gymnast and work out at least three hours a day.

Jaxon doesn't seem to notice as he walks next to me. "I hope it's okay that I'm walking you all the way to your room. I'd feel more comfortable making sure you get there all the way."

I bite my lip, trying not to smile as I keep following Lauren up the stairs. This is probably not the most ideal time to feel a sense of thrill at a guy looking after me, but I can't help it, so I'll just take it for what it is. Even if I never see him again.

"Where'd you get the fancy scrubs?" she asks when we get to the room and plops herself down on her bed.

I freeze as I realize I'm wearing completely differ-ent clothes. It never crossed my mind that she would ask where mine went. Before I can come up with an excuse, Jaxon's already ahead of me.

"I'm pre-med. I had some laying around."

My head whips over to look at him. "You are?"

Lauren makes another flirty sound. "I had no idea any-one on the football team was going to be a doctor."

"You're on the football team?" How did I not think to ask these questions before?

Lauren giggles. "You spent the night with him and you didn't know he was a pre-med football god? Must have been one hell of a night."

"I...I..."

"Third string doesn't exactly make me a football god," Jaxon interjects.

Lauren waves her hand dismissively at him. "You wear the uniform. It makes you a god."

"Yeah." He's obviously feeling uncomfortable with her flirting, which is making me feel bad. Or maybe he's just exhausted. Who knows. "Anyway, do you have a piece of paper?"

"Um…sure." I grab a stack of Post-it notes off my desk and a pen. He quickly uses it to jot something down and hands it back to me.

"There's my number. I know you don't have a replacement phone yet, but when you get one please use this. For anything." His eyes plead with me, and I can't help but feel like I made a friend in all of this.

I nod gratefully as he backs out the door.

"See you later, Annika. Nice to meet you, Lauren."

"Nice to meet you too," she says with a flirty wave of her fingers.

As soon as the door shuts behind me, her questions begin. "Why didn't you text me back last night? I was looking for you and you never responded."

"Yeah, um, sorry about that. I lost my phone."

She makes a face. "That sucks. But I'm glad you're okay. And I'm glad you ended up with that fine piece of ass."

My lips quirk into a small smile. Leave it to Lauren to jump to the best of conclusions.

"So, tell me all about it," Lauren demands, forgetting about the loss of my cell. "Was it good? Was he hung? How many orgasms did you have?"

"Lauren!" I admonish. "It wasn't like that."

She crosses her arms under her tiny chest and glances at Kiersten, like our snoring guest is the reason I'm tight-lipped. "She sleeps like the dead. Tell me everything before she wakes up."

And that's when the memories begin to assault me. The memories of what happened in the hospital. The memories of the camera between my legs. I close my eyes tightly, willing it all away, to no avail.

Suddenly, despite my exhaustion, the only thing I can think about is taking a shower and ridding myself of this filth. Grabbing the shower supplies off the shelf over my dresser, I continue to play it off, like the evening was much less life altering than it actually was.

"Forget it. You're not getting any information out of me."

Lauren huffs and climbs under her covers. "Fine. I'm going back to sleep. I'm glad you ended up with Jaxon though," she says through a yawn. "I hear he's one of the good ones."

Nodding, I don't say anything else in response. The only thing I can think about is showering.

I practically run down the hall to the community bathroom. Fortunately, no one else on my floor is awake because suddenly, everything is becoming more real, and it feels like I'm caving in on myself. I can hardly breathe, and my heart is pounding.

Frantically, I turn the shower on as hot as I can get it, which isn't scalding because of the uneven ratio of people to water heaters in this dorm. I wish it was scalding as I stand under the spray and begin cleaning every square inch of myself. I use double the amount of shampoo I normally do to get the lather as thick as I can, leaving the bubbles in my hair while I use my loofa to scrub myself over, and over and over, trying to scrub the filth and memories off me.

For the first time in my life, I shave all my pubic hair off until I'm completely bare, trying to get rid of any trace of whatever it was that was on me.

If I could, I'd scrub my insides, too, but I can't. So instead I get my outside as clean as possible.

Panic begins to overwhelm me when I realize that I'm naked and alone in a community bathroom. Yes, it's only women on our floor, but that doesn't keep the sudden terror I feel at bay.

Rinsing my hair of the shampoo and then conditioning as quickly as possible, I shut off the water and grab my towel, wrapping it around me as tightly as I can get it. Then I listen.

I listen for anything that sounds unusual. Anything that might give me an indicator of lurking danger. I know in my mind I'm being ridiculous, but the fight or flight feeling is so strong, I can't help it.

I thought I wanted out of that hospital. I thought I didn't want to shower with the doctors and nurses in the other room. I was wrong. I wish I had taken advantage of the safety in numbers while I was there, so I wouldn't feel this vulnerable now.

I'm pissed off at having this much fear. This is not who am I. Not who I want to be.

When I don't hear anyone in the bathroom with me, I relax just enough to throw my clothes on quickly and race out the door.

Pippa's words come back to me.

Your memories will come in waves. Your feelings will come in waves. Don't beat yourself up as you work your way through this. Whatever you feel is okay.

But it doesn't feel okay. Nothing about this feels okay. I just want to go to sleep and push it all away…sleep this whole nightmare away.

As I climb into bed, Lauren peels her eyes and takes in my outfit: baggy sweatpants and an oversized hoodie sweatshirt. "Aren't you going to get hot sleeping in that?"

Yes.

"No. It was really cold over there."

She thinks I'm talking about it being cold in Jaxon's dorm when really, I'm talking about the hospital. But she'll never know that as long as I can help it.

She shrugs and buries herself under her covers, me doing the same. Pulling the hoodie as far over my head as I can get it, I hide myself under my blankets, using them as protection from the outside world.

As sleep begins to take over, I realize my new reality is the two separate parts of my life…before last night and after last night. I'm only five minutes in, and the after is already proving to be harder than I expected.

ELEVEN

Jaxon

"Blue 52! Blue 52!"

My quarterback makes the call to switch the play, and I take a breath and get ready to launch off the line. I'm trying to concentrate, but Germaine has his eye on me. He's gunning for me. I can tell already.

"Hut, hut, HUT!"

The scramble begins behind me as I take off running. I don't get very far before Germaine catches up and blocks me from catching the ball. We jog to a stop as the whistle sounds and Coach starts yelling instructions. Thankfully, they aren't at me, despite not being at my best.

There is no way I'll be called to dress this weekend. Not with the shitty way I've been playing lately.

Germaine slaps my helmet, but with my lack of sleep, it feels more like a punch to the head.

"What's going on with you, Hart? Are you sick or something?" he asks as we make our way back to the line of scrimmage.

"Nah, man," I say as I roll out my right shoulder. I took a hit wrong yesterday, and it's still sore. Not sore enough to make a visit to the trainer. But one more issue to deal with. "I'm just tired is all. I gotta cut back on my time at night with the ladies." I waggle my eyebrows, but he ignores me.

"Don't bullshit me. You've been having fucking nightmares half the night for the last week." I stop walking. *I* knew I was having nightmares, but I didn't realize *he* knew that. "You need to get some sleep aid or rub some lavender on your feet at night or something… Where'd you go?" He spins around when he finally realizes I'm not beside him anymore.

I quickly catch up and try to play it all off. "Yeah, that's a good idea. I'll have to look into that."

"And buy me a fucking cup of coffee while you're at it. You're keeping me up at night," he adds, swatting me on the ass as I walk by, getting back in position.

"Red 71! Red 71! Hut, HUT!"

The quick snap throws me off my game this time, and I fall a full two seconds behind where I should be. So much so that Germaine intercepts the ball and takes off the other way. It should be easy to catch him, but I can't do it today.

"Fuck!" I bellow, getting really irritated at my inability to keep up.

"What the hell is wrong with you?" Steven Timen, one of the biggest douchebags on my team, yells at me. "Aren't you a fucking Hart? Isn't football in your blood? Stop bringing us down, man."

I get ready to bolt after him, all the anger and rage from the last week finally about to break free, but before I can, Germaine is in my face. "Don't listen to him, man. He's pissed that he got benched for this week's game because of grades." I take a deep breath, trying to control my anger. "He's just a dick who thinks being raised by the great

Jason Hart automatically means you're the next super star. That's not your dream, man. You're not a meathead like him. Let it go."

Looking him in the eyes, I nod once. Germaine doesn't say anything this time, just looks at me. He knows my issues with my dad better than anyone. Knows how much bullshit has sprung up over the years.

That's the great thing about having Heath Germaine as my roommate. He's my best friend and doesn't expect me to be anything I'm not. I help him study plays and know stats. He's a neat freak and keeps our room spotless.

The bad thing about having Heath Germaine as my roommate is he knows me almost too well...including my medical history, and I can see the concern for me building. Normally, it doesn't bother me. He's my best friend, and he doesn't make an issue out of it. But once my dad found out that he knew, he gave Germaine his phone number, with strict instructions to call any time, day or night, if I ever got sick. I was fucking mortified. Before I could tell Germaine to lose his number because I didn't need a fucking babysitter, he turned to my dad and said, "A buddy of mine had ALL in high school. I know what to look for." He never asked me about it again.

Even though he's never mentioned it, though, doesn't mean it's not in the back of his mind these days. I know him well enough to know he's wondering what a reoccurrence would look like and if he needs to make that all-important phone call now. Honestly, I don't know if I'd rather him think my health is at risk or to know that it's more likely my sanity falling apart.

I thought when I dropped Annika off, I wouldn't feel angry and upset. She's not dead. In fact, her injuries seemed pretty minor. I only spent a small amount of time with her, but she came off as strong and resilient. Hell, she kicked the social worker out of the room and had no qualms about getting into a car with me. Annika is fine.

But I'm not. I hate sleep because as soon as I doze off, the nightmares begin. Sometimes I relive that night over and over for hours. Sometimes it changes up and I'm too late, and Annika is dead. Sometimes I let my rage take over, and I kill her attacker in cold blood. Sometimes I can see her, but no matter how hard I try, I can't get to her. That's the worst version because when I can't get to her, I have to stand there and watch her be violated.

I never know what I'm going to see when I close my eyes, but it's never good. I tried going for a run before bed to exhaust myself, but it didn't work. So I stopped going to bed at all. Now, I stay up studying for as long as I physically can until I fall asleep with my head on my desk. Doesn't make a difference if I'm sitting up or lying down, though. The nightmares still come.

Somehow, I've made it through the last week of practices, but the longer I go without real sleep, the worse it's getting.

I shuffle into the locker room once we're finally dismissed. Everyone else jogged, knowing the last guy to make it to the showers is going to have his balls shrivel up from lack of hot water. I want to care, but I don't. I'm actually hoping a cold shower will do me some good. I have more studying to do, and I need something to wake me up before I go to the clinic and ask for a caffeine IV.

I barely make it through the doors when a deep voice calls my name.

"Hart! My office."

Germaine gives me a pointed look, and we both know Coach is calling me in because my practice has been off for days. If he's not even giving me time to strip down and shower off the funk, he's *really* not happy about my performance. No one wants to be in a closed room with an athlete before he's showered the body odor off. This must be really bad.

"Shut the door behind you," Coach Newsome instructs, tossing his clipboard on his desk.

As coaches go, Coach Newsome is tough but fair. When my dad first found out he was going to be my coach, he expressed approval in his training style and ability to pick a lineup. I'm not worried about him dropping the hammer unnecessarily. But reality is, I've been off for the last week. I'd be stupid not to be slightly concerned about what the repercussions are going to be. I worked hard to even get to third string, and I really don't want to be cut at this point. Not when I only have a couple more seasons left to play competitive football for the rest of my life.

"What's up, Coach?" I ask with more confidence than I actually feel.

He stands with his hands on his hips, not even bothering to have me sit down. "I got a call from the counseling department today."

Shit.

I rub a hand down my face. That's not at all what I was expecting him to say, and I think I'd rather be getting my ass chewed right now. I finally look at him, schooling my emotions. "Uh huh."

He looks around the room and breathes through his nose before saying anything else. When he finally speaks, it's clear he's concerned. "Why didn't you tell me, son?"

All I can do is stare at the floor while I try and put my answer into words, but what can I say? Because I didn't want him to know how ashamed I feel? Because I didn't want him to know that I'm not handling it as well as I thought I would? Because I'm still fucking angry at this guy, I look at every single person on campus, trying to decide if it's him so I can bash his face in before calling the cops?

I don't say any of that. Instead, I settle on, "Because it's not my story to tell, Sir. It's her story."

He nods once. "I can respect that, son, but you're part of that story. And from what I can see, you're not handling this all that well."

I can't deny it. I'm *not* doing well. But I sure as hell am not going to admit the truth either. This is something I need to deal with on my own. Without all these people looking over my shoulder, trying to get me to sing "Kumbaya."

When he realizes I'm not going to reply, he gets more forceful. "I expect you to answer their call, Hart. And I expect you to go to that appointment. I have more respect for you than for most of the guys on that field, and I like you being on this team. But you're starting to crumble, and I'm not going to run the risk of you getting injured because you think you're too much of a man to get the help you need."

"What? What do you mean—?"

"Don't even try, son," he interrupts, not buying my bullshit. "Your push off is too slow. You're practically jogging down the field. And don't get me started on how exhausted you look. Make. The. Appointment," he commands, leaving no room for misunderstanding.

Nostrils flaring and jaw tight, I nod in resignation, because I'm not getting out of this, no matter how much I don't want to talk to a shrink. Coach will follow up to make sure I go, and if I don't, well, I guess he can't really bench me since I'm not playing anyway. But he could kick me off the team, and I don't want that.

"Yes sir," I say through clenched teeth.

"Good. Get out of here. You probably have a voicemail to answer, and you need to take a fucking nap."

By the time I get back in the locker room and peel off

my sweaty pads, everyone else is done showering. My teammates lob playful insults my way about how small my balls are about to be and how they might call me "Jackie" since my penis is going to shrivel into a vagina. I laugh with them halfheartedly, my mind still not really into all of this.

Germaine is the only one who looks at me with real question in his eyes. I nod that I'm fine and thankfully he lets it go. I'm sure he'll interrogate me later, but for now, I can keep going through the motions.

After taking the world's quickest shower, I finally grab my phone out of my locker. I have one missed call and a voicemail. I don't recognize the number, but it's definitely from one of the campus administration offices. Coach wasn't kidding when he said I could expect a phone call soon.

I could return it right away, but I don't. I'm intent on putting this off as long as I can get away with. Instead, a text catches my eye. I don't recognize that number either. Opening it, it's the last thing I expected to see, but the only thing I was hoping for all week.

Hi. This is Annika. I finally got my phone replaced. Here's my number. This may sound forward, and there's no pressure, but would you like to meet up for coffee?

I blow out a relieved breath then look around, making sure no one saw my reaction. Quickly typing out a response, I suggest a time and place. I want to meet up with her more than anything.

Coffee and Annika are the only two things that might be able to get me through this hell I'm stuck in.

TWELVE

Keeping my head down, I cross the main quad to the coffee shop. Kampus Koffee is a staple for college life. Most students spend at least a few hours here every week. If they aren't standing in line to get a shot of caffeine, it's because they have a nice variety of couches to lounge on and tables to study at. It's also open later than the cafeteria and the snack bar. To top it off, they have the most amazing pastries. Perfect for a late-night carb load if you don't have a car to leave campus.

But getting here has been harder than I anticipated. I can't stop looking over my shoulder every time I hear someone behind me. Whenever I hear footsteps, I have to see who is behind me. Is he coming for me? Or is someone late for class and hoofing it?

I hate that I feel unsafe walking across campus. I've never felt this way before. But in the last week, it seems to be getting worse. I can't seem to shake the fear. It's to the point now where I only shower every couple of days, not because I don't need it. But because I can't. The thought of undressing in a public bathroom is damn near debilitating. Hell, I'm not sure I'd be able to get naked in a private bathroom with the doors locked and a panic alarm. It's so bad that the last time I had to wash my hair, I finally gave up the fight and showered in my clothes, which of course made me feel even more humiliated. And then angry for feeling humiliated.

I'm stronger than this. I'm more logical than this. I'm not a weak person. I was raised to be a fighter, but dammit, I feel like I'm losing this battle. I don't even remember what happened that night, but for some reason, I'm still shaken all the way to my core.

I'm sure part of my emotional state is my lack of sleep. Whenever I close my eyes, I have nightmares. Sometimes, it's that Ron guy following me out of the club. When I look at him, he smiles, and the wider he smiles the more distorted his face becomes, until finally I'm looking into the eyes of the devil himself.

Then there's the version of me being assaulted over and over. I'm not unconscious this time, I'm awake and aware. I feel every touch and every whisper of his breath. It's a continual loop until I finally wake up, not knowing if those are actual memories or my imagination at play.

And sometimes I see Jaxon in the distance trying to rescue me. But the more he runs and tries to get to me, the farther away he gets. All the while, I hear a sinister laugh in my ear as Jaxon gets smaller and smaller before he disappears completely.

To say I'm not doing well is an understatement. And if Jaxon is as observant as he was last time I saw him, he's going to pick up on it, which I don't want him to do. I don't want anyone to know.

Swinging the door open to the coffee shop, the bell

above me rings. Not that anyone can hear it. The place is packed. Glancing around the room, I see Jaxon sitting in the corner, playing on his phone. As I wait in line, I take the chance to get a good look at him.

He's not big for a football player. In fact, he's not big for any kind of athlete. His dark hair is cut short enough to run his fingers through it, but not long enough to be in his face. He rubs the back of his neck as he reads something on his phone. He doesn't have an imposing presence. He just looks like every other guy on campus. Yet for some reason, my whole body relaxes when I see him. It's almost an automatic response. Like one of Pavlov's dogs that were trained to associate food with the sounds of a bell. I associate safety with him.

"A salted caramel mocha, please. Medium." The barista writes my name on a cup before taking my money and moving my order down the line. It takes a few more minutes to get my drink, and I see Jaxon look up a couple more times, but he doesn't notice me. Why would he? The giant hoodie sweatshirt and baggy sweatpants I'm wearing are designed to keep me as invisible as possible. A fact I'm proud to remember from last year's psych class, but not proud to be living.

Lauren keeps harassing me to go to this on-campus clinic because I won't get dressed in anything other than the comfiest clothes I can find in my drawers. She's sure I have the flu. I got so sick of her nagging, one day when I came back from class, I finally lied and told her I went and sure enough, I was positive for influenza. I don't know what she thinks the symptoms actually look like since I had no fever, no body aches, and no vomiting. But I guess considering I've been lethargic lately and I have huge dark circles under my eyes, I can pass for someone with a serious illness. The room carries the overwhelming odor of

Lysol now from her "disinfecting."

"Hi," I say as I walk up to the table. He looks up, almost startled, and it takes a full second before he recognizes me. When he does, he immediately stands up.

"Hey, Annika. Hi." He reaches to give me a hug, but thinks better of it and backs away. "How are you?"

"I'm good," I respond, knowing I'm not telling the truth, but right now I'd rather pretend everything is fine.

"I'm glad you texted me. Have a seat." He gestures to the chair across the table from him and we sit down.

"I'm sorry it took a while to text you," I say as I get settled in my seat. "Lauren and I have opposite schedules, so I had to wait until she had some free time for her to take me to get a new phone since she has the car."

"No, it's okay," he reassures me with a smile. "I'm just glad you got a new one. And I'm glad you used my number. I've been worried about you."

He has?

"You have?"

"Yeah." He blows out a breath like he's finally able to relax too. I want to know why, what is he feeling? But I know where that conversation will lead, and I don't want to talk about it. Not yet.

Instead, I take a sip of my coffee and stick to a safer topic. "How is practice going? Ready for the game this weekend?"

He chuckles. "Uh, no."

"No?"

"Third string players rarely get a chance to suit up. And after my shitty practices this week, I'm sure I won't get called up."

I can't conceal my surprise. "Third string?"

He looks a little sheepish before he answers. "Yeah, I'm on the practice squad."

"But," I say, confused, "I thought it was only red-shirted freshman on the practice squad."

He blushes this time, and I feel bad that I put him on the spot. I didn't mean to make him feel lesser than, I've just never heard of a junior not being at least second string.

"Yeah well. I'm not really very good."

"No, I'm sure you're good," I backpedal. "You wouldn't be on the team if you weren't."

"Not really. I tell myself they keep me around because I work hard, and I like what I do. But mostly they keep me around because I have a knack for remembering statistics."

"What do you mean?"

He shifts in his seat and stretches his legs out, obviously gauging my reaction to this information. I'm sure he's used to girls who are no longer interested in him because he's not one of the "good" players. But that's not me. I love the game, not the players. Always have. And besides, that's not why I'm here. These days, I have more important things to worry about than how "important" the guy I'm having coffee with is. Like keeping my own sanity.

When he's finally satisfied I'm not going to run screaming, he explains. "I don't know if it's like a photographic memory or something, but I can remember a ridiculous amount of useless trivia facts. That includes just about everything there is to know about football. Yes, I'm third string, but part of my job is helping guys like my roommate…you know Heath Germaine?"

I nod my head. "Starting linebacker, right?"

"Yeah, that's him. He's my roommate. Anyway, I started following the opposing team's lineup and watching highlights of their plays, including their stats each week. I would make sure to tell Germaine as much information as he could absorb to help prepare him. When the coaches found out I was doing it, and it was working, they asked me to help out several of my teammates."

My eyes widen. "That is the coolest thing I have ever heard."

He looks taken aback at my words. "Really?"

"Yeah," which sounds more like "duh" as I say it. "Any meathead can throw the pigskin around. But only the really, really talented know how to put the bits and pieces of information together to create an actual strategy. You're like the next Peter Brand," I say excitedly, referring to the mathematical genius who helped change the way baseball teams are stacked.

Jaxon sits up and looks at me again. I can't tell if he's proud or embarrassed by my assessment, but I think he likes that I get it. I think he likes that I appreciate his talent. And it is a seriously cool talent.

"Well, yeah. I love the sport, ya know?" he continues. "Ever since I was a kid, I knew everything there was to know about football. It became me and my dad's "thing." When he was on the road, he'd call me just to ask who he was up against in the next game and how it was looking for him. I always knew the answer, so it became like a game to see if he could stump me. He never could." I see a flash of what looks like sadness cross his face, but it's gone quickly, making me question if it was really there.

Instead, I focus on what he told me, furrowing my eyebrows in confusion. "Wait, I don't understand. When your dad was on the road?"

"Yeah. He's retired from the pros now. My dad is Jason Hart. You've probably heard of him."

It takes about one second before my jaw drops. "Holy. Shit. Your dad was only the best defensive lineman in the history of the game! He was fucking amazing! I mean, he wasn't a Steeler"—an unexpected laugh bursts out of Jaxon—"but I try not to hold that against him, because he was amazing."

"Hold on." Jaxon holds his hands up to stop my rant. "Back up. We're in Texas. You're not a Chaps fan?"

I scoff. "Never! Steelers all the way, baby. I bleed black and yellow."

Jaxon throws his head back and laughs again, and I smile back at him, glad to have made up for my faux pas a few minutes ago and make him feel comfortable again.

"I can't believe you said that. My dad is going to get a kick of it."

"Why would your dad care?" I ask with a smile as I bring the now lukewarm coffee to my lips again.

"My dad was at the hospital…" His face falls, and I know I'm mirroring his expression.

It feels like a slap in the face when the realization hits me. It doesn't matter how much football we talk or if we talk about school or classes or life goals. The fact is, the only reason we know each other is because of a horrible night in both of our lives.

Jaxon looks at me, unsure how to continue, so I help him out.

"Your dad came up to the hospital too?"

Jaxon swallows hard before answering. "Yeah. I called and told him what had happened. He was in town that night, so he met me there and waited with me."

"The whole time?" I ask incredulously.

Part of me is already mortified that Jaxon was there for so long. Now that's multiplied, knowing his dad was there too.

But another small part of me can't help but want to fangirl a little over the fact that *Jason Hart* came to the hospital when I was there. It's a really weird mix of emotions and confuses me more.

"Yeah, my parents are great," Jaxon continues. "He

and my mom didn't want me to be alone so he jumped in the car before changing out of his pajamas," he adds with a chuckle. "When we finally knew you were awake and okay, he took off for home."

"Oh." I glance down at my cup, still trying to figure out how to process all of this. I finally say the only thing that seems right in this moment. "Tell him I said thank you."

"I will. And since we're on the subject…"

I grimace because this is the one thing I don't want to talk about. And yet, he's the only person in the world I *can* talk to about it, so I almost feel like I should. Even if it's only to feel a sense of camaraderie with someone else.

He leans forward and really looks at me. "How are you?"

"I'm okay," I respond brightly, though I swear he can see right through me.

"No, Annika." He shakes his head. "I don't want to know what you're telling people. I want to know how you really are. Because I'm gonna level with you. I'm not doing good."

I take another hard look at him, and I can tell he hasn't slept in days. He's got dark circles under his red-rimmed eyes. There's no telling how many cups of coffee he's had today. His cheeks are stubbled like he forgot to shave. His hair, while cut short, looks like he hasn't done anything except continually run his fingers through it. If I had been more observant and wasn't in my own self-preserving bubble, I may have noticed before now. He's right. He's not doing okay.

"I can't sleep," he says quietly. "Every time I close my eyes, I see that night again and again and again, and I can't save you. It's freaking me out, and I don't know what to do. I guess I'm hoping that if you're doing well, maybe I'll be able to let it go and do better too."

Weighing my options, I look at him again. I really want to tell him I'm fine. I really want to make him feel like he can let it go. But the selfish part of me can't do that. The selfish part of me needs someone to know I'm not okay either. The selfish part of me really believes misery loves company, and this man in front of me is the only one who will understand my misery. So, I say the only thing I can.

"I'm not doing well either."

If the slump of his shoulders is an indicator, he doesn't like that answer, even though it's the truth.

"I don't sleep at night, but when I do, I dream constantly," I begin. "I only shower when necessary, because it's a community bathroom and the idea of…" I squeeze my eyes tight, not able to finish the sentence. Even saying the words out loud makes me uncomfortable. "I just can't do it. I don't know how to get over this or even how to get through it. Right now, I feel like I'm only going through the motions."

"That's it," he adds. "I feel like I'm going through the motions, but I'm not really getting anywhere."

I nod in understanding.

His finger circles the rim of his cup absentmindedly as we tiptoe our way through this conversation. "Did you get a call from the dreaded counselor yet?"

HIs playful tone makes me laugh a bit. "I did. And I set up an appointment with a lovely woman named Neisa. I'll see her next week. You?"

He smirks. "Not only did I get a phone call and make an appointment with a lovely man named Harold"—the way he makes Harold sound like a pretentious old British man makes me giggle—"but the counseling department called my coach to get him on my case."

I gasp. "Did they tell him what happened?" I feel like I can't breathe. I didn't want to tell anyone. I didn't want anyone to know. Why is the counseling department making phone calls?

"They didn't tell him your name. I wasn't happy about it myself, but that's part of the deal when you're a football player, ya know? It doesn't matter I'm only on the practice squad. I still have to do all the physicals. Even the mental ones."

"I know," I say, feeling panicky by trying desperately not to show it. "It kind of sucks that they outed you like that."

My hand shakes as I pick up my coffee cup. I try to hide it, but I know Jaxon notices. His eyes whip up to mine, and I can tell he knows exactly what I'm thinking.

"I didn't tell him, Annika," he says reassuringly. "I didn't tell him your name or anything about you. Neither did Harold. I specifically asked him that question. My coach doesn't know. No one knows."

I smile sadly at him, trying to relax, but crossing my arms over my body, trying to shrink just a little instead. "I'll be ready someday, maybe, but not yet. Ya know?"

"Yeah." He nods. "Believe me, I know."

We sit in comfortable silence for a few minutes, neither of us sure what else to say. At first, it was kind of nice to just sit with him. At this point, if the only way I can feel relaxed is to sit for a few minutes in a weird coffee shop art deco chair, I'll take it.

But as Jaxon begins playing on his phone, it doesn't feel comfortable anymore. We're not on a date. We're not even really friends. Maybe this is his way of saying he wants me to leave. Before I can ask, he finds what he was looking for.

"I knew it. Seven o'clock Sunday. Did you know the Steelers are playing?"

I nod. "Of course, I knew. I'm a die-hard fan."

"Well then, you're in luck." He turns his phone around to show me the ad he's apparently been searching for. "Buck's Sports Bar has NFL Sunday Ticket and are going to be televising it. So," he continues, clicking his phone off, "wanna go with me? We're pretty pathetic lately, and maybe it'll do us some good to watch some football and get out in the world again."

My body tenses at the thought of his proposal. Two weeks ago, if he would have invited me to watch a game, I would have jumped at the chance. He's good-looking, smart, kind, and motivated. But now…now I'm not sure. The last time I went to a bar my entire life changed.

Like he can read my thoughts, he says, "We don't have to drink any alcohol. Hell, you can sneak in a six pack of bottled water in your purse."

"I don't carry purses unless my roommate forces one on me. I'm not girly enough."

He smirks. If that's my only reason for declining, he's not going to make this easy to get out of. "Then we'll have to sneak them in under our clothes."

As much as I'm hesitating, the fact that he understands what my concerns are without even having to say it *and* is willing to humor me, makes me want to go. I need to do this. I need to go out. I need to go out with a man. Even if it's not a date, it's a step to taking back control of my life.

"Yeah," I finally agree. "I'll go with you. If nothing else, it'll force me to shower and brush my hair. I'm sure my roommate will be happy to see I'm coming back from the edges of death for once."

He chuckles lightly. "For what it's worth, I've seen you on the edge of death, and you look way better than that."

I bust out laughing as his face turns flaming red when he realizes what he said.

"I'm sorry," he apologizes quickly. "I've always been

told the filter between what I'm thinking and what I say doesn't always work right."

I giggle again, glad that I haven't lost my weird sense of humor in this nightmare. "For anyone else, it might've been too soon. But coming from you, somehow it was funny."

He smiles and takes a drink of his coffee. We spend the next hour talking about mundane things that have nothing to do with anything. And yet it's everything we need right now.

THIRTEEN
Jaxon

I didn't mean to put her on the spot when I invited her out, but from the look in her eyes when I asked, that's how she felt. I couldn't help myself, though. Somewhere in the middle of that conversation, I realized we're the only two people who know exactly what happened that night. We're the only two people who are struggling with what we say and don't say, and if we're going to get through this, we're going to have to lean on each other.

Underneath all her nerves, anxiety, and baggy clothes, I could see anger simmering. I could see feistiness that was begging to come out. It still is. And I know if we can help hold each other up, she'll be able to come out stronger on the other side. We both will.

Plus—and I know it's the selfish part of me talking—I like her. There's something about Annika that calls to me. I could wax poetic and say she's like a siren calling to me in the night or some shit like that. But it's the truth. It has nothing to do with how beautiful she is, and she really is beautiful. Even with her hair pulled up high on her head and dark circles under her eyes, she's still a knockout of the All-American variety.

But that's not the main reason I like her. Nope. It's her strength and her resilience. She's surprised me at every turn. I don't know many people who could maintain a sense of humor under these circumstances. Hell, I don't know a lot of people who wouldn't just drop out of school and hide away. But she's not. She has determination and drive. And even if what's happening between us ends up being nothing more than friendship, even if this is nothing more than a mini support group, I want to get to know her better. I *need* to know her better.

Leaning against the red brick wall outside Buck's, I scan the crowd as I wait for her. Buck's is right on the edge of campus within walking distance of the dorms. I was glad to see they had the game on tonight because this is the perfect place to meet up. It's close enough to campus that Annika doesn't have to find a ride. But I have to remember it's far enough away from her dorm that when the game is over and it's dark out, I need to walk her back to her room. I don't mind. I hope she still feels comfortable with me after tonight.

I have no expectations, and if she changes her mind about hanging out with me, I can respect that too. I'm trying my damndest to be sensitive to however she feels, for as long as she feels it. Because dammit, I'm going need some grace too.

She's late. My watch says 7:05. Just when I think she's not going to show, I look up and see her coming around the corner.

For the first time, I'm seeing her with her hair down. She's even more beautiful with her long, straight brown hair fluttering in the slight breeze. She not wearing a stitch of makeup, and yet, those dark lashes make her eyes look big. And her pink lips don't need any color beyond what's naturally already there.

"Hey." I flash a wide grin her direction as I meet her at the door. "I was wondering if you were going to show."

Her cheeks blush as she admits, "It takes a few minutes to mentally prepare myself for showering. I didn't plan far enough in advance, I guess." I refuse to react to her admission. I don't want her to feel embarrassed or like I'm shocked. And I sure as hell don't want her to feel like I'm pitying her. Somehow, I know she'd hate that. Fortunately, it seems to work as she adds, "Plus I didn't want to come with wet hair. You should feel special. I don't use a blow dryer for just anyone."

Her wit is back, and it makes me smile. "Well thank you. I'll make sure to compliment your hair several times tonight to make it worth your while."

"A true gentleman," she says, smiling up at me playfully. We step through the doors and into the building. It's not a huge room, but it's big enough to have several flat screens around the room, a bar that spans the entire length of the place, and booths lining all the walls with tables scattered in between. "Do you come to Buck's often?" Her nose crinkles up like she smelled something bad. "Wow. That sounded like a bad pick-up line."

"That's because it *was* a bad pick-up line," I joke. "Thank goodness we already made plans to meet. That could've been awkward."

"It really could." We look around for a table and spot an open booth in the corner that we head toward automatically. "But for real, I come here to watch games all the time. Why have I never seen you here?"

I shrug. "One of my teammates has Sunday Ticket, and we make a party out of it at his place. Especially if there's an alumnus playing."

"Oh, I can only imagine the trash talk that happens."

She has us pegged. "You have no idea. It can get downright nasty. Honestly, I think I'd rather be here most times."

After we slide onto the red vinyl benches facing each other, a waitress shows up almost immediately. She's dressed in the normal game night attire: short shorts and a flannel button-up with one too many buttons open and tied at the waist to show a little skin and make bigger tips. Normally I might be attracted to her, but not tonight. Tonight, I don't even give her a second glance.

"What can I get y'all?" The squeaky baby doll voice that comes out of her is another good reason why I will *never* give her a second glance. "We got two-dollar drafts. You interested?"

"You have Shiner on tap?" I ask, trying not to poke my finger in my ear to block out the noise. Annika tries to stifle her giggle at my reaction.

The waitress never even notices, too busy tossing our napkins on the table. "Sure do. One Shiner or two?"

I look over at Annika, and she's wearing that expression again. I'm starting to figure out it means she's fighting her instincts to run screaming. I consider grabbing her hand and saying something reassuring, but she doesn't need me babying her. She doesn't want that. If she kicked the social worker out of her room to talk to me alone because Pippa was too overbearing, it's more likely she wants to power through this one on her own. So I let her.

"Um, I'll just take a water please."

"One water, one Shiner coming right up."

She walks away and for a fleeting second, I pray she doesn't return if I have to listen to that voice all night. But that second ends quickly and my concern switches back to Annika. I know having an open drink, even if it's just water makes her uncomfortable, so I'm surprised to see a gleam in her eye.

As she smirks, she reaches down into the front pocket of her hoodie and pulls out a bottle of water. I laugh at her victorious smile.

"Stealth mode," she says proudly. "Even without a purse."

"I'm impressed." I don't tell her it's not because she snuck in a contraband, but because she's still smiling.

The next couple hours are spent sharing a plate of loaded nachos, fried pickles, and some mozzarella sticks while we argue over the game. She's team Steelers all the way, which I'm trying not to hold against her, even though I'm pushing for the Broncos.

"Anyone can beat that asshole quarterback, Tim McGovern."

"What do you mean asshole quarterback?" Annika exclaims, throwing a broken chip in my general vicinity, missing me when I duck. "He has the best completion percentage in the league right now. And the lowest number of interceptions."

"Yeah," I scoff, "because he has a good offensive live, not because he has any actual talent."

She gapes at me. "I can't believe you just said that," she whispers harshly.

"What? It's true. Look at how many interceptions he threw before they got Randy Malone. Now that guy, he's pretty amazing, and he's what makes Tim look good."

Annika shakes her head a look of disappointment on her face. "I can't believe you would say that. You, the mathematical genius."

"Trivia genius," I correct.

"After all these years of memorizing, how can you say he's not one of the greats?"

I snort a laugh. "Being one of the greats means you can lead a team to victory even if that team sucks donkey balls. As much as it pains me to say it"—I rub a hand over my chest like I'm hurting—"the Steelers don't suck donkey balls this season."

"See? We do agree on that," she says happily. "The Steelers are going all the way this year."

I look at her with disgust. "Unfortunately, I agree with you."

"You do?"

"Yes. But I will never agree that Tim McGovern is one of the greats."

"Fair enough," she says with a shrug as she finishes eating her nacho and pulls the water bottle out of her lap.

"How'd you become such a big football fan?" Her knowledge of games and players is impressive. And not because of her gender. I might have to invite her to my fantasy football league. I may have met my match, and it sure would make it more fun to have a worthy opponent.

She swallows her water and crushes the empty bottle, dropping it on the pile of dirty napkins we've accumulated since we've been here.

"Football is huge in my family. My dad and brother and I are obsessed. You should see my dad's tailgating setup."

My eyebrows rise. She notices and points at me.

"That's the expression we get whenever we drive into the parking lot with his trailer and mobile grilling station hitched to the back of the truck. At first, security didn't want to let him use it. Said it was a hazard because it was too big. And then he gave them some brisket."

I laugh. "Let me guess…he won them over with his secret recipe."

"Passed down for three generations," she says with a laugh. "I'm gonna jump to the conclusion you don't get to do a lot of tailgating, being that you have box seats and all."

I can feel the blush creep up my face. She's right. There's no way my family or I could get away with hanging out in the parking lot of the stadium. "Nah. But we do get the best hot dogs in the house."

She grins back and me, licking her lips of the grease from our food. Wiping her hands on a napkin, she completely changes subjects on me. "Why'd you decide to get into medicine?"

Well, that was a giant topic leap. I have nothing to hide, but I brace myself for her reaction. "I had cancer as a kid." She stops chewing with the bottle halfway to her mouth. "I'm fine now, I'm considered 'cured.' But those experiences kind of shaped me, ya know?" She nods and gets back to eating. "Have you heard of the Heart to Hart Foundation?"

She thinks while she finished chewing and swallowing. "Now that you say that, I have heard of it. But I didn't put it together with your name."

I like that she isn't overreacting to this conversation. Most people want to ask all kinds of annoying, prying questions, not only about my previous illness but the celebrities I've met. I like that she's much more reserved.

"My pediatric oncologist is on the board of directors. He's a great guy and made my experience much more comfortable. I've always wanted to grow up and be like him."

"A good doctor can make all the difference in the world." I see a flash of what is probably a memory on her face. She tamps it down quickly, but not before I catch it. I can't help but hope her doctor was one of the good ones and made her feel comfortable. Maybe I'll ask her someday, but for now, we'll stick with safer topics Like cancer. Ironic. "So it's because of him you want to be a doctor?"

I shrug. "Him. My dad. My desire to help people. I spend my time in practice helping the other players get better using statistical data. I figure maybe I can use this weird gift of mine to do some good in the world."

She wipes her mouth with a napkin and leans forward, clasping her hands together and leaning on the table. "I think that's really admirable. Most guys in your position would follow right in their father's footsteps and use their connections to be an agent or manager or something. But to go out on a limb and do your own thing, that's really cool."

She gets it. I like that she gets it. I'm not my dad. I'm not his foundation. I'm me. I have my own dreams and goals. She has no idea how badly I needed to hear someone say it.

"What about you?" I ask, changing the subject. "What's your major?"

"Double major in kinesiology and physical therapy."

"Really?"

"Yep. I wanna be a trainer. Ideally"—she looks up at me and I can see it before she says it—"for the Steelers."

"No," I groan. "Who would want to touch those guys in the locker room?"

She smiles at my quip. "It's not about touching them. It's about working their muscles and joints, so they can be the best players they can be. It's about making sure they're in tip-top shape and are well-oiled machines. I wanna help with that. I'll probably never darken the doorway of that locker room, but it's still my dream."

"How come I haven't seen you on the field before?"

"You have to be a junior to get into the training program. You'll probably see me there next year. And maybe even in some classes, now that you've changed your major."

"I didn't even think about that; yeah, I'm sure some will overlap."

Our conversation is cut short when the commercial break ends, and the final quarter begins. We spend the next forty-five minutes watching the Steelers beat up the Broncos, much to her delight and my dismay.

When the game is over, it's dark out, and she has no hesitation when I offer to walk her home. The conversation continues with us talking about my siblings, her dad, and Lauren's last gymnastics meet when she fell on the beam and ended up with a bruise from the inside of her knee all the way to her groin. I've had big bruises before, but I admit when she showed me the picture, I've never had anything like that before.

We have a lot in common, and she makes me laugh. I still feel protective over her, but now, I want to keep getting to know her.

Lauren isn't there when we get to the dorm, leaving Annika all alone. She lets out a yawn, and I know I feel the same way. There's only so many nights without sleep a person can get. I know I should leave, but frankly, I don't want to leave her behind.

"I had a really good time," I say, trying to find a polite way to make my exit.

"Me too. You were right. I needed to get out and back amongst the people. I think next time will be easier."

"You're really impressive, you know that, Annika?"

She tilts her head in question. "Really?"

"I've never met anyone as strong as you. Anyone who refuses to be beaten down and takes life by the horns and makes it her bitch."

"I don't feel as strong as you're making me sound," she admits sadly. "I know it's going to take time, but I guess I need to fake it till I make it, right?"

"I need to learn how to fake it better."

"It sucks to be afraid all of the time, to not even be able to drink water at a bar. But more than anything, I'm pissed off."

I take a step closer to her. She doesn't even flinch. "Good. Be angry. Stay angry for as long as you need, until you feel like you've pushed through the hard parts. Coach always says to let your anger fuel you to be the best you can be."

"He sounds like a good motivational speaker." She yawns again, and I take that as my cue. But before I can head out, she stops me, putting her hand on my arm. The look on her face is almost pleading.

"This is gonna sound really strange, but the only time I seem to relax is when you're around." I understand exactly what she's talking about. "I know this sounds really forward, but I'm so tired." Her eyes close and her head drops in defeat. "Would you please stay the night with me? Maybe I'll sleep better if you're here."

My eyebrows quirk up, and she slaps my arm playfully. "Not for that."

"No, I know," I say with a laugh. "Just for sleep."

"Yeah. Maybe you being here will help me relax enough to sleep. And I think maybe you'll be able to sleep too."

I know I should walk out that door and tell her it's not a good idea, but she's right. Every part of me wants to stay, to make sure she's okay. Hopefully I'll be able to sleep as well.

She sits down on the bed and takes off her shoes. I follow her lead and toe mine off as well. Stripping myself of my sweatshirt, leaving just a white T-shirt underneath, I meet her at the bed.

Unsurprisingly, she doesn't take her big hoodie off at

all.

It takes some time to situate ourselves on the bed. We're both unsure of how much touch will make us uncomfortable, but it's inescapable because dorm beds are not big at all. Finally, after some maneuvering, we're lying comfortably, facing each other, her hands under her cheeks.

"Get some rest," I say as her lids are already getting heavy. "And Annika?"

"Hmm?" she mumbles.

"If you end up working for the Steelers, this friendship is over."

The sound of her light chuckle is the last thing I hear before drifting into the best sleep I've had in a week.

FOURTEEN
Annika

As I slowly come to, I realize for the first time in over a week, I slept through the night. No dreams. No nightmares. I didn't even hear Lauren come home.

I'm warm and comfortable. And I'm listening to the sound of a heartbeat in my ear.

My eyes blink open, but I don't dare move as the memories of last night come back.

I remember asking Jaxon to spend the night and him saying yes. He stayed. Jaxon stayed.

What I don't remember though, is how we ended up in a tangled mess of arms and legs. Not that I'm complaining. He feels solid underneath me, and as long as he doesn't know I'm awake, I could relax right back to sleep

"Good morning."

Busted.

I begin to move off of him, but before I can go anywhere he holds me tighter.

"Don't go yet." His voice sounds groggy and gravely.

I like it.

Without hesitation, I snuggle right back into him. "How'd you sleep?" I whisper.

"I don't know. I think I must still be dreaming." I bite back a smile at his answer, not just glad we both slept, but glad he doesn't regret staying.

A few minutes later, we're both more awake. As he stretches, I move off him, backing myself closer to the wall allowing him to roll over and resituate himself back on the bed. Neither of us is quite ready to get up yet, and somehow, in all the moving around, we end up face to face.

"Hi," he whispers, his brown eyes looking right into mine.

"Hi," I say back.

"What are you thinking about?"

I clap my hand over my mouth. "Morning breath."

He tries to hide a smile, but isn't very successful. "Does my breath smell that bad?"

"Actually, no. Does mine?"

"I don't know. My nose it stuffed."

I pinch his rib at the quip, making him laugh, still no odor to be detected. He pulls me closer to him and kisses me on the forehead. And suddenly, the sexual tension moves up a notch.

Jaxon licks his lips and looks down at mine, and I know exactly what he's thinking. It's what I'm thinking too. I really want to kiss him.

I'm attracted to this man which is strange under these circumstances. But he's so much more than the guy who saved my life. He's funny and smart and protective. I'm not sure if I have a hero's crush or if he really is that wonderful. Either way, I don't care right now. Right now, I just want him to lean in closer.

As if he can read my mind, he leans in slowly. Centimeter by centimeter until our noses are almost touching, and that's when the door flies open, and Lauren comes barreling in.

"Oh good. I see the love birds are finally awake." She's wrapped in her pink bathrobe, a towel on her head, smelling like her fruity body wash.

Rolling over to look at her, I spoon right back into Jaxon, who buries his head into my hair and wraps his arm around my waist.

"Good morning, Lauren. I didn't hear you come in last night."

"That's because the two of you were sleeping soundly." She drops the towel and begins combing through her wet hair. "Not that I'm complaining. It was much nicer hearing Jaxon snore than hearing you thrash around in your sleep all night." Jaxon stiffens behind me. "You must be finally on the mend if you're not having fever nightmares anymore."

Two of us in this room know full well those weren't fever nightmares. But neither of us are going to correct her. Instead, I respond with "Yeah, we both slept like the dead."

"Good. You needed it. Because we're going out tonight." She claps her hands together excitedly and smiles like she's won a trip to Disney World.

I, on the other hand, freeze because this is what I've been dreading. I knew eventually she was going to try to drag me out again. But I'm not ready. I'm just not. I didn't even want to go out in public with Jaxon last night.

But I did it. I powered through my anxieties, and I'm glad I did. Although I'm nowhere near ready to go out with Lauren. Not by myself and absolutely not to the kinds of places she wants me to go.

"Can't," I say, coming up with an excuse off the top of

my head as quickly as possible.

'What?" Her excited expression drops. "How come?"

"I have a big report in my American history class due tomorrow. It's worth a third of my grade, and I haven't finished it yet."

She huffs in frustration. "Come on, Annika. Can't you get it done early before we go?"

"I wish." I'm lying through my teeth. I don't wish that at all. What I do wish is that Jaxon would continue rubbing his hand up and down my arm like he's doing now. It's comforting and relaxing and maybe turning me on just a little bit. Which, again, is weird under the circumstances. But my body reacting normally to a man's touch is a good sign.

Unfortunately, it also makes it very hard to concentrate on this conversation with my roommate. "I-I'll do my best, but I wouldn't count on it. I have a statistics test in a couple days that I need to nail. I can't afford to work hangover recovery time into my schedule."

"Fiiiiiine," she breathes out slowly, rolling her eyes. "I'll give you a pass this time, but only because you went out last weekend." Looking over her shoulder, she winks at me. "And because I'm impressed to see a football player in your bed this morning."

I feel the rumble of Jaxon's chuckle behind me, making me elbow him in the ribs. "Don't encourage her."

"Oh, you can encourage me all you want." Lauren heads around the corner into our walk-in closet where she can have some privacy to get dressed. "There's more where that came from."

I roll back over and look at Jaxon again. The sexually charged moment is gone, but it's almost as nice just to see him still smiling.

He brushes the hair out of my face and runs the tips of

his fingers down my jawline, making me tingle all over. "Thanks for letting me spend the night," he says quietly.

"Thanks for humoring me and staying."

"I wasn't humoring you. I wanted to. It was nice sleeping next to you." I close my eyes, memorizing the feel of his fingers on my face. "I gotta go," he finally whispers again.

"I know." I *do* know. But that doesn't mean I like it. I enjoy being with him. I enjoy the comfort he gives. I enjoy the laughter he creates. The conversations we have. I don't know how it happened, but I have feelings for him. Real, genuine feelings.

I won't tell him, though. I won't put that pressure on him. I'm damaged goods right now, and we both need some time to sort things out.

Finally pulling away, he rocks himself forward so he can launch over me and out of the bed.

Stretching his arms over his head, my eyes catch a sliver of skin between his shirt and jeans. Oddly, it turns me on, which makes me excited. I'm not as broken as I thought I was. I'm nowhere near ready to go "there" but knowing my hormones aren't damaged makes me happy.

"Are you ogling me?" A flirty grin crosses Jaxon's face.

"Nope," I deny, shaking my head and crinkling my brow. "I was wondering how you could sleep in those jeans all night. Looks uncomfortable."

"Only for you, Annika. I only sleep in jeans for you." He leans over and kisses my forehead before snatching his discarded sweatshirt off the floor and pulling over his head.

And now I lie here, after turning into a puddle of complete and utter uselessness. That had to be the sexiest kiss I've ever had in my life.

"Is the coast clear?" he yells out to Lauren as he puts his hands over his eyes, shuffling forward. "Can I walk past that room to get out the door?"

"You're good, Loverboy," she responds, walking back in fully clothed. And by fully clothed, I mean in her team workout gear of a sports bra and tiny, skin-tight shorts. "Although I'm not quite sure how good yet."

I slap my hand over my face and Jaxon chuckles.

"I'll call you later, Annika. Bye, Lauren."

Once again, she gives him a flirty wave.

The door no more than closes behind him and she launches herself onto my bed. "Spill. The. Details," she demands while bouncing up and down. "How in the hell did that happen? Again! He's fucking hot, Annika. Please tell me you got it on with him. Please!"

I try to smack her in the face with my pillow, but she sees it coming and deflects it at the last second. "I don't have anything to tell. We haven't gone there."

"What?" she shrieks. "You haven't had sex with him yet?"

I look at her like she's nuts. "Some of us don't put out on the first date."

She sits back, acting way more offended than we both know she really is. "You say that like it's a bad thing."

"No, I say that like it's not *my* thing." I sigh dreamily and focus my gaze on the ceiling while I talk. "I don't know what's happening, Lauren. I ran into him at the coffee shop." Not totally the truth, but she doesn't need to know that. "We ended up going to a sports bar to watch the Steelers game."

"O. M. G," she says slowly. "He took you to a sports bar to watch a football game?"

I nod, smiling at her. "And he drank Shiner."

"He's like your perfect guy."

"You have no idea," I mumble, throwing my arm over my face. It doesn't stay there long as she pulls it away, looking me in the eyes.

"You really like him, don't you?"

I quirk my lips to the side, trying not to smile, but the look of excitement on her face finally has me caving. "I really do," I gush. "I have no idea how it happened. I didn't know him before last week. But, god, Lauren, he's just perfect. He's kind and generous, and he's smart. So smart. He comes from a football family, so he totally gets my obsession. He's just—"

"Hot," she interrupts, making me giggle.

"That, too. I don't know. I don't want to jinx anything."

"You spent the night with him twice now, so clearly he likes you too."

I understand her logic but that's not the way this relationship really works. I don't tell her all the ugly details, and there are a lot of them. But she's got one thing right—Jaxon Hart has gotten under my skin.

I just need to be careful this isn't some one-sided obsession on my part. I'm already mentally and emotionally broken. I don't need my heart to be shattered too.

FIFTEEN

Jaxon

Everything changed the night I stayed with Annika. For me anyway. It was almost a month ago, and I still can't get her out of my head. Not because we've spent at least a couple nights together every week since then. No, it's even more than I sleep so much better when I can feel her next to me.

Harold, my new counselor, warned me that I might end up having feelings for her—it's not unusual to mistake feelings of protection for love. But he's wrong about this. Sure, whenever I think about how she was assaulted it throws me into a rage. But I don't think about it that way anymore. Or at least not as often as I did.

Now I find myself only thinking about *her*. About how much I enjoy our daily texts and hanging out in the quad drinking coffee or at Buck's watching football. How she makes me laugh when she gets pissed when I pull ahead of her in fantasy football. How I'm looking forward to tailgating with her and learning how to cook brisket in the back of a truck.

I like being with her. She's everything I ever wanted in a girl. She's smart. She's beautiful. She loves football. She's interested in *me*, not my family, which is a big plus when you have a celebrity parent.

Plus, she's strong in her mindset and low drama in her emotions. She's literally the perfect woman.

But she's also still struggling. I know I didn't know her before the attack, but from the way she talks, I don't think she's ever been as insecure as she is now. She works hard at pushing through things that make her uncomfortable; I can see it in her eyes. She's determined to stop hiding behind the sweatpants and that damn bulky hoodie.

Which is why I'm surprised to see her in jeans and a long sleeve T-shirt, not the hoodie, as I fling the door to my dorm open when she arrives to study.

Gaping, I look her up and down before my eyes finally land on the scowl on her face.

"If you say one word about what I'm wearing, I will go back to my place and put the bulky clothes on again, got it?"

Trying not to smile at her feisty little threat, I close my mouth, nod once, and gesture for her to follow me. As she passes by, I can't help but notice how her clothes cling to her body. She's thin, but not skinny, with curves in all the right places. I tilt my head and bite my bottom lip when I see the way her jeans hug her ass. It's literally the first time I've seen the shape of it. I like it. She's got a bit of junk in her trunk.

The dude who sits at the sign-in desk, Mike or Mark or whatever the hell his name is, snickers, and I know I've been caught checking her out. I wink at him, feeling a strange sense of déjà vu about this scene, but dismissing it quickly.

"Second floor. Down the first hall," I direct as we walk to the stairwell. She glances over her shoulder, making sure I'm following right behind her, which I am, and I have the fleeting thought that I'd be willing to follow her almost anywhere.

It only takes a few seconds to get to my room and head inside.

"Nice place," she says as she puts her backpack on the floor and peruses the room. It's nothing fancy. Standard stuff—two desks, two small dressers, two twin beds that partially fold away to give us extra walking room when we're not sleeping.

And a fifty-inch TV hanging on the wall, courtesy of my roommate who refused to live here without access to Netflix. It's not like we watch it very much. But in hindsight, I'm glad he thought of it. Suddenly, I have visions of Annika snuggling in close to me while watching scary movies on my bed. Maybe Germaine was onto something.

"It's really"—she looks for the right word—"clean."

She seems almost apologetic for assuming it would be a dump. If it was just me, it might be. "My roommate is a clean freak."

"I can tell." She runs her finger from one side of the dresser to the next. "There's not even any dust."

I gesture to the door. "There won't be any on the top of the doorjamb, either. I'm not exaggerating that he has an entire bucket of supplies under his desk."

"Seriously?"

I nod. "He even mops once a week."

She plops herself on my bed. I like that she's comfortable enough to do that. "Man, I wish I had a roommate like that. I can't even get Lauren to pick up her dirty clothes half the time. I don't know how her workout clothes aren't moldy from leaving them wadded up on the floor, all sweaty." She sticks her tongue out in disgust.

"Well"—I clap my hands together—"as much as I enjoy hearing all about Lauren's gross laundry habits"—she giggles which makes me feel about ten feet tall; I love that sound—"we both have studying to do. You wanna take my bed or my desk?"

She twists her lips as she weighs her options, looking around the room. Gently bouncing up and down a couple times, she makes up her mind. "I'm comfortable right here. Can you pass me my backpack?"

We shoot the shit a little more as we get situated in our respective locations and tuck into our studies. Without having any overlapping classes, it's not like we can help each other. But between practices and work, which I finally went back to last week after requesting some extra time off, and her heavy load of science classes, it became obvious that I needed to get a little creative when it comes to spending time with her. Even sitting silently while we focus on our individual studies is better than not seeing her at all.

No, I haven't made a move on her yet. I'm waiting until I know she's ready for that. Until I know she likes me as more than a friend and won't get freaked out. I'm almost positive she has feelings for me, I just hope they aren't exaggerated because of how I helped her. That would suck; my feelings for her have nothing to do with that night. Nothing at all.

I drum my pencil on my desk to the beat of my homework music in the background, trying to focus on genetics, but my brain doesn't want to wrap around the minute details that go along with cell division. Like she can feel my frustration from across the room, Annika tosses a wadded up piece of paper at me.

Startled and not quite sure what's being thrown at me,

I bat it away long after it's already landed on my desk then turn to see what she's doing.

"Having a hard time over there, Hart?" She grins mischievously at me while pulling a stack of mail out of her backpack and sorting through it.

I groan. "How am I supposed to go to med school if I don't give a shit about mitosis versus meiosis and all the other bullshit that goes along with it?"

She furrows her brow and answers playfully. "Um, med school has more than blood and guts to it."

"I hope. I know I need to learn this stuff as the foundation to everything else, but jeez, man. This is not high on my excitement list."

She drops most of the mail on her lap, ripping open a thick envelope. "I bet you like anatomy and physiology better. All the bones and muscles and ligaments. It's awesome. But whatever you do, don't take it with Henderson. He totally gets off on making people cry in class."

"For real?"

She nods as she opens the packet of paper in front of her. "Yep. I watched some guy weep for almost forty-five minutes after Henderson ripped him a new one in front of everyone for answering a question wrong."

"Isn't that an upper-level class? How did you take it your freshman year?"

"I'm smart," she says with a shrug.

I snicker. "And modest too."

When she doesn't answer, I look at her closer. "Annika?" She still doesn't answer, her eyes glued to the papers in front of her, mouth gaping open. "Annika, what's wrong?"

"I don't… Holy shit. How could they…?"

She's not making any sense, but I know instinctively that something is very wrong. Jumping off my chair, I practically launch myself onto the bed, terrified of what she's looking at. She looks up at me, eyes huge, face devoid of any color.

"They're making me pay for it, Jaxon. I didn't do anything, and they're making me pay for it."

Snatching the papers out of her hand, I quickly read them over. It's a bill from the hospital for six thousand dollars for services rendered.

We knew it would come eventually, but holding it in my hands brings everything back again. And if that isn't jarring enough, right there on the front page is an itemized list. In big bold letters it says **Sexual Assault Kit - $1200.**

"Holy shit," I breathe, not believing what I'm seeing. How can they make the victim of a violent crime pay for her own evidence? She had GHB in her system. She was found behind a dumpster. She's the *victim.*

Seeing red, I crumple the paper in my fist and bang my hand on my forehead, trying to get the images of that night out of my mind again. Annika, half naked and unconscious lying in a puddle of who knows what in a back alley. The alarmed look on the guy's face when he realized he'd been caught. Hearing her groan and making the choice to save her life and let him go.

I let him go.

Realizing she is probably having similar thoughts, I try desperately to control my breathing, so I don't scare her. She was doing so well. I don't want to see her go back to hiding behind her sweats.

We were both doing so well.

Hearing her soft cries, I snap out of my red-haze fog to see tears streaming down her face. She looks shell-shocked and bewildered, and all I want to do is make it better for her. Taking her face in my hands, I speak gently, trying to calm her down. "It's okay, baby. It's okay. We'll take care of this, okay? You don't have to worry about it. Let me take care of it."

She looks vulnerable and timid. It kills me to see her like this. She's the strongest person I've ever met. The look on her face as she looks into my eyes crushes me. Her words crush me.

"I didn't do anything wrong, did I? Was I dressed too slutty? Should I have not been drinking? I didn't push him away, Jaxon. I never said no. It's my fault, isn't it?"

"No, baby, no," I say a little stronger, trying to get through to her, but not sure how. "Don't even think that. It's not your fault. It was never your fault. I was there, baby. You didn't say yes, okay? You never said yes. You didn't deserve it, and you don't deserve"—I throw the bill on the floor, wishing I could burn it on the spot—"you don't deserve that either. You know that, right?"

She squeezes her eyes tight, trying hard to believe me, but she's completely rocked to her core. We both are. It feels like a punch to the gut, which makes me pissed off to think about what it feels like to her.

I can feel her pulling away from me, caving in on herself emotionally. I've never seen her like this, and it scares the shit out of me. So I do the only thing I can think of to make her more comfortable; I cross the room to my dresser, pull out the biggest sweatshirt I own and help her put it on over her clothes. Then I lie down on the bed, pulling her as tight to me as I can to protect her. Her silent cries seem to last for hours until she finally falls asleep, exhausted from emotion.

I hold her all night long, even when she thrashes around, having nightmares again for the first time in several weeks.

SIXTEEN
Annika

That night in Jaxon's dorm was brutal. When I saw the hospital bill, the *detailed* hospital bill, in the envelope, I felt victimized all over again. I knew there would be charges from the doctor and the medication they gave me. But the rape kit?

All I could think about was that I was paying for people to take pictures of me. Private pictures of the private areas of my naked body. Pictures I didn't even want. They are billing me for my own humiliation and degradation. It pissed me off, but that anger took a back seat to how small I felt. All I wanted to do was hide. I couldn't get far enough inside myself to get away from it. I felt exposed, even sitting in Jaxon's room, only the two of us. I just knew, *knew,* that everyone else in that building, everyone on campus, had seen those pictures.

Obviously, I wasn't thinking rationally, but when you are feeling that kind of vulnerability, it doesn't matter. When Jaxon pulled his giant hoodie over my head and let me hide inside of it, I could finally let the sadness come out. Besides that first day when I came home from the hospital, I had never cried over my attack. It was cathartic to let go, to get it out. It felt like a weight had lifted off me somehow. That's not to say I wasn't embarrassed by my display. I'm not normally that emotional. I like staying on an even keel. Then I woke up the next morning after a terrible night's sleep, hoping Jaxon didn't think I was too much trouble to bother with anymore. That thought terrified me more than anything.

Somehow in all of this, I fell for him. In head-over-heels-let-me-have-your-babies love with him. I would never tell him how I feel. At least not now. There's still too much shit in my brain to make me a good girlfriend. But I'm hopeful that someday I'll heal more. Until then, I'll accept the comfort of his friendship. Because if he turned me away now, I'm not sure how I'd react. He's too much of the rock in my life right now.

I'm sure that's not exactly the makings of a healthy relationship, but it's working, so I don't care.

In the meantime, I continue to keep my head down, force myself into jeans each day, and plow my way through the fear. Jaxon's words from long ago have become my mantra.

Be angry. Stay angry for as long as you need, until you feel like you've pushed through the hard parts. Let your anger fuel you to be the best you can be.

So I do. I channel my anger into proving my emotions wrong. Into proving everyone wrong who would ever look at me with pity if they knew what I had gone through. And I function to the best of my ability giving fear and humiliation the figurative middle finger while I do it.

It's working for the most part. There's only one hurdle I still can't seem to get over—going out with Lauren. The idea of being at a club or party with only her at my back is debilitating. But that's not the worst part. The worst part is I can't go into public with her at all. Not even to dinner or the movies. I don't know if it's because she was there that night and didn't help me, which is ridiculous because there was no way she could have known what was happening.

My new therapist, Necia, says it boils down to basic association, and it should fade over time. Lauren was there that night. She's the one who pushed and pushed me to go that night. Her critical eye and opinions are why I wore that stupid dress that I'm glad I'll never see again. Association. All of it comes back to Lauren and that night.

Necia also warned that since Jaxon rescued me, I associate him with safety. I stared blankly with a look on my face that said "duh" when she told me that.

Still, as I sit on my bed staring out the window instead of at the textbook on my lap, I know I have to say something to Lauren. Blowing her off isn't working; the excuses are running out, and she's getting irritated. A showdown is coming, and I have to decide how much to tell her. I'm out of excuses and with tonight being Halloween, she is going to put on more pressure than usual, I know it.

My phone beeps with a text, giving me a breather from my wayward thoughts.

Jaxon: Bill is paid. If you get anything else from them, throw it away. Don't even open it.

My eyes widen in surprise at Jaxon's words.

Me: What do you mean the bill is paid?

Jaxon: Just what the word paid means.

They have the money so don't give them any more.

Me: What?? Jaxon, you don't have that kind of money!

Jaxon: No, but my dad has a foundation that does. And one of the umbrellas of it is solely to help people pay extravagant medical bills. He put in a call yesterday to the treasurer, and they had an emergency vote by email. Decision was unanimous. Your bill has been paid, and you never have to think about it again.

Tears well up in my eyes as I run my fingers over the screen of my phone. I can't believe after all these weeks, he's still taking care of me. I'm not his problem. This isn't his issue. And yet, he doesn't ever hesitate to try and make things better.

After taking a few deep breaths to calm my nerves, I respond.

Me: Thank you. I don't think you know what that means to me. I don't think you know what *you* mean to me.

His response is almost instantaneous.

Jaxon: I'd do anything for you, An-nika.

Trying not to swoon, I hold my phone to my chest and close my eyes tight, enjoying the feeling his words bring. Someday, I'll tell him how in love I am with him. Someday.

Before I can respond, another text comes through.

Jaxon: What are you doing tonight?

Me: Studying. Midterms are coming up. I want to get a jump on that. You?

Jaxon: Germaine is dragging my ass to a Halloween party at the Kappa Phi house.

Me: That sounds… Fun?

Jaxon: No, it doesn't. But I've put it off too long. I need to spend some "quality time" with my boys. That's his excuse, anyway.

Me: Don't you spend quality time with him every day at practice?

Jaxon: That's exactly what I said! Apparently, practice doesn't count as bonding time. Wanna go with us? We can make fun of all the slutty costumes together.

Me: Lol. And interrupt your male bonding? Hell no.

Jaxon: It was worth a shot. Gotta run before he steals my phone and doesn't give it back. Call me if you need anything, got it?

Me: *cue military salute* Yes, sir.

Jaxon: Smart ass. I'll call you later.

I click my phone off just as the door opens and Lauren comes sauntering in, the clack of her too-high heels practically ticking off the seconds before the inevitable conversation.

Spinning in a circle, she shows off her slutty wizard outfit.

"I'm not sure that's what JK Rowlings had in mind when she wrote Hermione's character," I quip.

She glares at me, hands on her hips. "Hermione grew up eventually. I'm sure she pulled out her short robe whenever they went clubbing."

"Hogwarts was out in the middle of nowhere. There weren't any clubs around."

She rolls her eyes and fluffs her hair in the mirror, making sure her wizard hat is staying put. "Then use your imagination. There's only a few ways I can think of to stay entertained when you're away at boarding school. Especially when your boyfriend is right down the hall." She winks at me, and her expression changes and her shoulders drop when she finally seems to notice I'm not dressed for a party. "Annika, we have to leave in like ten minutes if we're going to get there before the booze is watered down. Get a move on, girl."

"I'm not going," I say quietly, looking down at my book.

"What?"

Chancing a look up at her, I brace myself. Show time.

"I said, I'm not going."

She rolls her eyes. "That's ridiculous. Of course you're going out. It's Halloween, and you need the break. I even bought you a costume."

She tosses a small plastic package at me and the cover on the front makes my heart race and my breathing hitch. It's a slutty nurse costume, complete with a pillbox hat, fishnet hose, and a barely-there dress. Designed to show a whole lot of cleavage and a whole lot more leg, this "costume" is my worst nightmare.

"I figured with your major it was perfect for you."

"I appreciate you thinking of me," I lie, because in this case I really don't. "But I have midterms coming up and I front-loaded all my science classes this semester. You know that."

Whipping around to glare at me, I know she's finally going to snap. She may be my best friend and would do anything for me, but she knows I'm making up excuses and not telling her something.

"What is the matter with you lately?" she accuses.

"I don't know what you mean." More lies.

"Don't give me that bullshit. You know exactly what I'm talking about," she says, throwing her hands up in exasperation. "You've never liked going out. I know that. But lately, you've become a hermit. It's like you don't want to spend time with me at all."

"That's not true—" I try to deny, but she cuts me off.

"It *is* true. You don't like dancing. Fine. I might even be able to understand about going to a frat party. But you won't go to dinner with me, not even to the fucking cafeteria. It's like you don't want to be seen with me ever since you hooked up with Jaxon. Did I do something wrong? Or am I not good enough for you now that you're part of that crowd."

Her eyes well up with tears and I feel terrible. I never wanted to make her feel like this. "No, Lauren." I toss my book aside and move forward on my bed. "It has nothing to do with you."

"Then why don't you want to hang out with me?"

Hanging my head, I try to tell her the truth of what I've been going through. I want to admit everything so she can put the worry out of her mind. But I just…can't. "It's not you, Lauren. It's me."

Batting at a stray tear, she scoffs at me. "Great. Now you're pulling out the worst breakup lines known to man. You know what? Forget it." She grabs her matching glittery clutch off the dresser, throws her shoulders back, and stomps toward the door. "If you change your mind and decide I'm good enough to be your friend again, let me know."

I jump when the door slams behind her. Then the tears begin to fall at the realization of yet another thing I've lost.

SEVENTEEN
Jaxon

f it weren't for Germaine practically manhandling me out the door, I wouldn't be at this party. The idea of being in the Kappa Phi house, surrounded by slutty costumes on the girls and overly macho costumes on the guys and sometimes vice versa, didn't sound appealing. I'd rather be with Annika.

I knew she wouldn't darken the door of a place like this, especially with it being this crowded, but I needed to appease my best friend. So here I am. It's as bad as I expected.

Sure, I've had some laughs with my friends, slapped backs with some guys I haven't seen in a while, even struck up a few conversations with people I see on campus. But it doesn't hold the same appeal anymore, all because my girl isn't here.

I finally admitted it to myself the other day. I've fallen for her. I've fallen for her resilience and her strength. I've fallen for her calm demeanor. I've fallen for her drive and her motivation. I've even fallen for her loyalty to her favorite team, despite being sorely misguided on who the best team in the NFL actually is.

I've fallen in love with *her*, and I want to be where she is every minute of every day. I guess that's what it's supposed to be like when you fall in love.

My dad used to tell me parties were more appealing when he was playing the field. But once he only had eyes for my mom, that was it. No party could hold his attention compared to her.

He was right. I've smiled politely, made conversation with no less than three girls who have hung on my arm. But it doesn't matter how much cleavage the sexy devil shoves in my face or how many times the naughty nurse offers to take my temperature. They're still not the one I want.

The one I want is at home, dressed in baggy sweats without a stitch of makeup on, studying. Who knew that could be such a turn on?

A half-dressed girl stumbles through the room catching my attention. It's clear she's very, very drunk. She's laughing and smiling, but as I glance around the room, I realize I'm not the only guy watching her, and most of them are leering. It shocks me, knowing that any guy in this room could be a predator. I never noticed it before tonight.

"Why are you staring at that girl, man?" Germaine leans over and yells in my ear. "You kind of look like a creeper."

Taking a sip of my beer, I keep my eyes on her. "Dude, she is seriously trashed."

"Yeah?" he questions, obviously not understanding what I'm getting at.

"Where are her friends?"

"I don't know, man. We're all friends here." He slaps

me on the back, emphasizing his point. But he's missing mine.

"No, I'm serious. She's by herself, in a barely-there Halloween costume and is drunk off her ass. Who is watching her?"

I can tell by the movement in my peripheral vision he's giving me a sideways glance. "Dude. She's fine. She's in the middle of a roomful of people. What the hell has gotten into you?"

"Nothing," I huff. "I just…that's not really safe."

I can tell when it hits him by the "ahhhh" that comes out of mouth. "Dude, I get that you're on high alert after what happened outside your club, but it's not your responsibility to make sure everyone makes good choices."

He has no idea how much responsibility I feel, because I never told him. When the story broke about Ambrosia a couple days after the attack, he asked me about what had happened. I told him that all the staff had been made aware of the situation and more safety precautions had been put into place. Which was true.

What I didn't tell him about was my involvement. Or Annika's. That information is for me and me alone.

"Doesn't matter, man." I shake my head, suppressing my anger at his ignorance and refusing to take my eyes off her. "Things can change in an instant."

Fortunately, as the words are coming out of my mouth, another girl comes up to her. When the drunk chick sees her friend, a giant smile immediately crossed her face, and she wraps her arms around the sober girl who rolls her eyes and helps her walk away.

"See?" Germaine smacks my shoulder. "Her friends are here. All good. You can stop worrying now."

Blowing out a breath I try to agree with him, but I can't. Not because anything wrong is happening here, but because the only girl I want to keep my eye on tonight isn't with me.

Suddenly, I'm exhausted by all the people and noise. Downing the rest of my warm beer, I drop the empty cup on the table. "I'm not feeling it tonight, man. Are you okay if I head out?"

Giving me the once over, he jeers at me. "You lasted a couple hours before you had to go running back to your woman to get some pussy."

I punch him playfully as he ribs me. He's been doing it a lot lately. Every time I disappear, he knows exactly who I'm with.

"Hey, you wouldn't be making fun if you knew her like I do."

"I'd like to know her if someone would ever introduce me to her."

"Sorry about that." I rub my hand down my face, feeling guilty at the lack of introduction. "I'm not trying to keep her from you. Our schedules don't overlap very much."

"I know man, it's cool. Thanksgiving break is coming up. Maybe we can go out before classes start up again."

"Yeah. I think she'd like that. She's cool."

He claps me on the back again. "I don't doubt that. I've never seen anyone catch your eye like she has. Now get outta here. And don't forget to put a sock on the doorknob if you need a little privacy tonight."

I shove him while he chuckles and walks away, following behind yet another scantily clad co-ed who gives him a flirty eye and sway of her hips when she walks past him.

I roll my eyes. I'm glad to be out of the meat market business. It was fun for a while, but at a certain point, chasing tail is fucking exhausting.

The Kappa Phi house isn't a long walk from my dorm.

Which is convenient when you go to a party that has lots of booze. Not having to drive means not having to find my car in the mess of vehicles, none of which are parked in actual spaces. "No wonder people do the walk of shame," I mumble. I'd never be able to find my ride in this mess.

Pulling out my phone, I see it's only 10:30. Man, I really am pussy-whipped. I laugh at myself and shrug my shoulders. I may be pussy-whipped, but I have a phone call to make and hopefully a girl to get to.

Dialing her number, she answers on the third ring. "Hey, did I wake you?"

'No," she says, sounding all out of breath. "I was watching a scary movie."

"By yourself?" I chuckle.

"It wasn't the smartest idea. You called right as the guy was about to jump out, and it scared the shit out of me. Took me until the third ring to figure out where I'd thrown my phone."

The visual image makes me laugh. "You didn't break it, did you?"

"No, thank god. I'm still paying off this upgrade. I don't need to get another one."

That's my girl. Only someone as strong as her could joke alluding to how she lost her phone last time without losing her shit.

"Good, cause I'm not sure I could go for another week without talking to you."

"You know how to find me."

"Yeah, the problem is, you're never there."

She groans. "I know. This semester is about to kill me. Remind me to never take three science classes in a single semester again."

"Did you at least get any studying done tonight?"

"No," she grumbles.

I know that sound in her voice. She started with the best intentions, but something changed her mind. "What happened?"

"I had a fight with Lauren."

Her deep sigh doesn't surprise me. She's known it was coming for a while. Still, I try to be supportive of the hurt I hear in her voice.

"That bad?"

"It was a long time coming. I knew it wasn't going to be pretty, but I wasn't expecting her to think I have a holier-than-thou complex."

I stop in my tracks. "What? She said that?"

"She seems to think since you and I started hanging out, I think I'm more important than her. Like, I'm hanging out with the football gods, and she's just a gymnast."

I snort a laugh. "First of all, that's a load of bullshit. I'm hardly a football god. God of men, maybe." She giggles. "But certainly not a god of football. Second, I had a friend in high school who was a gymnast, and I stupidly challenged her to see who was stronger."

"Oh god. That doesn't sound like it went well."

"Yeah, you know where this story is going. We were equally matched on the pushups, which, by the way, was my choice. But when she tossed out the handstand challenge, it was over."

The boisterous laugh coming from the other end of the phone makes me smile. "You football players are stupid sometimes."

"Yeah, well. We get knocked in the head a lot." Swinging the door open to my dorm, I wave at that Mark or Mike guy at the front desk. I still don't know his name or what he even does besides sign visitors in and out. He just nods in my direction, barely looking up from his magazine. As I stomp up the stairs, I try to reassure her. "You and Lauren will work it out. Did you think about maybe telling her the truth?"

"NO!" Her answer is immediate and sounds final, so I don't push. "I just…I've made a lot of progress, I don't want to go backward again."

I understand her concern, even if I don't necessarily agree. "Fair enough. It's your story. You do what you feel is best."

"I will. Anyway, I don't wanna talk about this anymore. What are you doing the rest of the night?"

Now we're getting somewhere. "I don't know. I was thinking maybe I should come over, and we can watch those scary movies together and snuggle."

She can't see the flirty grin on my face, but it's there. One of these days I'll feel confident enough to make a move. Hopefully sooner rather than later. It's getting harder and harder not to kiss her senseless.

As I get to my door, there's some guy sitting in front of it.

"That actually sounds fun," I hear her say. "Why don't you come over?"

As I get closer to the guy, I wonder if he's homeless. His hair is greasy. Terrible acne covers his face. His clothes look a little disheveled. But then I realize, he's just a kid.

"What's up man?" I say with a nod of my head. "Yeah, that sounds great, Annika."

My attention is divided between my phone conversation and this teenager in front of me. Who is he, and what does he want? Standing up, he immediately digs his hands in his pockets, like he's nervous. "Hey. Um. Jaxon, right?"

I take a step back, thoroughly confused. "Hang on, Annika," I say into the phone and then swivel the microphone away from my mouth. "Do I know you?"

"Yeah, um…" His hands come out of his pockets, and

he nervously wipes them on his jeans. "I'm Kade. Kade Maxwell?"

I stare at him blankly. The name doesn't ring a bell.

"Okay, I guess you don't know who I am." Nervousness is coming off of him in waves. "My mom is Shonda Maxwell."

I shake my head slightly, still not making the connection.

"Oh God. This is awkward."

It really is. He's nervous and jittery, and I can't help wondering when the last time he bathed was.

"Okay, I'm gonna rip the bandaid off. I'm your brother," he blurts out.

I freeze and stare at him, trying to register his words. *My brother?* No, my brother, Matty, is at home with my parents and my sister, Lucy.

When I don't say anything, he goes one step further.

"Um…my mom and your dad had an affair, and here I am."

I immediately swivel the phone back in place. "Annika, I gotta call you back." Clicking the phone off without waiting for a response, I brush him out of the way to open the door and gesture him inside the room.

As soon as the door closes behind us, I turn to him, hands on my hips, glaring. "What the fuck are you talking about?" I demand.

He looks taken aback, but recovers quickly. "Okay, that wasn't quite what I expected you to say." He's still nervous, but there's also determination there. The attitude doesn't overshadow the fact that he's greasy and unkempt, and smells a little. I'm not sure how this kid thinks he could at all be related to my dad.

His words come out in a rush. "Like I said, my mom and your dad had an affair, and I'm your brother, and I came to see you, because I've been saving my money because I wanted to meet you."

"How old are you?" I finally ask him.

"Fourteen," he says shyly, looking at the floor.

I bang my fist gently on my forehead as I do the math, but it doesn't add up. "I don't believe you." His eyes whip back up to mine, stunned. "My dad didn't even meet my mom until I was seven," I explain. "By that time, you would have already been born, and let's face it, statistically speaking, women who get knocked up by a football player, a star player at that, typically want massive amounts of child support. It would have already been sorted out by the time my parents met."

He relaxes like the explanation makes perfect sense. "Oh, no man, not that dad. Austin."

My entire body freezes as I do the math again. He's fourteen. That's six years younger than me. My dad died when I was five. That means he would have been born just a few months after my dad died…

Seeing the look on my face, he fumbles around in his back pocket. "Sorry, here…" He pulls a paper out of his pocket and unfolds it. "It says right here on my birth certificate."

Handing it to me, I inspect the words in front of me. There, plain as day, it says his name: Kayden Austin Maxwell. Father: Austin Mitchell Bryant.

"Holy shit," I breathe as I collapse onto my bed. All I can do is stare at the paper. It's true. He's my brother. "What the fuck?"

Slowly pulling myself back together, I look up at him again. It's clear he's not Jason's son. But could this be true? Could he really be Austin's? I have no idea. I remember my dad. But that was through the eyes of a five-year-old. He could have been tall or short. I don't have any real frame of reference. He was just "normal" in my eyes.

"Okay, I need you to explain this to me, because I have no idea what the fuck is going on, and it's kind of freaking me out," I finally say.

"Yeah. I can see you are either under informed, or I know way too much."

I snicker humorlessly. "You're fourteen. You probably should have been sheltered from some of this shit." The words come out harsher than I intend. But right now, I'm really pissed and the only one here is him. Unfair? Yes. But he should have expected it by coming here like this.

"All I know is my mom and your dad, *our* dad, were having an affair when he died. I don't know anything else other than that. Except I was born seven months after his death.

I take a deep breath, calming myself. Regardless of how I feel, I have to remember he is a fourteen-year-old kid who came looking for me. I suspect he's looking for some of the same answers very soon, like how the fuck this happened in the first place. "Where do you live?"

"Up in Dallas."

My eyes widen. "How'd you get here? That's a six-hour drive."

He shrugs and digs his hands into his pockets again. "I've been saving my birthday and Christmas money for a few years so I could get a bus ticket here."

"Ohmygod," I breath as I wipe my hand down my face. "Are you shitting me?" He shakes his head and looks at the floor, face turning red from embarrassed by my pointed questions. I realize I can't kick him out. He has nowhere to go, and he's a kid. I may not want to deal with this right now, but I'm not going to be an asshole. Instead, I ask, "You hungry, man? That must have been a long bus ride."

He relaxes a little and even smiles. I find myself inspecting his expression, trying to find any trace of resemblance. "Uh, yeah. Kind of, I guess."

I grab a bag of popcorn off the shelf over my desk, pop it into the microwave, and pull a bottle of water out of the fridge, tossing it to him. He fumbles around with it for a few seconds before finally getting a grasp on it. Clearly, he didn't get his athleticism from my side of the family. I chuckle at the thought as I pull out my phone and text Germaine.

Find a place to stay tonight. I've got company.

His response is almost immediately.

Get 'er done!

I don't bother correcting him. I don't need him up in my business until I get this sorted out.

Kade and I make small talk for the next couple of hours. I ask him about school and what he likes to do. He asks about college and what it's like to be out on your own. We get to know each other a little bit, both of us still unsure how all this is going to work and where we go from here.

When he's finally settled into Germain's bed, snoring slightly, I grab my phone and quietly step out into the hall, pulling up the number of the one person I need to talk to the most.

He answers after the first ring. "Jax. What's wrong?"

"Dad. We need to talk."

EIGHTEEN

Annika

I didn't hear from Jaxon for the rest of the night. I didn't hear from him the next day either. I texted a couple of times to see if he was okay but the only time he responded it said "Yeah, I've just got some shit going on." That told me nothing. And it told me everything I needed to know.

I have been utterly stupid.

I misinterpreted everything. Jaxon was my friend, nothing else. Anything deeper than that was a fantasy in my own mind. Necia had warned me that many survivors develop a hero's crush, but I didn't believe that's what was happening. In hindsight, having never been in love before, I guess I didn't know how to tell the difference.

Admittedly, the whole scenario makes me sad. I spent longer in the shower than normal last night getting all the tears out without anyone knowing. I was oddly proud of myself for staying naked in a community bathroom shower longer than absolutely necessary. Baby steps, right?

But now, I feel empty. I'm strong and I'll get through it, but it sucks to know that the person who was my closest confidant, who I thought could potentially be my soulmate, well…I was wrong.

Keeping my head down as I walk to Kampus Koffee, I barely register his voice.

"Annika."

Maybe I'm more heartbroken than I thought. I'm hearing Jaxon's voice everywhere I go. Clearly, I'm delusional. Necia is going to have a field day with this one.

"Annika, wait up." His voice is closer now, and I look over to see him jogging toward me. "Hey, didn't you hear me calling you?"

His smile is huge, like nothing is different, and I haven't spent two days waiting for my phone to ring, my heart breaking.

"I…" I stumble over my words, confused by how happy he looks to see me. "I'm sorry, I didn't know you were calling me."

He chuckles lightly. "Who else do I know named Annika? You're it."

Kissing me on the top of the head, I take a step back and look at him.

"What?" he asks when he sees the perplexity on my face. "What's wrong?"

"I haven't heard from you in two days."

His shoulders fall and he looks sheepish. "Yeah I've had some pretty intense personal shit come up."

I wait for a second and then gesture with an "and?"

"And, I don't know. I don't want to talk about it."

Suddenly, my hurt is replaced by anger, and my back stiffens in an involuntary response. "Oh, you don't want to talk about your personal stuff."

"It's too fresh, ya know?"

"Really?" I'm trying to keep my emotions under control because this is possibly the most hypocritical he's ever been with me.

He finally seems to register my anger, and his confusion is clear. "What? It's hard to talk about. You of all people should understand where I'm coming from."

A humorless laugh burst out of me. "Okay. I get it."

"Get what? Annika, what do you get?"

"That I don't want to talk about my personal shit either, but I do because that's what friends do. They trust each other and share with each other, but clearly I misunderstood what's happening here." I gesture back and forth between us. "I'm going to get some coffee. When you'd like to reciprocate our friendship, feel free to let me know."

I turn to walk away, but he grabs my arm before I can get anywhere. "What are you talking about?" Dragging me out of the way of prying eyes, he leans me against the wall. "Why are you mad at me? I don't understand what's happening."

I sigh and look at the ground, unwilling to meet his gaze. "I'm not mad at you. I'm mad at me, okay? I just misunderstood this whole friendship. Just ignore me."

"Misinterpreted? Annika, you've gotta help me out here."

Confessing my feelings for him was not high on my priority list this morning, but I owe him an explanation for my behavior. He's been nothing but kind to me. He deserves to know the truth of my outburst.

"I thought that you kind of liked me. And I kind of like you too. A lot. Okay more than a lot." His brown eyes look back and forth into mine, and he leans in closer to hear what I'm saying. "But I think I over-exaggerated the connection."

"You didn't over-exaggerate anything."

"Jaxon," I say quietly, "you know every detail of the most intimate, personal, disgusting thing in my life. You know every part of that. If you can't share the same kind of personal ugly about you, then you don't feel about me the way I feel about you."

Understanding crosses his face, and before I can ask him to move out of my way so I can leave and end my humiliation, his lips come crashing down on mine. A squeak comes out of me at the unexpectedness, and then I melt into him as his hands cup my cheeks. His lips are soft and warm and plump. His tongue tastes slightly of coffee and bacon and, well, of Jaxon. He kisses me and kisses me and kisses me, until the only thing I can hear is the sound of our breathing and some catcalls in the distance. Those whistles are what finally make me pull away.

Pressing his forehead against mine, he says, "Don't listen to them, listen to me." He licks his lips, and I close my eyes, enjoying the feel of his body up against mine. I didn't realize how much I craved this kind of closeness, this kind of touch, until now. "I have wanted to kiss you for so long. But I needed to know you were ready. I needed to know I wasn't pushing you too quickly. I don't ever want you to feel unsafe with me. That's why I haven't made a move until now."

"Really?" The word comes out like a breathy sigh.

"Really. But now that I know how you feel, if I have your permission, I'm gonna kiss you again, and I'm going to kiss you a lot."

"Okay." I wrap my arms around his neck. "Kiss me again right now."

He chuckles lightly against my lips before granting my wish. There's no tongue this time. Just deep satisfying kisses, until my lips feel swollen. Only then does he pull away. "Come on. Let me buy you some coffee, and I'll fill you in on what's going on."

"No, Jax. You don't have to tell me. It's your story to tell…"

"No. You're right. I like you, Annika, and I want to be with you. This isn't one-sided for me. I trust you implicitly, and I need to do this with you."

Biting my lip doesn't deter the smile that crosses my face as he leads me into the building. Jaxon likes me. He *likes* me, likes me. And he's going to kiss me. A lot if I have my way.

As I claim the same table we sat at when we first met here, he stands in line for our coffees. I want to text Lauren and tell her what happened, but I'm afraid she'll think it's too little, too late. So I don't.

"Salted caramel mocha, right?" He hands me the largest size cup they have. Oh yeah. I definitely want to kiss him again.

I blow on the steam and take a sip while he gets settled. I'm curious what has him so frazzled that he disappears from my life for two days after months of texting every few hours.

"When I got back to my dorm the other night," he begins, "this kid was sitting outside my door."

"Uh huh." I take another sip, not sure if this is actually the best coffee I've ever had or if my surging hormones are making it taste better than normal. But it's truly the best I've ever tasted.

"He claims he's my brother."

He drops that bomb right as I'm swallowing, causing me to spend the next several minutes choking. I hold my hand up to make him wait while I cough, grateful I didn't spit the coffee all over him instead.

"How…he…what?" I croak out when my throat is finally cleared.

Jaxon chuckles. "That's the reaction I had. It took me a little bit to sort out what he was telling me. But it turns out, my dad had an affair."

My eyes get huge, in spite of my attempts to not over-react. "Holy shit. Does the press know yet?"

"No," he shakes his head vehemently. "Wrong dad."

I tilt my head and furrow my brow. "I'm sorry, I'm not following you."

Like he's just had a lightbulb moment, he says "Oh shit. We've never had this conversation." Putting his coffee down, he leans forward. "Jason didn't meet my mom until I was seven. They got married when I was eight."

"Oh, I didn't realize he was your stepdad."

He shakes his head. "No, adopted dad. That's why the football gene skipped me. We don't have any actual genetics in common." I don't like the expression on his face when he says that. It's like he lost a little confidence in himself. The look disappears quickly, though, as he continues. "My birth dad died in a car accident when I was five."

"Oh, Jaxon, I'm sorry."

"Me, too. He was a good dad. But apparently, he wasn't a very good husband," he says, staying on track with his story. "He was having an affair when he died."

"Oh shit," I exclaim louder than I intended. Looking around the room to make sure no one noticed my outburst, I lean in closer as he keeps talking.

"I, of course, didn't know anything about it until this kid, Kade, showed up at my doorstep, claiming to be my brother."

"Do you think it's true? Does he look like you?"

"I don't know. That's the thing. He's..." Jaxon pauses, and I can tell he's trying to phrase his next statement the right way. "He's kind of...weird. It's like no one ever taught him hygiene."

I look at him quizzically. That was not what I was expecting him to say. "You're gonna have to explain more."

"He dresses kind of weird, like really geeky. It was like he'd just come from ComiCon."

I scowl. "Hey, don't make fun of the Con. I went once. It was fun."

He bites back a laugh before deadpanning, "Yes. I'm sure it was."

"Excuse me." I slap his arm playfully. "You can't tell me you don't love *Star Wars* as much as the next guy. And *The Walking Dead*. And *Game of Thrones*…"

"Okay, okay, fine." He stops. "Bad example. But if you saw him walking down the street, you'd assume he lived in his mother's basement, playing video games and only venturing out for Pokémon Go."

I chortle. "Don't you think you're being a little judgmental? He's just a kid."

"I'm not trying to be. I'm trying to explain why it was hard to wrap my brain around us being related. Like, how much of who I am is because my dad Jason taught me. I don't know that anyone ever taught this kid basic social things. My other dad, *our* dad, was dead so obviously, he didn't. And if his mom was having an affair with a married man, I don't know what she could be like. But I couldn't begin to tell you when the last time was that he washed his hair. He obviously doesn't wash his face. And I had to loan him my deodorant because when he took off his shirt to go to bed, the smell was overwhelming."

My heart squeezes at the thought of Jaxon's brother probably spending most of his life alone. "That's really sad, Jaxon. What if he really is your brother, and he's been neglected all his life?"

"I had the same thought. At first I was mad that he showed up out of nowhere saying he was my brother. Then

I was mad that no one told me. Why didn't anyone think it was important for me to know? It was eye-opening talking to him. We're both really good at math and science. Apparently, I got that from my dad's…um, Austin's side. It made me think if Austin was still alive and Jason never came into the picture, would that be me? I can't seem to wrap my brain around it."

"I get it. I think about that sometimes. If my mom was alive, would I be more of a girly girl? Would I know how to do makeup, or would I like jewelry? I was raised by two men. I don't know."

"Wait." Now his facial expression mirrors the exact one I was sporting a few minutes ago. "Your mom died?"

I snort a laugh. "I guess we haven't talked about that either. Yeah, she died when I was a baby."

"Oh," he says nonchalantly. "Welcome to the dead parent club."

We slap high five over the table like it's no big deal. Reality is it's a *very* big deal to lose a parent, but for us, it's been long enough that it's part of our normal.

"Okay," I say, getting back to his story. "What happened? Did you ask your parents about it?"

"Yeah. As soon as Kade went to sleep, I called my dad because if I have an extra brother, someone has to break it to my mom that Austin was having an affair. No way is that going to be me. He's the husband. That's his job."

I nod in agreement. "Sounds reasonable. What did he say?"

"She already knows."

My eyes widen. "She knows you have a brother and never told you?"

"No, she didn't know that part. At least she didn't until yesterday. She knew Austin was having an affair. She was getting ready to file for divorce before he died."

I resituate until I'm sitting back in my chair as I absorb all this information. "God, Jaxon, every which way this totally sucks."

"I know.

"What happens now?"

He shakes his head and takes another sip of his coffee. "I put Kade back on the bus yesterday. Do you know the whole time he was with me, not once did his phone go off? No one was looking for him at all. Not even his own mother. I asked him if his mom knew where he was and he said no. He didn't tell her he was leaving, and she didn't notice he was missing."

My heart breaks. I know I don't talk to my dad and brother as much as I should, but I know if I disappeared suddenly, they'd look for me. They'd notice if I was gone. Makes me miss them. I should call them today.

"I talked to my parents yesterday." Jaxon clears his throat, like he's bracing himself for the next bomb he's about to drop. "They want me to get a DNA test."

"How come? Your first dad is dead. Does it even make a difference at this point?"

"I don't know," he says slowly. "I think maybe they're worried he wants money or something. I need to think about it though, ya know? If he isn't my brother, that's the end of it, but if he is, what then?"

It's a valid question, and one I really don't have an answer to, but I throw out my thoughts anyway. "You know, if no one really cares about Kade, maybe that's why he came looking for you. It sounds like he's lonely, and he's looking for a connection somewhere.

"Your parents are probably right about the DNA test, just to be on the safe side and to make sure nothing shady is going on. But no matter what that test says, there's still connected history there, even if it's not a direct link. Maybe you should just keep in contact with him. Text a little. Be his friend. Teach him how to use soap."

A laugh bursts out of him. I like seeing the smile on his face even in the middle of a personal crisis.

"I thought about that. Maybe I need to make an effort here. If my life had turned out a little differently, if my mom was a little less involved, and my dad had never come along, that could be me."

My heart swells with more love for this man than I felt before. His natural compassion for people is astounding. After a few seconds of silence, though, I have to lay it on the line.

"Jax."

"Hmm." He looks up at me.

"If you ever disappear on me like that again, I don't know if I can take it."

He reaches over and grabs my hand. It's the first time he's intertwined our fingers, and my whole body warms at his touch.

"I'm sorry," he pleads. "But can you do me a favor?"

"Anything," I say, and I mean it.

"Come with me to buy more deodorant. I gave it to Kade as a parting gift."

I laugh, pushing his hand away from mine. "Come on, you dork." I stand up and grab my backpack. "I don't know if I'll be able to get close enough to kiss you again if you stink."

He chuckles and grabs my hand again as we walk out the door.

I don't care what Necia says, this is definitely not a hero's crush.

NINETEEN

Jaxon

"**J**axon!"

The shriek is ear piercing but at least gives me time to drop my bags and brace myself. Lucy, my eight-year-old sister, is tiny compared to everyone else in this house. But when she comes barreling down the stairs and jumps on you, let's just say she's been known to knock a few people over.

Sure enough, as she comes racing down the stairs, jumping and wrapping her limbs around me, the breath is knocked right out of me.

"Hey, Lucy-Goosy!"

She giggles at the nickname I've been using since she was a baby. "I'm glad you're here, Jax. Come up to my room! I need to show you my new Barbies. And I got all the movies now."

"All of them?" I ask playfully. "Because I think there's a new one out."

Her eyes get wide. "There is? Which one? Is it the

Swan Lake? Cause I have that one."

"No, I think it had something to do with being a rock star."

She shakes her head at me in exasperation. "That's not a new one. I have it, and I know all the songs."

"Huh," I pretend to be thinking hard, not because I actually make a point of keeping up with Barbie, but because I love seeing the delight on her face. "I guess I'm behind on my movie watching. We'll have to get some popcorn and snuggle on the couch, and you can catch me up sometime this week."

She wiggles out of my arms then bounces up and down in front of me, her energy taking over. "Really Jaxon? Really? Because I got a new big giant Barbie blanket we can snuggle under. And I even got a new Barbie beauty salon. I can do your hair and I can paint your nails and I can put makeup on you—"

"Whoa, whoa, whoa. Slow down there, Lucy. You can do my hair, but I draw the line at the makeup."

Her face falls. "Why?"

"Because I don't trust your brother or your father not to take pictures and use them as blackmail."

She puts her hands on her hips. "Well that would just be mean. Besides, Mommy already has pictures of Daddy in my makeup."

A laugh bursts out of me. "Really. I might need to get a copy of that. I'm sure all of his Instagram followers would love to see it."

"They already did." She turns to skip away. "Mommy posted it, and it went viral. Daddy was soooo mad."

I chuckle as I follow her into the kitchen area to find my mom. "I'm sure he was."

As I come around the corner, it looks like the kitchen has exploded, which explains why the house smells like cookies. There's flour all over the counters and sugar, butter, vanilla—all kinds of ingredients are strewn everywhere. Mom looks like a mess with her hair pulled up and specks of dough stuck to her shirt.

"There's my boy," Mom says when she looks up and sees us, wrapping her arms around me. "I'm glad you're home for the week."

"Me too," I mumble into her hair as we embrace. "Hey how come I never saw that picture of Dad in makeup that went viral?"

Pulling away from me, she turns back to the batch of cookie dough in front of her. "Because it wasn't up that long. He made me take it down once Deuce called and started harassing him about it."

"Deuce harasses him about everything."

"Yeah, but it got really bad when the lipstick stained his lips a berry color. Took three days for it to finally fade." We both laugh at the visual image. I can only imagine his scowl when he realized his lips were going to be bright pink until it wore off. "Anyway, it took you awhile to get here. Was traffic bad?"

"It wasn't horrible, but it was definitely heavier than normal because of Thanksgiving," I say, sitting on the bar stool at the counter. What I don't tell her is I also got a late start because of this morning's make-out session with Annika. Some things a mother doesn't need to know. I also don't tell her I took regular breaks on purpose, extending my six-hour drive to eight.

Things still aren't fantastic with my dad. Sure, he's helped me out with getting Annika's hospital bill paid, and he clarified a bunch of information about the affair. But we still haven't gotten to the crux of the issue—his disappointment. I have a bad feeling it's going to come to a head this week.

Pushing that all out of my mind, I focus on two of the most important ladies in my life right in front of me.

"So, Lucy-Goosy, when do you go back to school?"

She frowns. "Tomorrow."

I look at my mom, furrowing my brow. "They're not out for the whole week?"

Shaking her head, she explains, "They only have half the week off this year. Supposedly, when the calendar vote went out, the majority of the parents voted for half a week at Thanksgiving, which could get us out for summer a couple days early."

"Supposedly?"

She glances up at me. I know that gleam in her eye. She doesn't believe the *supposedlies*. "The school district Facebook page is a wealth of information. It's been blowing up lately with people who don't believe the tally was accurate."

"That's a bit of a conspiracy theory, don't you think?"

She shrugs. "The superintendent's daughter is getting married in the Bahamas and the dates would have overlapped if the other calendar was implemented. The entire affair is non-refundable, and he would have lost out on a lot of money if the other calendar was used. Who knows if it's true, but it makes for some interesting gossip."

"Isn't that what vacation time is for?"

"Like I said, lots of conspiracy theories running around."

My mom has never been one for drama, but the longer her kids have been in this school district, the more hoity-toity she realizes people can be. Now she sits back and laughs at some of the obnoxiousness. She may have married into a whole bunch of money, but that's never changed who she is. She couldn't care less that we have a large house or that my dad can afford to take us all overseas for vacation. She doesn't give a shit about designer clothes or handbags. She just is who she is.

It never occurred to me when I was young that she went from struggling to make ends meet to starring in a season of in *Real Housewives of Dallas* practically overnight. But she did. It never changed her, and I like it that way. It keeps us all grounded.

"Mama, can I have a bowl of ice cream?" Lucy climbs up on the school next to mine and scoots as close to me as she can get.

"No, baby. It's almost bedtime."

"But Moooom," she whines. "I'm hungry."

"Tell ya what." She puts her mixing bowl down and shakes out her arms. She must have been doing this for hours. "If you're really that hungry, I'll let you have a bowl of cereal."

Excitement runs across Lucy's face. "Can I have the Fruity Pebbles?"

Mom sighs in resignation and probably with exhaustion. "Only because Jaxon is here, and it's a special occasion. Can you grab the cereal for me, Jax?" She gestures over her shoulder. "There should be a new box on the top shelf."

Standing up to grab Lucy's snack, I can't help to poke fun at my mom. "You know with how much sugar is in there, you might as well have given her the ice cream."

"Please don't remind me. I'm learning to let go of my failures as a parent," she jokes.

"What are you doing anyway?" I ask, as she rolls out more dough.

"I'm a football mom again. There's always a fundraiser happening."

Cringing, I remember all the times she spent volunteering when I was in middle and high school. Raising money for the football team became almost a full-time job. Bake sales. Donation requests. The list was never ending. "Only a few more years Ma, and you won't ever have to do it again."

She chortles. "Not sure what I'll do with all my free time."

Before I can toss out any ideas, the backdoor flies open and Matty comes racing in. He's wearing a grass-stained practice uniform, his face flush from exertion.

"Jaxon!" he yells when he sees me and ambles toward me quickly, like middle schoolers do when their bodies are growing faster than their balance can keep up with.

Despite the fact that he's almost as big as me, I'm still quicker. Getting him in a headlock, I ruffle his hair while he wraps his arms around my waist and fake punches me in the ribs.

"Boys, quit," Mom yells. "You're going to get sweat all over my cookies!" She sounds mad, but we all know she's thrilled to have everyone home again.

"There's the man we've been waiting for."

My dad's voice booms through the room. Releasing Matty, I look up at him, gauging Dad's reaction to my presence. He looks happy to see me, but still somewhat cautious. Apparently, we both feel the same tension—like there are all these unspoken words, and no one knows where to begin. So I just go in for a hug.

"Hey, Dad."

He slaps me on the back twice, pulls me back, and gives me the once-over. I roll my eyes, but for the first time, I don't hide my irritation as I say, "I'm fine, Dad."

He flinches at my anger. "Oh! No! You look good, son." It's the first time he's said that to me in a very long time, and I'm not sure how to interpret it. Is he pacifying me, or does he finally understand how annoying it is that he can't let my previous illness go?

Glancing at my mom, I can see her torn between focusing her attentions on my siblings, when all she really wants is to monitor our conversation.

"How's Annika?"

I can't hide my pleasant surprise at Dad asking. She's the one thing I could talk about all day.

Smiling shyly, I answer with, "She's good. She's real good. I mean, she's stressed because she front-loaded all her science classes, but I'm hoping a week off with her dad and brother will do her some good."

He doesn't say anything in response. He doesn't have to. I already know by looking at him that he really wants to poke fun at me for being a pussy-whipped fool. I wait for the banter to start, but Mom chimes in before it happens.

"I'm glad she's doing well," she interjects. "With everything she's gone through, it's nice to hear she's handling it well."

I bristle at the reminder of those first days when Annika wasn't doing well at all. I don't want to go there. Don't want to talk about that. "Yeah, well, she's the strongest person I've ever met in my life." Deflecting the conversation before it gets too intense, I redirect my attention to my kid brother, who is also binge eating Fruity Pebbles. "How was practice, Matty?"

"It was great!" he says between bites. "They wanna move me to running back."

"Really?" I chuckle when I hear my dad grunt in frustration.

"Not everyone can be a defensive lineman, honey," Mom says, wiping her hands on a towel and putting several cookie sheets in the oversized oven.

"Dad was pissed," Matty exclaims. "He got in the coach's face, yelling about how I was born to play defense, and he better get his head out of his ass if he wants to have a winning team."

"That is not what I said," Dad defends, but none of us believe him. Instead we laugh at what the scene probably looked like when a middle school coach was trying to calm down a stage dad.

Matty points his spoon at him while he chews. "You did too. You said Hart men are destined to be football greats." Matty looks back at me. "Deuce was standing right behind me. Trace and I were so embarrassed."

I roar with laughter. "Deuce was in on it too?"

Matty nods, clearly happy at his ability to entertain us with his story.

Catching my dad's eye, he's looking at me with a weird expression on his face. "Well, I mean, Hart men can do anything they want to do. There's no shame in being a doctor instead."

"Jason," Mom chides quietly, but it's too late. The mood in the room has already changed. It went from being happy-go-lucky, to stiff and uncomfortable.

I don't know what his problem is. I can't tell if he's trying to be supportive or if he's masking his disappointment, but a line in the sand has clearly been drawn. There's Matty, the one genetically designed to be Dad's mini-me. And there's me, who is Hart in name only.

Shaking my head, I glance away, refusing to look at him again, instead focusing on my chattering siblings. When it's time for them to go to bed, I offer to tuck Lucy in, mostly so I can go upstairs and get away from my parents.

After being coerced into reading three Barbie stories to Lucy, and talking shop with Matty, they're both finally down for the night. I can hear my parents still talking downstairs, and I'm sure they're waiting for me to spend some time catching up. But It was a long drive, and if I'm going to deal with this shit for the next several days, I need to pace myself. That's my excuse for avoiding, anyway.

Flopping back on my bed, I tuck one arm under my head and use the other to pull out my phone and send a text.

Me: I miss you already.

Annika's response is immediate.

Annika: I miss you too. More than you know.

A smile crosses my face as I doze off, not even bothering to change out of my jeans.

TWENTY
Annika

Normally, I like going home and hanging out with my dad and brother. It's nice having family time, and they're fun to be around. Plus, Thanksgiving break is right smack in the middle of football season, so we watch a lot of games. It's the one thing we've always been able to bond over, no matter what. We are the true epitome of a football family.

The three of us make it a point to go to the grocery store and stock up on all kinds of football food before every big game—from chips and queso to Bagel Bites to mozzarella sticks. My dad even likes to grill fajitas. We do it up big, inviting friends over and having a party every time the Steelers play.

What I wasn't anticipating this year was dating someone and how much I would miss him. Being away from Jaxon has been much harder than I thought it would be. Since we don't live in the same town, it's not like I can drive thirty minutes and meet him somewhere. We're a good four hours apart. Even for Texans who are used to driving long distances, that's still a hike.

It helps that we're texting every day and calling when we can. But it's still hard being without him.

I can tell from the tone of his voice when we do talk that he's really missing me too. But he needs this time with his family. He needs to hash out some things with his dad, especially now that Kade has appeared in his life.

"Annika."

I look over my shoulder as my dad tosses a newspaper down on the kitchen counter. My hands are greasy from cutting up Velveeta for the queso so I can't see what it is he's reading. I assume it has to do with football, since I'm making more game day food right now.

"What's up, Dad?"

"How well do you know this Hart boy?"

I've been waiting for this question. The minute I accidentally mentioned I was dating someone, there was no stopping the inevitable. I offered up few details about Jaxon but did try to make sure they understood I was happy and he is great to and for me. Of course, my brother, Damien, took that as his invitation to jump online and search for everything he could find about Jaxon Hart.

My dad wasn't too pleased to hear he's the son of a former pro-football player. For a man who doesn't follow Hollywood news or pop culture, his opinions on professional athletes and their behavior off the field is well-known. In his mind, football players—all athletes—are great to watch on the field, and they're fun to cheer for, but they don't always make great men. Faithful men.

I reminded both my dad and brother that Jason founded an organization that's sole purpose is to help people. That he puts others before himself every day. My brother found out about the foundation during his googling efforts. My dad was impressed with the mission of the foundation, and the work they've done to match patients with bone marrow donors, as well as helping to relieve the stress of medical bills on families who fall through the cracks otherwise.

Dad made a "hmrph" sound and walked away when he knew he couldn't argue with my logic.

"Like I told you before, Dad, we're getting to know each other."

"That doesn't tell me anything." He crosses his arms, a stern look on his face. "What are his intentions with you?"

"Are you kidding me, right now?" I ask with a laugh. "What are his intentions? This is not 1950."

"1950 was a much easier time to raise girls, if you ask me," he spouts. I roll my eyes because no one asked him. He wasn't even born back then, but I've been hearing this spiel my whole life. "The girls wore long dresses and none of those jackasses touched them."

I quirk an eyebrow at him, careful not slice myself with the knife as I look away from my meal prep. "No, the jackasses touched them back then, too. The girls were just sent away to deal with their *stomach tumor*," I say, making quotation marks with my fingers, "when they got knocked up."

"Hmrph." I don't have to look to know his mustache fluttered when he made that noise.

"Now, I trust your judgement and know you'll pick a good man," he says, as I throw the cheese in the crockpot. "But you never know. Some of them are real good at being charming, but only until they get what they want."

I snort another laugh. "Not that it's your business, but Jaxon hasn't tried anything with me, and we've been dating for like two months. Are you happy now?"

He takes a step back, clearly shocked. "He hasn't?"

"Nope. Except for some making out." Dad's face turns

red and I backpedal playfully. "I mean with very chaste kisses to the cheek after walking me to my door from the library. He's dreamy!" I clasp my hands together and hold them to my chest as I mock his antiquated ideas.

He gives me a look that says not to patronize him. I chuckle and level with him.

"Jaxon has been very respectful, Dad. Our relationship is not about that. He's pre-med. I'm pre-physical therapy so we have similar interests. He's third string on the football team, most times doesn't dress out, so I'm taking him tailgating in a couple weeks."

I'm not lying about that part. When Jaxon suggested borrowing his roommates truck so we can head to a game early, I squealed with delight. I'd kind of given up on the idea of participating in my favorite past-time activity this season, since I'm still a little leery in crowds. Since Lauren and I are on the outs, I might have to find a new tailgating partner anyway. But with Jaxon beside me, that covers all my bases. I can't wait.

"The only bad thing about him"—I see my dad bracing himself as I sigh with over-exaggerated disappointment—"he's a Chaps fan."

"That son of a bitch!" Dad yells, banging his fist on the counter. "Doesn't he know we bleed black and yellow?"

"I know. I told him," I agree with a shrug. "Don't worry. I'm working on him. It's going to take a little time since his dad is a retired Chaps."

Dad points right in my face. "I told you this kid was trouble. You keep your eye on him. If it weren't for that damn foundation, I'd have no respect for either one of those Hart men."

Laughing, I can't believe the ridiculousness of this conversation. "I know, Dad. But really, you'll like Jaxon. Give me some time, okay? It's still new. But I promise when the time is right, I'll bring him home for you to meet him."

"I just"—he runs his fingers through his hair, eyes following me as I piddle around the kitchen—"want you to be careful, Annika. Have you see the news lately?"

Grabbing the can opener to open the Rotel for the dip, I keep my hands busy. I have no idea where he's going with his, but my gut tells me it's not going to be good. "I don't watch the news, Dad."

"You should. Sexual assaults are up in your town."

"Really?" I try really hard to sound nonchalant, despite my heart beating rapidly. I have to force myself not to bristle, and I will my breathing to stay calm. "How do you know that?"

"Apparently the police are doing some digging." He taps his finger on the newspaper. That's what he was reading about. "There are an awful lot of girls ending up in the hospital full of that date rape drug."

Breath, Annika. Just breathe, I think to myself, trying to keep my hands from shaking and praying I don't slice myself on these cans. I'm barely paying attention to what I'm doing, just going through the motions as I try to keep myself calm.

"Lots of girls," he continues. "One of them was even dragged outside of a club and raped behind a dumpster, Annika. I don't want that to be you."

Ohgodohgodohgod. Keep breathing. Keep breathing.

"I just...I would feel better if we went over some of your self-defense moves. Maybe had a practice round or two with your brother."

I nod my head but don't say anything. I don't want to practice. We've gone over those moves for so many years, partly for fun, partly because it was the only way they knew how to teach me to protect myself. We did it so much in high school, those moves are like second nature to me. But what they don't seem to understand is there's not a lot of self-defense that will protect you when you're drugged and unconscious.

But I don't say any of that. Instead I nod my head in agreement. "Yeah. You can pull out the mat before I leave, and we can go over some moves."

"I need Damien to go extra hard on you. I don't want you to be the next victim. I don't think I could handle that."

I had thought about telling my dad about my attack this week, being honest and getting more support. But after this conversation, and seeing my dad's face at the thought of me being harmed, I know there is no way. It will crush them. "I get it, Dad. We'll practice for a bit, but not today since we're about to have guests. Where is Damien any-way?" I deflect, not sure I can handle much more of this conversation.

"He ran to the store for more beer."

I smile and nod at him. "Okay, good. I'm almost fin-ished here. Just need to throw the potato skins in the oven and dump the chips in a bowl. Is the living room set up, or do you need help moving furniture around?"

"Nah, you finish up here. I'll get the grill going. Those fajitas aren't going to cook themselves." He squeezes my shoulder as he passes by, grabbing the marinating meat and heading out the door.

As soon as his back is turned, I clutch my heart and release a deep breath. I love being home with my family, but I don't know if I can have another conversation like this one.

Snatching my phone up off the counter, I type out a quick text to the one person I know who can calm me down.

Me: Quick. Tell me something that will get my mind off my dad wanting me to practice self-defense moves.

With as fast as his response comes through, I'm guessing he's been looking for a distraction too.

Jaxon: My little sister forced us all to play beauty parlor, and I don't know how long my nails are going to be bright pink.

He attaches a picture of him, his dad, and a kid I assume is his brother, Matty, all sporting the world's messiest manicure. It makes me laugh out loud and immediately a sense of calm comes over me.

Me: You guys are super pretty.

Jaxon: You think that's good? You should see my toes.

Wiping my eyes, I can't stop the giggles. I'm still not looking forward to my dad pulling out that mat, but at least I'm calm enough again to get through the rest of the day. It's almost scary how Jaxon can do that for me. I just hope I can reciprocate it someday.

TWENTY-ONE
Jaxon

Every time I come home to visit, I work out with my dad. It's been that way ever since I left for college. But this morning's workout was awkward, to say the least. I went with Dad and Matty, meeting up with Deuce and Trace. It was like being the fifth wheel on a double date. The boys paired up and did their own thing, under the watchful eye of their dads. And the two retirees went through the motions of maintaining their physique. Neither of them is as solid as they used to be, but they aren't slouches either.

The only thing that made it bearable was Deuce's incessant chatter and jokes. Where Dad clammed up whenever we talked about my role in football, Deuce had no problem ribbing me, which is the way I like it. Yes, he pokes fun, but there is no doubt in my mind Deuce has mad respect that I stay on the team, despite the very real possibility that I'll never actually play a college football game, just because I love the game.

Dad doesn't seem to get that. No, he stayed quiet for the two hours we were at the gym. Even Deuce noticed Dad's abnormal demeanor and asked if he was getting laid enough. Then he laughed his ass off at my gagging sounds.

Now that we're home and Mom and Lucy are off on their annual Black Friday shopping trip, there's no buffer between us and the obvious distance. I need to get out of here, so I can get out of my head.

Me: What are you doing this afternoon? Wanna hit a movie with me?

I'm not expecting Kade to answer right away. We've texted back and forth a lot the last week or so, just random shit. He really is as into comics and video games as I suspected. But I'm also coming to the realization that Annika was right—he has no one.

Based on our conversations, no one realized he came to visit me, and he disappeared for almost thirty-six hours. Not his mom, not his teachers. He didn't even have any friends who were looking for him. It makes me sad for him. But it also makes me feel sad for me. He's my *brother*. For the most part, I've been surrounded by loving and supportive family my entire life, while my dad's son has been all alone. It's not fair.

Kade: Hell, yeah! Marvel just released the newest one. I've been dying to see it.

I snicker. Yeah, he's a total comic book freak. But at least we have something in common—I have yet to be disappointed in the big screen version of the characters.

Me: Cool. I can be there to get you in

about an hour. That gives you plenty of time to shower and get all gussied up for the ladies.

Kade: See you then.

Ok, there aren't actually any ladies we're going to see, but I'm not quite sure how else to encourage his hygiene habits. Maybe it's not my place to say anything, but clearly no one else has. And if he wants to make friends, maybe smelling a bit better will help.

Shoving my phone in my back pocket, I grab a Tupperware of cooked chicken breasts out of the fridge and make a plate to tide me over until I get some movie theater popcorn.

"What are you up to?" Dad saunters in the room, going for a plate too. When he puts it by mine on the counter, I snag another two chicken breasts with my fork and pop them on his plate. Working out makes all of us hungry.

"I'm heading out in a bit. Kade and I are going to a movie."

I don't have to look to know his whole body just stiffened. I can practically feel the concern rolling off of him.

Looking him in the eye, I challenge him with, "You gotta problem with that?"

He sighs and shakes his head. "I just want you to be careful. I don't trust his intentions."

"You've never met him. You have no idea what his intentions are."

After placing one of the plates in the microwave, he leans against the counter and crosses his arms. "I'll give you that one. But Jax, don't you find it weird that he randomly comes out of the woodwork fourteen years later?

It just makes me wonder if his mother put him up to it because she needs money."

"Seriously?" I sneer. "My brother finds me after all these years because no one else bothered to enlighten me on the subject, but you automatically assume it has something to do with you and your money? He's my brother."

"You don't know that yet. And besides, you already have a brother. He's upstairs playing video games."

Finally, I snap. "I. Am not. A HART!" I yell.

My dad reels back like he's been slapped, which should make me feel bad. But he doesn't get it. I look at the floor when I speak again because I don't want to see the look of hurt on his face. I may never be able to explain this to him again.

"I am a Hart because of nurture, Dad. You've raised me to be who am I since I was seven years old. But there's another part of me. The Bryant part. It's not perfect. It sure as hell isn't athletic. But it's *me*. And if you can't accept that part of my life, that part of my history…" I run my hand down my face in exasperation. "If you keep dismissing that part of me like it's irrelevant, then you're not the hero I thought you were."

I chance another look at him. Except for the tick in his jaw, he hasn't moved.

Pushing my plate aside, I grab my car keys. "I gotta go. I've got somewhere to be."

I don't bother waiting to see if he'll stop me. I leave, slamming the door behind me.

• • •

The *snick* the door makes sounds louder than normal because of how quiet it is in the house. I guess everyone is asleep since it's close to midnight. Everyone except my dad.

The light from the TV tells me exactly where he is—sitting on the couch in the living room with his feet up on the coffee table, watching ESPN. What I didn't expect was the bottle of Johnny Walker Black sitting next to him.

"Gift from Henry Davidson?"

Making a sound of satisfaction when he swallows, he lowers his glass and pours two fingers in a second glass I hadn't noticed before. "It's good stuff. Try it." He hands me the extra glass.

Bringing it to my lips, I try not to grimace from the smell. The burn on the way down my throat is even worse.

"Must be an acquired taste," I say through my cough as I beat my own chest.

He gives me a half-hearted smile. "I should have picked up more Shiner when we were out today."

"I was born and bred in Texas. It's almost a requirement to drink it."

The rumble of his chuckle is the only response I get before we go back to sitting in silence. I guess that's better than fighting with him, but I don't like how awkward things are between us. He's my dad. He's a great dad. I just don't know when I became such a disappointment to him.

"I fell in love with you when you were seven years old."

His words cut through the silence like a knife. Choosing my words less carefully than I should, my automatic reaction is to banter.

"That sounds creepy, Dad."

He looks at me and smirks. "Someday when you're a father you'll understand what I mean by that. It's the only way to truly describe what it feels like to be a parent. I love football. I love my mom. I love my job. But I'm so in love with my kids, sometimes it hurts to breathe."

"Then why are you disappointed in me?"

There. I said it. I laid it on the line and put the ball in his court. We may never have a chance to hash this out again. I'm ready to have this conversation and be done with it.

His expression isn't what I expected. He looks...sad. "I've never, ever wanted you to think I'm disappointed in you."

"Well, you have a shitty way of showing it." I take a breath to gather my thoughts. "I'm not yours. I know it. I've always known it. I'm not able to follow in your footsteps. Not in football. Not in business. I'm not who you want me to be."

"That's not true," he vehemently denies, pointing at me. "You are exactly who I want you to be. And you have always been mine."

"Really? You're not at all disappointed I'm not going to be working in the industry?"

He looks back to the TV, not making eye contact, and I know I've nailed it on the head. It hurts, I admit. I don't like being a disappointment to him.

"It's not that."

"It's not?" I challenge. "You won't even talk to me about Matty's games. Mom is the one who tells me when he's accomplished something, not you. Sure, you start telling me. I hear the excitement in your voice, see how proud you are in every gesture. Then you you look at me, your disappointment shows all over your face. You clam up and pretend it never happened when I'm around, because it's just a reminder that I'm lesser than."

He looks stunned that I would call him out. "That's not what happens at all. I just..."

"You just what?"

"I don't ever want you to think I'm prouder of him than I am of you. Or that I love him any more than I love you."

"You have a really bad way of showing it."

Our eyes make contact and hold, like we're vying for control. For the first time in maybe my entire life, he's the first to look away.

"In this family, you're either allowed in on the celebrations or you're treated like you don't deserve to know." I spew out the words, not with malice, but with all the hurt I've felt over the years. "That's not keeping me from feeling like Matty is more important. That's drawing a line in the sand. You've made it clear I'm either a part of football in this family or I'm not part of the family completely."

"Jax—"

"No" I cut him off. "I was in that hospital room with you every time Dr. Bates reminded us of the side effects of my treatments—potential growth issues, potential heart issues, potential sexual issues, potential dental issues. I knew, *knew,* any dreams I had of going pro were dead before we ever got the all clear on the cancer. But Dad, they were the dreams of a nine-year-old boy. Those dreams die for almost everyone. You're one of the very few who had them come true."

His cheeks are flushed, and I'm not sure if it's because he's angry or ashamed. But now that I'm on a roll, I can't stop.

"I don't keep playing football because I have a dream or because I'm trying to win your approval. I play football because it's fun. I have friends on the team. I get the best seats in the stadium when I dress out and sit on the bench. And Dr. Bates said I need to exercise for the rest of my life. Why not have fun doing it instead of getting used to a row machine and treadmill already?

"I've never strived for greatness in the game. But you know what I have strived for greatness in? Math, science, and statistics. Those are things I enjoy, that I'm not only good at but are also attainable. You missed that part, didn't you? It wasn't an extension of your dreams, so there was no reason to notice that part of me until I changed my major."

He points his finger and interrupts my rant. "Now that's not true. I've always known you were good at that stuff. That's why we talked about you being an agent."

"No, *you* talked about me being an agent. I went along with it for a while because maybe, just maybe, I'd be included in this family if I did."

"That's not fair—"

"You're right. It's not fair. It's not fair to me." I shake my head, exhausted from the emotion of this conversation. "I was the only Bryant left until Kade came along, and you remind me of that every single time you shut me out of the Hart side."

Taking a deep, calming breath, I suddenly have the need to be alone to put myself back together.

"Look, Dad, you've been the best father a kid can ask for. Always. But you have to sort this shit out. If you're trying to protect my feelings, or whatever, stop. It doesn't work and the only thing that happens is you shut me out. My dreams are mine. Just like Matty's dreams are Matty's. None of them are yours. Support us and encourage us. But for the love of Christ, stop trying to manipulate them."

I turn and walk away, unwilling to see how badly my words hurt him.

"Jason, tell him." I stop dead in my tracks as I hear my mom's voice calling from their bedroom door. "Tell him the truth. Stop trying to protect him from your own insecurities and level with him." Her breath hitches, and I know she's trying not to cry, but I refuse to turn around. "I'm tired of the two most important men in my life struggling to get along because they keep skirting around their issues."

I hear their door close, and I assume she went back to bed. My dad clears his throat before speaking. "It's not disappointment. It's never been disappointment. It's always been fear."

His words make me lose my breath. "Fear of what?"

He sucks in a couple breaths, like he wants to answer, but it takes him a few tries before he finally gets his words in order. "Before Matty was born, I was afraid of how that would change our relationship. I knew I loved you all the way into my bones, but with him being my biological child, I didn't know if it would feel different, ya know?"

Whether he wants them to or not, his words make my gut clench. I'm afraid of what he's going to say. No kid, even if he's an adult, wants to hear that his father loves his siblings more. Even in these circumstances. As much as I stand to lose, as much pain as I may face, I can't walk away. I have to listen.

"But then he was born. And not only did I have so much love for him, but the love I had for you grew. I didn't know I could feel that strongly about anyone. I didn't know those feelings could intensify. But they did. And it happened again when Lucy was born.

He takes a sip of his drink, and I hear the empty glass hit the table as he puts it down. "Then Matty started getting really good at football and you…"

"Didn't?" I offer, finally turning around.

He gives me a pointed look. "Found other interests. My entire life has revolved around football. I didn't know how to talk about math and science, but I didn't want our relationship, our closeness, to change.

"As Matty gets older, I see so much of myself in him. The same drive, the same determination. It's actually weird how much alike we are."

"And I'm like Austin, the man you hate."

I expect him to agree with me. To say he has a hard time not seeing the man he hates whenever he looks at me. But he doesn't. Instead, he shrugs.

"I don't know. I never met Austin."

"But you don't dispute that you hate him."

He sighs. "Hate is a strong word. From everything I know, he was a wonderful father to you, and I will always be grateful for that. But I have a serious lack of respect for the way he treated your mother. When she hurts, I hurt. So yes, if I think too much about it, it still makes me angry."

"And with Kade showing up, now you have to think about it more."

"I admit, it's been harder to put out of my mind recently. Mostly because I had to see the look on your mom's face when that old wound opened up."

I cringe and squeeze the bridge of my nose between my fingers. "I didn't want to tell her, Dad. I don't know that I could have seen her crushed like that. I still remember how much she cried before you came along, and I was only six."

"It wasn't your job to tell her, Jax. She and I are a team. It's my job to support her through bad times like it's her job to support me during bad times. But you're missing my point."

Sitting down next to him, I prop up my feet on the table in front of us and stare blankly at the TV, mirroring his pose.

"Yes, I'm excited about seeing Matty's future. I'm excited for all the possibilities. And I'll admit, I'm a bit of a stage dad."

The comment makes me chuckle. "I'll say. Did you really tell the coach Hart men are destined for football greatness?"

He groans and rubs his face. "Yeah, that wasn't exactly my finest moment." Turning to me, he gently punches my leg with his fist. "Jax, it's not that I don't want to talk about Matty with you or that I'm trying to exclude you. Hell, you're the one person I want to talk to about it! You get it. You have such a love for the game that I want to share it with you like we used to. But I'm fucking terrified that somehow I'll screw up my relationship with you by staying too focused on football. Or that I'll make you feel that I don't love you as much as I love him. When I see you, it's a reminder not to let my excitement take over."

That's it? That's what this whole issue has been? "You're trying to tell me you have been having your own version of adoption issues?"

He shrugs and turns back to the TV. "That's what my therapist calls it," he says quietly, and my head whips over to look at him.

"You're…in therapy?" All my life, my dad has been the strongest man I know. The one who holds everyone together. To hear that he's been getting professional help himself, it feels like I've been doused by cold water. Of course, it also makes more sense as to why he was adamant about me getting therapy after Annika's attack. He knew it would help, because it helped him.

He rubs his finger on his lip before answering me. "I know things have been off between us for a few years, and I don't know how to fix it. You used to look at me like I hung the moon, and now you look at me like…" He shakes his head but doesn't finish his sentence. "I didn't know how to fix it so I started seeing someone in the area. Apparently, this rift isn't that unusual in families like ours. I guess there are a lot of parents out there who have both biological and adopted kids, and sometimes the lines get blurred of how to feel and how to react to things. I've never, ever wanted you to feel less than, so I overcompensated and ended up doing the exact same thing I was trying to avoid. I have to live with that guilt. The fact that I caused my child an enormous amount of hurt by trying to keep him from being hurt is a tough pill to swallow."

"You do know how ridiculous that sounds, right?"

"You know how ridiculous I feel? Although not that any of us should be surprised. I'm not always the sharpest knife in the drawer. Your mother has quite a few examples, even from way back when we first started dating." We both chuckle, both of us seeming to feel the tension leave the room for the first time in a while. "I'm sorry, Jaxon. I never meant to make you feel less than. I've never been disappointed in you. Not once."

"Not even that time in high school when I drank half your vodka and filled the bottle back up with water?"

"Okay maybe once. It took me forever to figure out why my vodka went into the freezer as a liquid and came out as a solid."

We laugh again and spend the next few minutes sitting in silence, both of us wrapping our brains around this conversation. It never occurred to me that my dad would be afraid of losing me. That he struggles with his own adoption issues like I seem to be struggling with mine. In some ways, it's a weird kind of bonding moment.

Clearing my throat, I decide it's time to make my own confession. "I've been thinking about the foundation."

He stiffens just slightly, and I know it's because he doesn't trust where this is going. "What about it?"

"Dr. Bates is getting up there in years, ya know?" I look over at him, and he's watching me, with a ghost of a smile. "You're probably gonna need to replace him at some point. Maybe even around the time I get through my oncology residency."

His lips quirk up. "I'm not sure I could get Dr. Bates off the board if I tried."

"Maybe. But it might be cool to have someone with the latest training working alongside him and all his experience. Maybe he could *mentor* someone to take the reins."

He puts his arm around me, clasps my shoulder and squeezes. "I'd like that."

Finally, *finally* we're on the same page. It feels good to clear the air, although it still is kind of mind-boggling that a parent could struggle with their own version of adoption issues. That never even crossed my mind, and I'm not sure I totally understand it. But I guess until I adopt a child of my own, if I ever do, I'll just have to take his word for it.

And I wonder briefly, if that means he'll back off about me spending time with Kade and let his concerns go. I chuckle to myself. Not likely. But that's a fight for a different day.

TWENTY-TWO
Annika

I never thought I would be glad to use a community bathroom again, but I had to get out of my dad's house. I love him. I love my brother. But for the first time ever, I was uncomfortable being in my childhood home.

Maybe it was self-defense training I was practically forced to do, but most likely it was Jaxon not being there. In such a short amount of time, he's become a huge part of my life, and I miss him when we're not together. So when I hear his knock on the door, I have to stop myself from racing to answer.

I don't try very hard.

Swinging the door open, I try to calm my breathing as I look at the face I've missed.

"Is Lauren here?" He looks almost as desperate as I feel to be wrapped up in him.

I shake my head. "No."

"Where is she?"

"She won't be back until tomorrow morning."

That's all I say before he crashes into me, kissing me so passionately, I might just pass out. Kicking the door closed behind him, he pushes me up against the wall, plunging his tongue into my mouth while I tug on his hair.

Running his hands down my back, he grabs my ass, making me gasp. He immediately stops, but when I kiss him again, he knows it's the green light to continue. I can feel his biceps flexing as I run my fingertips down his arms, his chest, his stomach, and push my hands under his shirt where I feel his warm skin on my hands.

Pushing his shirt up, I'm desperate to get closer to him. He doesn't hesitate, instead ripping it over his head, pausing only long enough to smile at me before going in for more kisses.

His abs seem to go on for days and oddly, the smattering of dark chest hair he has turns me on more than I expected.

"Bed," I mumble against his lips, and I feel us swivel as we clumsily make our way around the corner and fall onto my mattress. His warm hands slide under my shirt, and he pulls back, watching my reaction. I bite my lip and nod, and slowly, together we rid me of my sweater.

His lips feel so good against my skin as he kisses down my neck, down my chest, over the swell of my breasts. When he pulls the cup of my bra down and takes my nipple in his mouth, I whimper, the sensation of his tongue flicking the peak overwhelming.

My eyes roll back, and I hold him close as his hand explores my stomach, my back, my hips. And when his hand finally makes its way over my leg to the apex of my thigh, I freeze. He rubs over my jeans and my breathing picks up, only this time it's not because of anticipation and pleasure.

This time it's fear.

"Get off me," I whisper quietly, trying not to freak out.

This is Jaxon—JAXON. The man I love and trust more than anyone else in this world. But it's like my body has disconnected from my brain, and I can't feel anything but afraid. He doesn't seem to recognize my freak out, enjoying peppering kisses on my bare skin, so I say it louder. "Get off, get off, GET OFF ME!" I yell and push him away with all my strength. He bolts upright, off the bed, hands raised in front of him as tears stream down my face.

"I'm off. I'm off, baby." He's trying to sound calm, but I can hear his own fear. "I'm not going to touch you, okay? It's okay. I'm off. You're okay."

Embarrassment and anger course through me as I curl into a ball on the bed and sob into my pillow. I thought I was doing well. I thought I was moving on and had pushed through the hard parts. I was wrong. "When will it go away, Jaxon? When will I not be broken anymore?"

He grabs my shirt off the floor and tugs it over my body, helping me get my arms in the sleeves before grabbing a blanket off Lauren's bed and tucking it in around me. It's like he knows I need to hide under the covers, hide from my fear, even if it's stupid and only for a few seconds. Then he sits next to me on the floor, far enough away that he's not touching me, but close enough that I can feel his warmth and comfort. Instinctively, I reach for him, never opening my eyes. Just the feel of his hand clasping mine makes me feel better.

"I'm sorry," I finally whisper when I run out of tears and get control over my emotions again.

"You have nothing to be sorry for," he murmurs into my hair, kissing me on the head. "And you're not broken."

I sniff and wipe my nose on my sleeve, which is super sexy and one more thing to be embarrassed about right now. "I don't know what happened. It's not like I remember anything so why did that freak me out?"

He runs his thumb over my palm gently. "It's going to take some time. That's the first time we've gone that far. One step at a time, ya know?"

I smile half-heartedly. He's…perfect. Rolling to my stomach, I cross my arms and rest my chin on them, sighing as I confess why this is probably on my mind again. "My dad made me practice self-defense moves with my brother."

"He did."

Nodding, I sigh again. "I didn't want to. I didn't want to put myself in a position where I might freak out, ya know? But he was adamant about making sure I can protect myself."

"No wonder it all came back to you right now."

Turning to look at him I ask, "What do you mean?"

"He took away your choice. You could have told him no, but that would have opened up questions and a conversation you didn't want to have, so you did it anyway. Sound familiar?"

It does. It so does. Everything that happened at the hospital was with my consent, but not because I wanted it. And it was horrible.

"I think you're onto something," I say, stroking his hand with my thumb. "It doesn't help that I almost told my dad."

"You did?"

Nodding, I sigh again. "I couldn't get the words out. He showed me this article about how"—I swallow hard and push through—"rapes are up in this area."

"Wait." Jaxon turns to look at me, concern written all over his face. "What do you mean they're up in the area?"

"I don't know. I didn't read the article. I know I should be aware of that stuff, but I couldn't."

"No, of course not, baby. I didn't mean to insinuate

that. I hadn't heard that, is all. I need to let Paul know," he mumbles as I flip over on the bed and stare at the ceiling.

"He was worried about my safety—my dad. I didn't want to crush him."

"I think," Jaxon says as he clasps my hand again, "you don't have to tell him if you don't want to. My dad said something this week about loving his kids so much it's hard to breathe sometimes, and I think that's probably the way your dad feels about you. So unless there's a reason for him to know, you don't have to feel guilty about not sharing it with him. Like, if your life was physically altered in some way, you wouldn't have a choice, ya know? But maybe part of the reason you don't want to tell him is because you know he probably doesn't want to know."

I smile at him, his words giving me the freedom to let go of the guilt of keeping my dad in the dark. "He really does want to think self-defense is enough. If he realized it was completely out of my control, it was just random, he would never get over it. But I don't want to talk about it anymore. It's depressing me. Let's change topics. Did you and your dad finally have a real conversation?"

He chuckles. "Yeah, we had it out finally."

Feeling stronger now and missing him next to me, I hold up the blankets, silently inviting him back under the covers, even as my heart still races. "Will you snuggle with me? A week is too long without lying next to you."

He grins. "You sure?"

Nodding, I move closer to the wall to make room for him. He doesn't waste any time, kicking his shoes off and climbing in next to me, pulling me close and situating my head on his shoulder. Once we're comfortable, I get back to our conversation.

"You were saying you had it out with your dad. How did it go?"

He doesn't say anything, and I know he's trying to put the conversation into words. After a few minutes of relaxing against each other, he finally says what's on his mind. "I knew I was going to die. When I was nine years old, I knew it was coming."

The heaviness of his confession is not at all what I was expecting. "That must have been scary."

"It wasn't actually," he continues, rubbing my arm absentmindedly. "Between the cancer and the chemo and the mouth sores, I was in so much pain. I was kind of looking forward to it."

I stay quiet, waiting for him to continue. I can tell he has a lot on his mind.

"I never told my parents," he admits. "It would crush them to hear it. But it's true. I remember being in that hospital bed. I remember resigning myself to the fact that I was going to die and was going to go live with my first dad in heaven.

"Then all the sudden, I was well. And I was happy about it, but my mindset had already changed. It's like I got this second chance at life, but all my childhood dreams were already gone."

Shifting my position to see him better, I say, "Everyone's childhood dreams disappear eventually. Yours may have changed sooner than most."

"That's exactly what happened. Everyone else always seems surprised football isn't in my genes, but come on. I'm five-eleven. I don't know if its genetics or if chemo stunted my growth, but either way, I'm nowhere close to being big enough for the pros. I don't care because I never wanted that career. But when I didn't die, I kept doing things I loved. Not just football and video games, but even at school. And I liked doing math and science. I never really knew where that came from, but now I think it's the

Bryant part of me that gives me those strengths. Like that whole nature versus nurture thing. Jason raised me to have a certain moral code and way of seeing life. But Austin gave me the proclivities to certain interests."

"You think your dad understands that now?"

My head moves up and down when he shrugs. "I think so. I think he's having his own adoption issues right now, which is super weird." I giggle at the confusion he clearly feels. "But I guess he's so much larger than life, he has a hard time relating to someone normal like me."

I poke him in the ribs. "I don't think you're normal. I think you're just as extraordinary as he is."

Jaxon turns to look at me and I can't help but caress his cheek with my hand and lean in to kiss him again. We both know sex is off the table for now, but it still feels good to kiss slowly and with feeling.

"I'm sorry you have blue balls now," I whisper against his lips, making him laugh.

"No worries. I wasn't far enough along for that anyway."

Crinkling my brow, I ask, "You mean you weren't turned on?"

"On no. I was turned on. It's just"— red-faced, he runs his fingers through his hair like he's nervous—"sometimes it just takes my body longer to react than normal."

I lean up on my elbows to get a better look at him. "I don't understand."

"Just another fun long-term side effect of chemo." Wrapping his arms around my waist, he snuggles his face in my shoulder, hiding like I did a few minutes ago. Looks like we both need to take a minute when forced to face our humiliations.

"Wait." I punch his shoulder lightly trying to get him to look at me. "What does that mean? Like, you can't get it up, or…"

He sighs and pulls back to look at me, despite his embarrassment. "I can get it up. Sometimes it takes a while. And sometimes it takes me a while to…uh…finish."

I blink several times, wrapping my brain around this new information. "But, why only sometimes."

"That's the part I don't know," he says with a shrug. "I haven't figured out if it's when I'm tired or stressed or what. But the good thing is I've learned how to be patient, so I'm a very giving lover." He wiggles his eyebrows up and down, an ornery look on his face, and I can't help my belly laugh because of it.

"But seriously, Annika." His voice seems to drop an octave and takes on a serious tone. "That means we don't have a choice but to go slow when we decide to go there. And I promise, we'll get there."

I smile shyly before leaning up and kissing him again. I'm lucky to be able to love this man. Even through the biggest struggle of my life, he's everything I need.

TWENTY-THREE
Jaxon

"**S**eventeen! Eighteen! Nineteen! Come on, Hart!,"
Germaine yells, me groaning through my last
leg press. "Give it all you got! Twenty!"

My eyes squeezed tight, I yell my relief as I finish and
lock the machine in place. A week off for the holidays really did me in. I knew I should have pushed harder during
the workouts with my dad. I didn't, and now I'm suffering
for it.

"What's the matter with you?" he asks as I climb out
of the leg press machine and begin adding another seventy pounds for his turn. "You stay up too late after we
got home last night? Don't think I didn't notice you never
came home after walking Annika to her dorm."

I chuckle at his razzing. He has no idea Annika had a
freak-out moment yesterday, or that the whole reason we
went out with him was because we had decided on a whim
to get out of the dorms and cool off with some wings and
beer. Since Germaine was back in town, I asked him to join

us. I'm glad I did because they hit it off. I mean, *really* hit it off.

They talked so much shit to each other about football that I just sat back and let them go at it, waiting to see who would come out on top. It was hilarious how mad they would get while arguing and debating over the best players and best teams. It was great.

When we got to her door, I gave her a quick kiss and turned to leave, but she asked me to stay. I knew we weren't going to pick up where we left off earlier, but spending time with her is what I love. We settled in to some chick-flick that we never made it to the end of, both falling asleep. I'll never admit that to my nosy roommate, though.

"Don't be hatin'," I reply as he gets settled into the weight machine. "Just because I have a warm body to keep me company at night doesn't mean you can get all jealous."

He pushes the weights up with a grunt and holds them there while he finishes his thought. "I'd say you were wrong, but I admit it…I'm jealous. She's a cool girl." Then he grunts again as he begins to work his legs.

Twenty reps later, he continues. "Loves football. Loves beer. Loves wings. Seriously man, where can I find a girl like her? She got any friends?"

I laugh out loud, thinking about how exact opposite Lauren is from Annika. Come to think of it, Lauren and Germaine might actually get along.

"Oh, she has friends all right." I huff out as I re-rack the plates now that we're done. "But there's only one Annika."

"I guess I'll just have to keep sorting through the pussy before I find what I'm looking for." He slaps me on the back as we walk to the next station.

Leg day is always the roughest. Especially when Coach

works sleds into our routine. I fucking hate the sled. Dragging that shit stacked with two hundred pounds of weight on it is not my idea of fun. Today is going to be harder than normal after binge eating Thanksgiving dinner.

As we attach the shoulder straps in preparation, he asks about Kade.

"What did you do over break? Just hang with the fam? Did you see your brother?"

"Sure did."

"How'd that go?"

"It went well." I grab more plates to add to the sled. Shit. This is gonna be heavy. "We went and saw a movie and then to the mall for a little while. He's uh…never really had anyone teach him about style before. I helped him out a little bit."

Germaine wraps the straps around him, setting himself up to go. "I guess he didn't get your pretty boy genes then, huh? Trying to show him how to be the ladies' man you are?"

"Shut up," I joke, pushing down on the sled with my body weight so he can't move it. "He's fourteen. Give him a couple years to become studly like his older brother."

Finally looking over his shoulder to see why the sled isn't moving yet, he glares at me. "Get off, asshole. You're gonna make me throw my back out trying to pull you." Turning back around and getting into position, he adds, "And fourteen is a sucky age. You couldn't pay me to go back to high school. That shit was terrible." He grunts as he begins a slow jog to the other side of the room, dragging over two hundred pounds behind him.

When he makes it back and we begin the switch for my turn, I ask what is sure to be a loaded question. "How was it with your sisters?"

He shoots me a glare, making me laugh. Germaine is

the oldest of four, and the only boy, so he has a strong protective instinct over his sisters. But none of them are pushovers, and none of them listen to anything he says, so he gets irritated when he goes home for any length of time.

"I met Jackie's boyfriend." He doesn't even bother hiding his distain. "He's a total fucking douchebag. Bucked up to me when I told him I'd break his dick off if he hurt my sister."

I chuckle. "I might buck up to you too, if the family jewels are on the line. My boys aren't going down without a fight."

"Not my point," he argues. "You wanna show respect to the girl? Show respect to the family, man."

"Don't you think you might be a little bit overbearing?"

He cocks his eyebrow. "Jackie is seventeen years old. Maggie is fifteen. And all of a sudden my little twelve-year-old baby sister Amy has boobs, man. Boobs! What the fuck am I supposed to do with that?"

"Uh, nothing? They're her boobs, not yours."

He drops another weight on the sled, ensuring it makes a "bang" as it hits the bottom. "You just wait until Lucy is wearing a bra. No way you're gonna keep from going ape shit when you see some guy checking her out."

Pointing at him, I say, "That will never happen. She's going to stay eight years old forever."

He just laughs. "That's what I thought. It's all fun and games until it's your little sister."

The thought of my Lucy-Goosy, who spent hours doing my hair in little ponytails this past week, becoming a teenager is the motivation I need to pull the damn sled across the room and back.

Almost an hour later, we hit the showers, listening to the banter of all our teammates as they discuss their week off. Everyone was disappointed when the team didn't get picked for a bowl game this year, but from the laughter in the locker room, they got over it.

Pulling my shirt over my head after finishing up my shower, I grab my phone out of my locker. A text and a missed call.

"I think I'm gonna go out to eat, maybe check out Buck's and see what's on cable before hitting the books," Germaine casually mentions while getting dressed. "You guys wanna come along?"

Opening my text, I see it's Kade. He's sent me a meme referencing Star Wars. "Yeah, maybe. I'll have to see what Annika's up to." Turning the phone around to show him, I add, "I can honestly say I have no idea what Kade is talking about half the time."

Germaine looks confused as he tries to understand what the hell he's reading. Finally, he gives up with a shake of his head. "Like I said, you couldn't pay me to be fourteen again."

Chuckling, I close out the text and hit the button for my voicemails. It's from my dad.

"Hey, Jax, it's Dad. Listen, I know you're probably in practice right now, but you said something a few weeks ago about the foundation posters being outdated. We were tossing around some marketing ideas today, and I had a thought. What if we did some new pictures with you as an adult, and something about how Hart to Heart is helping keep dreams alive? I don't know. I'm sure the team will come up with something more catchy than that. But give people a reference point to how long we've been around, and maybe throw some statistics about how many donors have been added to the registry. That means you'd still be one of the faces of the Foundation. If you're opposed to it, that's okay. But just think about it."

He pauses just as I hear a beeping noise. Looking at the screen, a number I don't recognize is trying to call in, so I ignore it. I'm too busy listening to how nervous my dad sounds. I know it took a lot for him to even pitch the idea to me. He's definitely trying to mend our relationship, and he's put the ball in my court.

"Anyway, you're right when you said you're not a kid anymore. You're an adult. And it's totally your choice, but you have an awesome story of a child with leukemia growing up to be a pediatric oncologist. I think it could really encourage people. Just let me know. Love you, son. Don't push too hard...er...never mind. You know what's best."

I chuckle. He's trying hard to let go of his overbearing nature, but that's one thing about my dad. When he loves someone, he loves them fiercely. When I think of it that way, it's not as annoying. This time.

"Call me when you can."

When the message ends, I quickly click over to my texts and type one out to him.

Me: Got your message. Great idea. I'm in. I'll call when I can to hash out the details.

Pausing, I think for a second before adding something I haven't said in a while.

Love you too.

Just as I press send and get ready to shove my phone in my back pocket, it alerts me of another message. I quickly open it up as I grab the rest of my stuff. Until I hear who it's from. Then I freeze.

"Jaxon, this is Detective Bellerini. I interviewed you the night of the attack behind Ambrosia. We got the guy."

My legs give out, and thankfully, there's a bench right

behind me so I don't end up with my butt on the floor. They got the guy. The guy who raped Annika. They got him.

"I need you to come in at your earliest convenience. I'd like to go over some of your statements and verify some of the details. And I need to let you know what happens next. Give me a call at this number as soon as you can."

I drop the phone from my ear before he can give me the number. My brain is running a thousand miles an hour. Who is he? Who is this asshole that assaulted my girlfriend? And do they have enough to keep him locked up?

I barely register Germaine's voice when he asks, "Dude. Are you okay?"

"They got the guy." It comes out like a whisper, but I'm pretty sure I'm in shock. I can't think. I can't move.

"Got what guy?"

I blink a few times and look up at my best friend. The one I've kept everything from, but who is about to find out all the details anyway. Getting the guy could mean a trial. A surge of adrenaline jolts through me, and all I can think is I have to get to Annika.

Jumping up, I turn back to my locker, waving my hands as I talk. "The guy. The *guy*, Germaine. The guy from behind Ambrosia that night."

"What are you talking about?"

I look down when my phone makes a noise, and I realize I never ended my call. "Here, listen." I hand him my phone as I grab all my shit, shoving my wallet and my keys in my pocket.

Germaine listens to the voicemail, and I know when he puts together the importance of this call. "Holy shit, they got the guy. But why are they calling you…?" He pauses as realization hits. "Holy shit. You're the guy who found her?"

I clench my fists and look at the floor, nodding once.

"Why didn't you tell me?" He looks legitimately hurt, but I don't have time to make it right. If I just got this call, Annika either already got a similar one, or it's coming soon.

Instead I give him my default answer. "It wasn't my story to tell."

He rubs his hand over his short hair, still putting it all together. "Your nightmares a couple months ago. Your lack of focus. It was all about this, wasn't it?"

I nod again and grab my phone from him, shoving it in my back pocket. "I gotta go man. I gotta get to Annika. She's going to be freaking out."

"What does she have to do with this?" The words are barely out before I see the final puzzle piece fall into place. "Holy shit. It was Annika? Annika was the girl who got… who you found?"

My jaw clenches as a wave of anger runs through me. Not at Germaine, but at knowing how difficult this is going to be on her. On us both. Giving him a pointed look, I slam my locker and prepare to bolt. "It's her story to tell. Please keep it to yourself." He nods in agreement, still looking shell-shocked. "But I promise, we'll talk later."

Then I bolt out the door, not looking back.

TWENTY-FOUR
Annika

It's still tense around here. Too tense. I've tried to talk to Lauren since she's gotten back from break, but she doesn't seem interested in talking to me. I can see the hurt by my lack of attention in her eyes when she looks at me. And she doesn't look at me very much. Mostly she ignores me.

It makes me sad to know our relationship has suffered this way because she hasn't done anything wrong. Then again, neither have I. Still, the more time that goes by, a giant void grows between us, and it's filled with this horrible secret I haven't been able to tell her. I know I should, so she knows none of this is about her, but the thought of her knowing my deepest humiliation makes me freeze up.

In general, I'm doing better, though. I'm not as afraid. I can go out in public alone again. I still have a hard time with crowded places. But on campus, I'm doing fine. So tonight, I'm going to use my progress to show her that things are okay.

With Jaxon still at practice, I'm dressed and ready to go. And as soon she gets in from her late afternoon class, I'm going to see if she wants to go to dinner with me. Just me. In the dining hall so she can see that none of this has to do with me not wanting to be seen with her.

As I wait I try to concentrate on my clinical biology class, but I'm too busy bouncing my knee to get anything done.

When I finally hear the door open and shut behind her, I stand up and smooth my hands down my pants. I'm wearing jeans and a long-sleeved shirt. *This is good*, I remind myself. *I've made a lot of progress. This is just one more step. And it's a step I need to take. Lauren deserves it.*

Coming around the corner, she sees me standing there, waiting for her. She quickly looks away, knowing I'm not letting this go anymore.

"What's up?"

"Um, I was getting hungry. I wanted to know if you would like to go eat with me in the dining hall." I cringe when I realize it sounds like I'm asking her on a date. What an awkward way to start.

She freezes, looks up at me again, but with indecision on her face. I can tell she doesn't trust why I'm asking so she's hesitant to say yes. Finally, after what seems like an hour, but is probably only seconds, she turns away and laughs. "Let me guess…Jaxon isn't done with practice yet."

My shoulders drop because she's right, but she's not going to believe he has nothing to do with this. "No, he's not. But I wasn't waiting on him. I was waiting on you."

She whips around and crosses her arms over her chest, cocking out her hip. "How come? Finally decided I'm good enough to hang out with again?"

I close my eyes and will my frustration away. "No," I

say, biting back the snarky comment that wants to come out. She has a right to feel like I've dismissed her, because I have. It was with good reason, but I know it's been painful for her. I hold my tongue and instead calmly say, "That has nothing to do with it. I just wanted to have dinner with my best friend."

She stands there for a few more seconds trying to decide what to do and how to respond. "Yeah. I don't think so. I think the minute that your phone rings, you're going to be off with your new friends anyway. I don't need that kind of bullshit in my life."

"Lauren, that's not—"

"Save it." She holds her hand out to me. "I've been through this before. If you don't like me, that's fine. Don't like me. But don't patronize me too, okay? I can find some real friends."

"Lauren, I *am* your real friend—"

"No, stop. This is not how friends treat each other. I went through this in high school. I'm not doing this again."

"Lauren, would you listen to me—"

"No! There's nothing you could say to make this better right now—"

"Lauren! I was raped!"

As soon as the words tumble out of my mouth, I know I can't take them back. Lauren stumbles back and her eyes get wide. The bravado she had deflates as she whispers, "What?"

Taking a deep breath, I steel myself to finally tell her the truth that has been between us all this time. It's ugly and dirty and terrible, but I already dropped the bomb. Now I have to answer her questions, no matter how much I don't want to say it out loud. "I was raped."

Her face pales and I can see the questions in her eyes, but all that comes out is "When?"

"The night we went out."

She looks off to the side, and I can practically see the gears turning in her head. "The night at Ambrosia? When Kiersten was here?"

I nod.

"By who?"

"I don't know." I sink down on my bed, shoving my hands between my thighs as I curl into myself. I refuse to put on a sweatshirt. I refuse to hide from this. Not in front of my best friend. But I can't look her in the eye either.

"What do you mean you don't know?"

"He said his name was Ron."

She's quiet again, thinking, and I know she's trying to figure out if we know anyone by that name. What she doesn't realize is if we had, Jaxon would have already figured it out and found him by now.

"I...I don't understand," she finally says, slowly collapsing on her bed across from me. "You...you spent the night with Jaxon that night."

I shake my head. "He drove me home from the hospital. Jaxon is the one who found me."

"Found you?" she quips. "What do you mean *found you*? Where were you?"

I close my eyes tight again before answering. "Unconscious behind a dumpster."

"What?" she shrieks. "What the hell, Annika? What happened? Tell me. I need to know."

Her voice is getting more high-pitched and hysterical. This is the reaction I knew would happen, but it wasn't what I was trying to avoid. I was trying to avoid more humiliation by protecting myself from having to talk about this over and over again. But now, here I am. Talking about it. I might as well go all out.

"Apparently I was drugged."

She opens her mouth to say something, but nothing comes out. Her eyes widen as she takes in the information I'm giving her.

"Jaxon found me and called the cops. When I got to the hospital, they tested my blood and found a bunch of drugs in my system. The police think someone put something in my drink and then helped me outside when I got sick. I don't remember anything after that."

She sits back, and I can tell she's in a state of disbelief. In shock. And who can blame her?

Taking a second to process her thoughts, she looks at me and says, "Annika, why didn't you tell me?"

It's a valid question, but the only thing I can do is shrug. "I didn't want you to know?"

"How come? I'm your best friend. I would have helped you through this."

I laugh humorlessly and look at the ceiling. "Lauren no one could help me through this. Don't you understand? I'm the one who's always telling you to be safe. I'm the one who broke Martin Rawson's nose at Homecoming when he tried to grab my boob. This wasn't supposed to happen to me."

She comes over to sit next to me and grabs my hand as I bat away a stray tear. "That is a load of bullshit," she says, turning to look at me. "You're the strongest person I've ever met. You're the smartest person I've ever met. But Annika, there is nothing you can do if someone drugs you. Nothing." She looks away suddenly. "Except, remember there is safety in numbers so someone always has your back, and I didn't. I was there, and I didn't even notice."

Now it's my turn to look at her. "No. No Lauren, do not go there."

"But it's true. You never texted me back when I was trying to find you, and I just assumed it was because you'd hooked up with someone and were busy. I saw the police outside the club, and it didn't even cross my mind that it would have anything to do with you. And then when you came home with Jaxon that morning and you were wearing his scrubs—" She stops and looks at me. "They weren't his scrubs were they?"

I shake my head. "No. But he really is pre-med."

She giggles softly and looks back at me. "I'm sorry Annika. I'm so sorry. I'm the world's worst friend." Tears cascade down her cheeks and mine are quick to follow.

"There is no way any of us could have anticipated this," I say, tucking a stray lock of her hair behind her ear. "We're taught to be careful when we're at a frat party. We're taught to be careful when we're alone with a guy. But we were in a crowded room full of people. In a business. Together. Safety in numbers and all that shit. But did it matter? No! I didn't even turn my back on my drink for that long. It was half a second. Half a second to wipe the booze off my leg. Half a second is all it took. You can't be responsible for every half-second of everyone's life. Hell, I can't be responsible for every half-second of my own."

She sniffs and itches her nose with the back of her thumb. "I just, I can't believe you've gone through all of this alone."

I smile shyly at her. "I mean, I haven't exactly been alone."

She perks up a little at my implication. "Jaxon really is that amazing?"

I nod and smile. "Yeah. He's been with me every step of the way. Hasn't told a soul, and he's been so respectful. Hasn't pushed my boundaries but encourages me, ya know? Like, he encouraged me to get back into public again. Encouraged me to get back out of my dingy sweats and into regular clothes."

Her eyes widen. "You didn't have the fucking flu, did you?"

I can't help but laugh at that. "No, I'm sorry. I never even went to the clinic."

"Damn, this room smelled like Lysol for weeks after I disinfected."

The giggles take over, and we laugh for way too long over something that isn't really that funny. But we needed this. We needed to clear the air, and we needed the comic relief. It's nice that this is no longer a wedge between us.

"I'm sorry I didn't tell you before, Lauren. I needed time to process it, and at a certain point, it seemed like too much time had passed."

"I get it." She pulls me in for a hug. "But if you ever keep something like this from me again, I will kick your ass. I don't care how many self-defense moves you know."

I laugh into her shoulder, enjoying having my best friend back.

The feeling is short lived when someone bangs on our door.

"Annika!" we hear Jaxon yell. "Annika, let me in!"

She looks at me quizzically. "What the hell is his problem?" She jumps up and heads for the door.

"No idea. He sounds panicked, though."

He bangs again. "Annika, let me in. It's important."

"Hang on, Loverboy," Lauren calls as she picks up her pace. Opening the door, she starts with "What's got you—?"

But he races past before she can finish her sentence and runs straight to me. "Annika, are you okay?"

He's on his knees in front of me and that has me on high alert. "Why? What happened?"

"Did you get the phone call yet?"

I grab my phone off the counter and sure enough the

light is blinking indicating a voicemail. I quickly open the call log and look at the phone number, but don't recognize it. "I guess. Who is this from?"

"Don't listen to that yet." He grabs my phone and tosses it on my bed, clasping my hands in his before he says the words that turn everything upside down again. "They caught him. They caught that Ron guy."

My vision begins to swim and my breathing gets heavy. Suddenly Lauren is sitting next to me, rubbing circles on my back while Jaxon cups my cheeks, holding my gaze. "Breathe, baby. Breathe." I concentrate on breathing in through my nose and out through my mouth, trying not to pass out as he keeps talking. "They want us to come down to the police station, okay? But I'm going with you. You're not going to do this alone."

"They got the guy," I whisper, concentrating on looking at him while I try to ward off the fear coursing through me.

"Yeah, they did," he confirms. "It's almost over, baby."

He stands us both up, wrapping his arms around me. All I can do is inhale his scent. Thinking too hard makes me want to hyperventilate.

"She just told me," Lauren says over my shoulder while I just keep breathing.

"Good," Jaxon responds. "It's going to take all of us to get through whatever comes next."

I hold him tighter, taking just a minute to gather my strength. Right now, all I want to do is hide, but I won't do that anymore. I won't.

It's time to take back all my control.

TWENTY-FIVE
Jaxon

The chairs in the police station waiting room are not at all meant for waiting. They're hard plastic and are making my back hurt. We've been waiting here for close to an hour and the irony of this moment is not lost on me.

We started this entire ordeal with me sitting in an uncomfortable hospital chair waiting to find out if Annika was okay. Before I even knew her name or who she was.

Now, we're sitting here together, on equally uncomfortable police station chairs, waiting to find out if this nightmare is almost over.

Except for getting in and out of the car, I've not stopped touching Annika since getting to her dorm room. The look on her face when I told her the news…fuck, I will never forget that. It was part fear, part sadness, part humiliation, and a whole hell of a lot of anger.

Reaching out her hand, she places it on my shaking knee. "Stop," she says quietly, stopping my bouncing.

"You're making me more anxious."

"Sorry," I mumble and rub my hand down my face. I'm trying really hard to be strong here, but the anticipation of what's coming has me on edge. The scenes from that night keep flashing through my brain, and I have a bad feeling we're about to plummet right back into nightmares. I'm praying that's not the case, but regardless, it might be time to set up another appointment with my counselor, Harold.

I only agreed to meet with Harold after Coach gave me an ultimatum. I went, I participated, and I felt better. Then I stopped going. Now I realize that might not have been a smartest idea. Like maybe I've been pushing all these issues aside instead of dealing with them. Or maybe this is how everyone feels, even after years of waiting for answers.

A door slams in the distance, and my ears focus on the squeaky footsteps. Looking to my right, I see him coming towards us. It's the detective I talked to outside of Ambrosia. I'd recognize him anywhere. Bushy mustache. Big beer belly. A little bit of waddle to his walk. *Why do police departments always have one guy who looks like a walrus?*

There is no doubt in my mind he's coming for us, so I stand to greet him, pulling Annika up with me.

"Jaxon, nice to see you again." He puts his hand out for me to shake, me mumbling my greetings in response, then he turns to Annika. "I'm Detective Bellerini. Sorry we haven't met before. I took over the case a couple weeks ago when the lead detective retired."

"Annika. Annika Leander," she replies, her voice strong.

He looks back and forth between us for a few seconds, clearly confused. "I didn't expect to see you here at the same time. I assume that's not a coincidence."

Annika smiles shyly at me. I know how much she hates

explaining herself. It makes her uncomfortable for people to know this much about her. She prefers to keep her private life private. "No, we uh, we've been hanging out for a couple months," she says by way of explanation.

The detective just nods. "It's actually not terribly surprising. Over the years I've seen my fair share of people who've been thrown together due to a tragedy, and they end up having very happy lives together. Funny how fate works that way."

I put my arm around Annika's shoulder and squeeze her to me. He just said the exact opposite of what our counselors have been warning us of. It's nice hearing from someone outside the therapy session that this *does* happen. People do fall in love amidst tragedy. This is real.

"I'm assuming y'all are here for the same information. If you wanna follow me, I can do this once with both of you, or I can split you up. Totally up to you." He looks back and forth at us again, waiting for a decision.

Annika reaches down and grabs onto my pant leg, like she's worried I'll take off without her. "We want to do this together, please."

He nods again. "Follow me." He turns around, squeaky shoes going back down the same hallway he just came from.

Once we're settled into his small, bare office, in chairs that are much more comfortable than the ones in the waiting room, he pulls out a file. "We got a call about a week ago from a girl who was assaulted at a frat party."

Annika gasps next to me and my jaw drops open. He certainly didn't waste any time before jumping right into that information.

"I'll leave out most of the details. What I will say is somehow, someway, she was coherent enough to call her mother. Girl happens to be a local, and when she told her mother where she was and that she felt funny, her mom called her own brother, who's a cop, and they tracked her down."

"How'd they do that?" I ask. It all sounds too easy, too simple.

"The brother happens to be a cop in this department." *That explains it.* "Wasn't hard to track her phone. Found her at the Kappa Phi house pretty easy."

"Kappa Phi?" I exclaim, stunned.

"Yeah. You know the place?"

"I was there at Halloween." I was this close to the scene of yet another crime. Visions of the drunk girl I saw come back to me. All I can do is pray that the rapist wasn't there that night and she ended up home safe. I feel Annika bristle next to me. She knows I was there.

"I can't say much more about that," he continues. "The guy isn't part of the fraternity, so we can't hold them responsible. Anyway, when the mom and her brother got there, they searched the rooms and found her upstairs, passed out cold. The guy who assaulted her was still there."

Annika gasps, throwing her hands over her face.

"What the hell?"

"He was in the bathroom trying to dispose of some evidence, but he was in cuffs before he could. It was a lucky break, one we've been waiting for. Once we collected DNA evidence at the scene, we were able to link it right back to him."

"Holy shit," I exclaim. "That seems too easy."

"It wasn't easy. It was lucky. Sometimes luck is all we have to go on. I wish it would have been sooner, though." His face falls slightly. "The girl called her mom before the attack, right as she was starting to feel sick. From what we can figure, he didn't see her make a phone call before she passed out or he probably would have altered his plans. It's just unfortunate we didn't get there sooner."

The weight of his words hang heavy in the room. They finally cracked a case they've been working on, but it came at the expense of yet another girl being raped.

Annika clears her throat before speaking. "Um, my dad had said there was an increase in sexual assaults in the area." I grab her hand and intertwine our fingers. She squeezes. "How did you know that this is the guy who… who…how do you know I'm involved?"

"That's a good question," Detective Bellerini answers kindly. "There's a bit of a backlog of getting all the sexual assault kids processed. However, yours had been done. When we ran the DNA into the system, yours popped up as a match." He sighs like he's choosing his next words carefully. "Look, I shouldn't be telling you this, but I feel like you have a right to know."

I sit up straight, immediately on alert. This feels like information overload now.

"The DA is taking this case before the Grand Jury because we want this guy off the streets. But I'm not done investigating. My gut says there's more. And I want to find them."

Annika gasps again and my head drops. Before he continues, I recognize that her breathing is getting irregular. I look up and see the fear on her face. Grabbing her face in my hands, I force her turn toward me.

"Annika, look at me." Tears are streaming down her cheeks and my heart breaks, knowing this is the beginning of what is going to be a rough few months.

"Baby, look at me." She holds my gaze. "You're okay. You're safe. They got him, honey. The police got him." She tries to smile, but it comes out like a sob. I continue to stroke her hair and rub my thumbs over her cheeks as she works on getting her breathing under control.

Detective Bellerini sits quietly, giving her a moment to pull her herself back together. When she finally opens her eyes, I can see the fiery determination has come back. She will not let this crush her. She refuses. I smile and nod once, because I get it. She doesn't need me to ask if she's okay. She is absolutely okay. She's shell-shocked and probably afraid of the near future. But she's ready to help the police in any way possible.

Pulling away from me and turning back to the detective, she confirms my assessment. "Sorry about that."

"No apologies necessary." He leans forward on his desk. "Just part of the job."

"What happens now?" Annika asks, ready to face the future.

"He's been sitting in holding for the last week. The judge denied bond until the DA has more evidence. Now that we've collected it all, he's gonna sit for a while. We're hoping the judge will think he's dangerous enough to keep him locked up, but it could go either way. We'll have another hearing tomorrow where the District Attorney will present everything to the Grand Jury, and we'll go from there."

"What do we need to prepare for?"

"The Grand Jury will want to hear both your testimonies." I grimace at his words. "It's not going to be a picnic, but they try to be respectful, especially since neither of you are the ones on trial."

We sit in silence absorbing all the possibilities. Annika scooches forward on her chair, looks the detective right in the eye, and asks, "What is his name?"

In all of this mess, I never even though to ask that question.

Detective Bellerini looks back and forth between the two of us. When he seems satisfied that we won't have any more emotional breakdowns, he opens the file on his desk. "Jonathan Ronald Campone."

"Ron," Annika says quietly.

"Excuse me?"

"He introduced himself as Ron."

He nods. "Doesn't surprise me. Guys like this usually use an alias when they're on the prowl. Got a mugshot here if you're interested in seeing it."

As much as I don't want to see his face, I absolutely want to see his face. He turns the file around and flips the page, and there's a mugshot. Sure enough, he has blond floppy hair hanging partially in his face, just like I remember.

We stare for a while, memorizing his features. He better hope he doesn't bond out, because if I see him out somewhere, I'll be the next one in jail.

Of course, I don't say that. Instead I look at my girl who is narrowing her eyes, staring at the picture. I know she's riffling through her memories, trying to see if anything triggers at all.

"How come we haven't seen him on campus before?" I finally ask. "He doesn't look familiar at all."

"He graduated a couple years ago so he's not on campus anymore. It's also part of the reason I'm still digging."

As much as I hate it, I understand his meaning. College is the first taste of freedom for many of us. Hell, it was my first chance to get away from my parents and figure out who I really am. For someone like this Ron fucker, that means a new crop of potential targets every single year.

Finally satisfied, Annika pushes the file back across the desk. "Thank you."

He nods and closes the file, immediately putting it in the bottom drawer of his desk. "Here's the thing." The detective leans back in his chair. "You two are dating?" We nod simultaneously. "Jaxon, if this goes to trial, you're an eye witness so you'll probably be called to testify. The DNA that was collected puts him at the scene of the crime. Annika, unless you want to, you can make a very good case against testifying."

"Why?" she asks, just as confused by that as I am.

"Partially because we don't need you. Sure, you could tell us what you remember up until you blacked out, but we've got enough DNA. You don't have any memories. I know at first it seemed like a curse because the lack of memory didn't give us anything to go on. But in this situation, consider it a blessing. Also, being that this may be considered a serial rapist case, be prepared for the media to swarm. Jaxon I'm going to try my hardest, but I can't guarantee I'll be able to keep your name out of the papers."

"Shit." I pinch the bridge of my nose. Not because my head hurts, but because this is bad news.

"Oh, it's not that bad," Detective Bellerini tries to reassure us. "Usually they'll try to contact you a couple times, maybe write a story about what a hero you are. But it goes away pretty quick."

"You don't understand," Annika says, rubbing my back like I'm the one that needs comforting right now. "His dad is Jason Hart, the retired Dallas Chaps."

Detective Bellerini freezes for a moment before blurting out, "Well, that's definitely going to put a kink in things. In that case, you need to let your family know pretty quick this is coming. Annika, you may need to let yours know too."

I don't have to look to know she grimaced. She really, really doesn't want to tell her dad.

"Typically, journalists won't print the name of the victim, but that doesn't mean they won't connect the two of you. And once they connect the two of you…"

"Everyone on campus will know your name. Annika," I turn to look at her, apology in my eyes. "We've got a lot to figure out with this one. I'm sorry."

She looks at me like I've lost my damn mind. "Why are you sorry? You didn't do anything."

"I'm sorry the secret you've been keeping is about to be outed."

Her lips quirk to the side and she sighs. "I really didn't want anyone to know. But now that I know I'm not the only one, if this is the price I have to pay to make sure his ass is behind bars for a long, long time, I'll deal with it."

I hold her gaze, finding truth in her words. I think after Lauren's reaction and everything the detective has told us, she feels like this horrible thing can finally be used for some good. It's going to take a minute to wrap our brains around it, and it won't be easy, but we're ready. We're ready to help take this asshole down.

TWENTY-SIX
Annika

I don't really notice anything as I stare out the car window. Everything is a blur. It kind of mirrors my thoughts because that's what they are right now—a blur.

All this time, I've been wanting to know who this Ron guy was, wanting to help put him behind bars, wanting to get justice for myself and maybe hoping for a little revenge.

Now that the ball is rolling, now that it's beginning to happen, I'm frozen. I can't move forward. I can't go back. I'm just stuck.

Jaxon's on the phone next to me. I think he's talking to Germaine, based on the conversation I'm not really listening to. It's more like white noise as my thoughts run at a rapid pace.

Will I have to testify before the Grand Jury? Will the jury believe the evidence? Is this Ron guy dangerous? Are his friends? Do I need to warn Lauren?

"Nah, dude, we're okay." Jaxon turns on the blinker.

I'm not sure where we're going. I don't care. I'm content to just drive. It means I don't have to think too hard. "We'll be back tomorrow." Jaxon chuckles.

I love that sound. It makes my whole body feel warm. "I'm serious, man. We need some time to process through this, ya know? It was kind of a shock. We need to be alone for a bit."

My ears perk up. I don't really know what he means by alone time, but it finally registers where we are as he pulls into the parking lot of a hotel. Not a run-of-the-mill motel, but a swanky hotel. Sometimes I forget that he comes from money, and when we end up places like this, it surprises me.

"Yeah, dude, if we need anything, I'll call. I promise. Yeah. Thanks for checking in. I'm sure we'll need you later, but we're doing okay now. Okay. Bye."

He drops his phone in the center console and turns to look at me. "How you doing, baby?" he asks gently.

I lean my head against the head rest and look at him. "I don't really know," I admit. "I think maybe I'm still in shock. Is that possible?"

A small smile crosses his face. "I think I would be surprised if you *weren't* in shock right now. That was a lot of information to process."

I bite my lip as I think about everything Detective Bellerini told us. It wasn't only me. It's not only me. There's another girl. Another girl who became a victim to that asshole. Another girl who is living the consequences of his actions. And that's just the one they know. Are there more? Are there more girls out there?

"I wonder if," I begin and then pause. I'm having a hard time forming coherent sentences. My thoughts are too jumbled. "I wonder if anymore girls are going to come forward once this hits the news."

Jaxon brushes the hair off my forehead. "Probably. But that's good, right? That means more evidence against him. Maybe more charges. We want him to have as much time behind bars as he can get."

"Yeah." I nod absentmindedly and then realize I haven't talked to Lauren yet. "Oh shit. I need to call my roommate." Looking around the car, I realize I don't know where my phone is, but apparently, I don't need to.

"I already texted her."

"You did?"

"When we first got in the car. I didn't want her to worry." He pulls my phone out of the door pocket next to him and hands it to me. "I texted her from your phone. Told her that I was taking you away for the night. I hope that's okay."

"Yeah, it's fine." I take my phone from his outstretched and clap it tightly to me, then look out the window again as more thoughts race through. "I don't want to tell my dad," I whisper.

Seeing the emotion on my face, Jaxon puts his hand on the back of my neck and squeezes reassuringly. "I know, baby. I know. And you still don't have to if you don't want to."

I shake my head. "No, I have to. My dad's going to see your name in the paper, and he's going to put it together. Can you imagine if he pieced it together without it coming from me?"

Jaxon chuckles and the sound centers me somehow. "We'll figure it out. Maybe you can send him a letter or something. Something to tell him you're okay and he doesn't have to worry."

It's actually not a bad idea, and I tell him as much.

Forcing myself to fully re-engage, I look around. "Why are we here anyway?"

He shrugs. "I didn't feel like going back to campus. I love Germaine. He's the best roommate a guy could ask for. But I just…I felt like we needed to process this together. It's been you and me from the beginning, and I wanted us to have some time. So we're here." He gestures with his hand like he's Vanna White or something. "We're going to get some room service. We're going to wear fluffy bathrobes. Maybe we'll sit in the Jacuzzi whirlpool tub. You can leave your underclothes on if you must." I quirk a smile. He always knows how to make me smile, even when things are tough. "And we're going to just chill for the next twenty-four hours."

"Twenty-four hours? We have class in the morning."

"You're honestly going to try and convince me you'll be able to concentrate on those classes right now?"

"Okay, no. Good point."

"Come on. Let's get our relaxation on."

Jaxon makes quick work of checking in, despite not having a reservation. It's amazing what you can get accomplished when you have a black AmEx card. A girl could get used to that. But only on special occasions. We wouldn't want to be greedy.

When we finally make it to the comfort of our room, I'm astounded by how beautiful it is. Maybe it's nothing special, but to me the palette of greys and blues is calming, comforting. There's a giant king-sized bed in the middle of the room and a small sitting area off to the side. It's not massive, and it's not overly ornate. But it's exactly what I need.

I feel myself calming, knowing we're isolated from everyone we know. It doesn't matter what's happening in the outside world. Doesn't matter if the news has already broken. No one can get to us here. And I realize how exactly right Jaxon was. How he knew exactly what I was going to need before I did. It makes me appreciate him so much more.

The flip side, though, is there's nothing to distract us. Nothing we need to concentrate on. Nothing that needs our focus. Which isn't necessarily a good thing. All there is to do now is think about the information overload and what's coming in our future.

"So," Jaxon claps his hands together, jolting me out of my spiraling thoughts. "We can order a movie. We can order food. Hell, we can even order some baggy clothes from the gift shop downstairs." I realize, we don't have any clean clothes. We might have to take advantage of that credit card after all. "Today is all about you and what you need. What do you want to do first?"

I weigh my options, but there's only one thing I can think of. "I really want to take that bath you were talking about."

"Works for me." He walks to the bathroom, calling out to me over his shoulder. "Do you want it really hot or luke-warm. I can make it however you want, babe."

"The hotter, the better." I follow him into the large bath-room. It's good sized with a garden tub, and I'm thrilled to know I can soak for as long as I want to. But I don't want to soak alone.

As he turns on the water, chattering mindlessly about things I'm not paying attention to, I start peeling off my clothes, slowly and in spite of my lack of confidence. I completely disrobe until I'm standing naked behind him.

"Okay, the bubbles are going. I think that's hot enough for you—" He turns around and freezes when he sees me. I watch as his pupils dilate, and it gives me a thrill to know he's turned on. I was wondering if he'd still want me, even after all of this. Again with the ridiculous thoughts, but I can't help it. Seeing him react to me gives me some of my confidence back.

"Holy shit, Annika," he breathes.

"I don't want to just take a bath, Jaxon. I want to take a bath with you."

He licks his lips and swallows hard. I know he's conflicted—wanting to make sure of my intensions.

"I need this, Jaxon. I need to know I'm still desirable. I need to know…I need to know I'm not broken."

Holding my gaze, he says the words that make my heart swell. "You've never been broken to me."

Slowly, walking up to him, I grab the hem of his shirt and pull it over his abs and his chest. He finally moves and helps me get his clothes off. Before I know it, he's standing naked in front of me for the very first time.

I can't help but peruse his body with my eyes, and to my surprise, he's very definitely turned on by me.

My gaze snaps up to meet his, and he blushes. "Told ya. It has a mind of its own. I have no idea why sometimes he works quickly and sometimes not."

Smiling back at him, I take his hand and lead him over to the tub. We climb in, him sitting behind me, my back to his front, and he wraps his arms around me, kissing me on the neck.

We sit there, soaking in the water, not speaking. There's nothing to say. Right now, we just have to lean on each other. So that's what we do.

He begins peppering kisses down the back of my neck, and I feel the goosebumps rise. I slide my hands up the back of his calves and up his thighs as high as I can get them. That's when his hands begin to roam too.

"I want this to be right, Annika," he whispers in my ear and a stray tear rolls down my cheek.

"I want it to be right too," I admit. "But the only way that's going to happen is to push through the first time. You know as well as I do that the first time will be hard. The last thing that was inside me was…was him."

"Oh baby," he whispers in my hair and holds me tighter.

"I need the last person inside me to be you."

He understands that it's not just an invitation, but a request. His hands begin to peruse my body again. I close my eyes and concentrate on staying relaxed. Staying in this moment right here, with Jaxon, no one else.

When his fingers tug on my nipple, a gasp comes out of me.

"Was that a good sound or a bad sound?" He's so concerned, it makes my heart swell.

"It was a good sound. Keep doing that."

He plays with my breasts, tugging on my nipples and rubbing them with his palms. One hand finally runs down the length of my stomach and when he gets to where I really want him, he stops.

"You have to help me out here, babe," he says. "It's your body. You need to be in control."

Tears are flowing freely now, but they're not tears of fear or sadness or embarrassment. They're tears of love. Of such overwhelming love, my heart could explode.

I take my hand and grab his, moving them down so his fingers brush my clit. Gently, I move our hands until he's rubbing circles in my most sensitive areas. My breathing hitches, and I can feel myself building. But this is not what I want. This is not what I need. I need him inside me. Any part of him. I need him to take the past away.

I tug on his hand again and our fingers move down farther, guided to my opening. He takes that as his invitation and pushes two fingers inside me. He groans as I clench around him, letting my body take over, doing all the work.

I can feel his erection digging into my lower back, but

he makes no move to further this along, content to just let me feel. He merely follows my lead.

As his palm continues to brush my clit, I increase my upward thrusts. It takes only seconds before I cry out, reaching up to thread my fingers through his hair, as my orgasm overtakes me. It's strong and intense. The first orgasm I've had in months.

Coming down from the high, he continues to kiss me softly, but suddenly I feel such desperation for him, I can hardly stand it.

"Jaxon."

He continues to pump his fingers in and out. "Hmm."

"Jaxon, I need you inside me."

"I am inside you, baby," he says, still not letting up.

"No, I need *you* inside me. Now."

He stops his ministrations and pulls his fingers out of me. "Babe, I had no idea this was even on the table today. I don't have any condoms."

"I don't care. I don't care about any of that. I just need you inside me, Jaxon. I need it," I plead, tears coming harder now, and I'm desperate to make him understand. Desperate to be a normal girl again. A normal girl who can have sex with her boyfriend without freaking out. I'm desperate to get the first time out of the way so that every time from here on out, the memory I have is of Jaxon. The memory I have is of the man I love, not the man who tried to take everything away from me.

"Baby." His voice is calm as he tries to talk sense into me. "We'll get there, honey."

"No, you don't understand." Turning around, I straddle him, ignoring the water that spills over the side. I grab his face between my palms so he has to look me in the eye. "You don't understand. I need this. I need this so I can be okay. I need you inside me. Nothing between us. No barriers, no obstructions, nothing. I need it to be just us."

I can see how conflicted he is, and in the back of my mind I understand completely. I'm asking for something really stupid. I am asking for him to take a huge risk. I know the risk I'm taking by not having safe sex. But in this moment, I don't care. Nothing else matters. My entire life was upended, and I've been doing well, but right now, right now I need him to make it all go away. The only way he can do that is by giving me this.

He takes a deep breath and brushes my cheeks with his thumb. But then he nods.

"Really?" I ask in disbelief.

"Yeah really. Come on."

We climb out of the bath and he takes the time to dry me off with a big fluffy towel. Then he guides me into the bedroom and over to the bed. Taking my hand, he pulls me to him, and still naked, our skin still glistening from the water, he kisses me senseless. His tongue invading my mouth. His hands exploring my body. And I'm all here. Nothing is going through my mind except the way he is making me feel. The way he's making me want.

When he lays me on the bed and pushes inside me, I gasp with the feeling of fullness.

"Open your eyes." I immediately obey. "I don't want your mind going anywhere it shouldn't. This is me. You and me. Always."

I nod and hold his gaze as he moves again. Soft gentle pushes to start with, and when I match him thrust for thrust, he begins plunging harder and faster. Until finally he looks me right in the eyes and says, "I love you, Annika."

I dig my hands into his hair and pull him to me, kissing him hard. "I love you too," I whisper against his lips, almost immediately feeling stars explode in my brain. I throw my head back and moan, enjoying the feeling that overtakes me.

Seconds later, Jaxon tenses and says "Oh fuck. Oh fuck you feel good. Fuuuuuuuuuuck!" He pushes one last time. Our hips practically locked together and right now, it's like he's taken everything dirty inside me, and made it clean again.

He collapses onto me, his head on my chest. We lay quietly as I run my fingers through is hair.

"I mean it, Annika," he says after a while. "I love you, so, so much."

I hug him tighter and kiss the top of his head. "Good." Relaxing back into the bed I quip, "Who knew I'd ever fall for a Chaps fan."

He chuckles before his breathing evens out and we fall into a deep, restful sleep.

TWENTY-SEVEN

Jaxon

Going bareback was possibly the stupidest decision I've ever made in my short adult life. I knew I was being dumb, even in that moment. But seeing the look on Annika's face and the desperation that was rolling off her like waves, I understood what she needed. I understood why it was important. So I gave her the only thing I could in that moment. I gave her me.

I wasn't totally off my rocker. Was it stupid? Yes. But risky? Not as much as it could have been. That's one of the other long-term side effects of chemo. There's almost no chance that I can have kids. It's possible, but considering all the other issues I have in that area, I figure there's a good chance I'll be saving up for a sperm donor someday.

Not that Annika having my baby would be the worst thing to ever happen to me. Shit, the whole situation got me thinking about how much I wish that would happen someday. Not when I'm in college and twenty-one years old. Hell no. But someday. I'm pretty sure she's my one.

In fact, I'm positive she's my one. There's not one else out there like her.

In that moment, while it was stupid, I also knew the worst thing that could happen is our future being bumped up by a few years.

And I admit, when she called me a few days later to tell me she started her period, I breathed a sigh of relief. I didn't let her know that. She's been back and forth with her emotions lately so I calmly said, "Okay." And let it go. No feeling happy that she wasn't pregnant. No feeling sad that she wasn't pregnant. Just "okay."

But now, as I sit here staring at the envelope in my hands, I'm thinking about my family all over again and wondering how bad I want those fertility treatments someday. My opinion might sway if I'm the last Bryant after all.

"Why are you staring holes in the mail?" Germaine asks, looking up from his desk where he's been studying. "You look like it's done something to offend you."

"It may have," I mumble, not taking my eyes off it.

"What do you mean by that?" He wheels his fancy office chair he brought from home over and snatches the envelope out of my hand before I can react. Whistling slowly through his teeth, he looks up at me. "DNA results are back. That was fast."

I puff out a sigh and run my hands through my hair. "I paid for the rush shipping. I didn't expect it to rush that fast."

Over Thanksgiving, while we were out, Kade and I talked about doing a DNA test, to put all the questions to rest. Not because we doubted his paternity, but because we both knew how it looked. For fourteen, he's pretty astute in his observations. I guess that happens when no one pays much attention to you. You learn how to people watch. And somehow, he knew showing up on my doorstep would have everyone freaked out.

Everyone in *my* life anyway. I still don't know if his mom has any idea I'm around.

Germaine hands it back to me and prods, "Well? Are you going to open it?"

I bite my lip and contemplate his question. "I don't know that I want to know."

"Care to explain why?"

"What if it says he's my brother? What if it's positive? That means my dad had an affair and that baby was left to fend for himself. My brother was left to fend for himself."

"You can't think about it that way, man." Germaine crosses his arms over his chest and swivels his chair back and forth. "You've got to think of it like you've got fourteen years to make up for, and you're off to a good start. Besides, what if it's negative?"

"That's the other thing I'm worried about. What if he's *not* my brother?"

Germaine shrugs. "Then he's not your brother. Problem solved."

But it's not problem solved. He's still fourteen. He still has no one. "I don't know." I rub the top of my head again. "I don't know what I want the test to say."

"It's a tough one, that's for sure. But the first step, man, is actually opening the envelope."

I think about it for a second, but I know what I need to do. Pulling out my phone, I dial his number.

"Hey man? What's going on?" Kade says excitedly on the other end of the line.

"Hey, not much. How's school going?"

"Good. Good! Remember that girl, Melissa? The one in my computer class?"

I chuckle, remembering how he thinks she's the most beautiful girl in the world, but she won't give him the time of day. I'm hoping now that he's discovered the Axe Body Spray line, things are going better for him. "Sure do. You got an update?"

"She talked to me in class." He sounds thrilled by this turn of events, and I can't help but smile for him. "I mean, it was just to ask for my help, but dude. She knew I'd know the answer. That means she knows I'm smart, right?"

I chuckle again. "Yeah she does. You're not invisible anymore. Just don't overdo it with the cologne."

"Hell yeah! I don't know why no one told me about this stuff before."

I clear my throat, and while I have the nerve I blurt out, "Our test results came in."

He goes silent on the other end for a few moments. "What did it say?" I can tell his excitement has turned into nerves. He sounds kind of like I feel.

"I haven't opened it up yet. I thought maybe we should do it on the phone. Together."

"Yeah. Yeah, good idea." He blows out a deep breath, and I can practically hear him stretching his neck as he prepares himself. "Okay. Let's rip the Band-Aid off. What does it say?"

Taking my own deep breath, I slide my finger under the lip of the envelope. I can see Germaine watching me as I pull out the letter that's been folded into thirds and open it. I don't even skip ahead, just read it aloud.

"In the interest of Jaxon Bryant Hart and Kayden Austin Maxwell DNA with 99.9% accuracy is NOT a match."

Kade gasps and my heart plummets. Not a match. We're not a match. He's not my brother. I look up at Germaine who is sitting there open-mouthed, shock on his face.

All three of us sit in silence as we try to wrap our brains around what I just read. Kade and I are not brothers. With 99.9% accuracy, we are not brothers.

Am I happy about that? I don't know. My responsibility to the situation is over, so maybe.

But once again, I'm the last remaining Bryant.

I don't know how to feel.

"But…" Kade says, clearly as stunned at I am, "but his name is on my birth certificate."

I know I'm shaken up by this news, but I only knew about the possibility for a few weeks. I hadn't really gotten attached the idea of it. But Kade, this kid, not only did he just lose the brother he thought he had for his entire life, he just lost the only man he knew as his father. And it happened in two seconds flat.

"I don't know man. I don't know how this happened."

"She…she told me he was my dad."

I can hear his emotion rising, and I can't think what to say except, "Are you okay?"

"No, I'm not okay!" His voice cracks with emotion. "For my entire life, I thought my dad wasn't around because he was dead. But really, it's because some asshole out there doesn't want me."

I can practically hear the tears in his voice, and my heart is ripped to shreds.

"You don't know that, Kade. He might not know."

"Oh, I'm sure he knows." He sniffs. "If you met my mom, she's not shy. I'm sure everyone within a hundred-mile radius knew the second she found out she was having me."

"Listen, man," I lower my voice, trying to calm him down, "this doesn't change anything between you and me."

The sobbing on the other end of the line breaks my heart.

"But it does, Jaxon. It's okay, you don't have to have anything to do with me anymore. I won't bother you again—"

"No, Kade. Wait! Don't you hang up that phone."

Germaine is still looking at me, waiting to see how I'll handle this, and I know he can tell it's gotten emotional on the other end. Hell, with as emotional as Kade is, I wouldn't be surprised if he can hear it clear across the room.

"Listen to me. We might not share DNA, but we share a connected history. Regardless of what this test says, my dad and your mom had an affair, and you were born. That means something. I don't know what other men were involved, but I know what it's like to lose your dad. I lost mine when I was five. Right now, what you're feeling, is because you just lost yours."

His sobs continue, and now my own eyes are filled with tears. Damn. Can things get any crazier around here?

"Don't you dare disappear on me, Kade, okay?" I plead. "I come home all the time, and I'm still gonna see you. We're still gonna go out. No one has to know this. No one. You and me, we can keep it a secret."

"Why?" he asks. "Why would you do that for me? My own father doesn't want me."

"Because you're worth it, Kade. Because we're this close to getting that Melissa girl to notice you."

Germain chuckles and swivels his chair back around, turning his attention back to his studies.

"I don't care what this test says. You're still my brother."

"Yeah," he says quietly with a sniffle. "Yeah, okay. No one has to know yet. Just let me wrap my brain around this first."

"Okay."

"Listen, um, I think I need to go, like, drown my sorrows in a game of Halo. I'm gonna let you go, okay?"

"Yeah." I wipe the tears out of my eyes. "But you call

me when Melissa talks to you again okay?"

"Okay. Thanks Jaxon."

We hang up, and I drop my phone to the floor, digging the heels of my hands in my eyes. Someday, I'll have to tell my dad about this. Someday.

But today, I'm going to pretend it didn't happen. Today, Kade is still my brother.

TWENTY-EIGHT
Annika

Sitting on the hard wood benches in the courtroom, we wait. Again. That's all we've been doing for the last several months, so I really shouldn't be surprised.

Laughter catches my attention and I look over to see a bailiff chatting with some random member of the court like my life hasn't been on hold for so long. Like Jaxon's life hasn't been on hold.

But I suppose working here, you get immune to how difficult this process actually is. How much it drags. Even now, it feels like we've been sitting here for hours, when I know it's only been fifteen minutes or so. Not that it'll make a difference.

The justice system is not all like you see on television. The district attorneys don't sit around in their expensive clothes, piecing together their plans for court, while coming up with some aha moments that will make the case go off without a hitch. Nor are they in court the next day.

Oh no. The DA usually looks pretty disheveled, has

way too many cases on his or her plate, and things get scheduled. And then rescheduled.

And then rescheduled again.

There are depositions. There are inquisitions. There are lots and lots of media. At least in cases like mine.

We had been warned that things were going to be hard, so the first thing I had to figure out was how to give my dad a heads-up. That was, by far, the hardest part of this process.

Multiple times, I tried picking up the phone to let him know, but I couldn't do. I didn't want to hear the sound of his voice when I spit out the words. And frankly, I wasn't sure I could get the words out anyway.

With Jaxon's help, I sat down the night after our trip to the police station and wrote my dad a letter. I told him all about that night. I told him all about Jaxon's involvement. And I told him how I was stronger than what had happened to me and was already in the process of healing.

I fretted for several days after dropping the letter in the mail. When my phone finally rang and his number came up, I knew he finally knew.

When I answered the phone, he didn't say a word. He didn't have to. I heard him crying on the other end of the line, and it was clear his heart had been broken. We didn't say anything for a long time, the two of us sat there sobbing. We were on opposite ends of the phone line, yet it felt like he was right there with me.

Finally, when he pulled himself together enough to speak, the first thing he said was, "Damn that Jaxon Hart. I didn't want to be a Chaps fan."

I laughed out loud when he said that, and I knew we were going to be okay. We talked for a little while. I refused to give him more details, knowing they would all come out in the newspaper anyway, except to say I didn't remember. That seemed to help him out a lot. I think if I had had a memory, it would have been worse for him. At least this way, I wouldn't live with memories for the rest of my life.

Now, he sits next to me, his knee bouncing up and down as we wait for this to finally be over so we can move on.

Jaxon sits on the other side of me and appears to be much more calm. Much more pulled together. I know it's an act, though. He's as nervous as I am. The difference is he spent years in the public eye and knows what to do. His knowledge came in really handy as this process unfolded.

By the time the news media caught wind that a rapist had been caught, Jaxon, his family, and their entire team of managers and PR reps were fully aware of the situation. They knew Jaxon's involvement with the case. And they knew Jaxon's involvement with me.

I was warned that it was inevitable my name would come out. At least locally. It doesn't matter if the press was ordered to keep the victim's names quiet, when one of the victims is dating the guy who stopped the crime in action, and that guy happens to be the son of one of the most beloved retired players in the history of the NFL, it was bound to happen.

Rumors circulated all over the internet, and my name was one of those rumors. It was never in any official journalism capacity. But it was in blogs. In chat rooms. On social media. People put it together, and it was humiliating.

Part of the evidence that was released publicly was every sick detail about what had happened. Now people knew that information. It made me nauseous all the time.

But then a funny thing happened. People started to come out of the woodwork to thank me. At first, I didn't know what was going on, but then I realized women were feeling empowered. They were feeling a sense of connection.

Men, guys I knew who had never given me the time of day, were suddenly feeling enraged that women could be treated that way.

Women I didn't know would come up with tears in their eyes and share their story, thanking me for having the strength they didn't have.

I didn't like the attention, per se, but Jaxon and my therapist encouraged me to embrace it. To recognize that this horrific thing I had gone through could make a positive difference in the world. If I'd had my way, I would have made a positive impact another way. But since I didn't have my way, I started looking at the positives.

I still don't have to remember what happened that night. I never regained my memory, and I hope I never do. But that doesn't mean I can't allow my story to be used to encourage others to come forward. Jaxon has suggested we work together to lobby for rape kits to be paid for by the state, versus being charged to the victim. But that's more responsibility I don't want to bear at this point. I'm not ready.

We got through the spring semester waiting for the trial to be set. The DA wanted to push it forward quickly, but the defense attorney always had a reason to wait. Finally, the judge had enough and scheduled it for trial.

In mid-July, in the middle of the heat, in the middle of the summer semester, the trial began.

Originally, I agreed to testify as a last result. But, thankfully, the facts spoke volumes and all the DNA results said more than I ever could. Then, there was Jaxon's testimony. As an eye witness, his testimony was vital to prove the attack wasn't consensual, in case the drugs in my system weren't enough evidence. While Jaxon didn't see that Ron guy's face (and to this day that's what I call him), he saw the attack. He saw me unconscious, and he saw him on top of me. And according to the media, it was Jaxon's testimony that made the difference.

I didn't go to court the day Jaxon testified. I wouldn't let my dad go either. But Jaxon's dad did. He refused to let Jax be in that room without being there for moral support. And even though he's biased, he says Jaxon's emotions helped the jury see beyond the DNA and clinical side of things. If I know him, his love for me and disgust for what happened, for what he saw, helped the jury members see the victim's side of things.

They got to see his shock, at finding me half naked behind a dumpster.

They got to see his anger when he realized I was unconscious and that Ron guy ran.

They got to see his confusion when he had to decide between keeping the perp pinned to the ground or saving my life.

And then the DA took it one step further and the jury got to see Jaxon talk about how many nights he held me while I had nightmares and how many times he held me while I cried.

Of course, the defense attorney tried to rip that story to shreds. Since Jaxon didn't know me before the attack, he had no idea if I was an emotional basket case before. He may have discredited Jaxon a little bit, but not enough to make a difference.

The trial wasn't long, but it was still nerve-wracking. Finally, after what seemed like forever, he was found guilty of two counts of aggravated sexual assault of an unconscious person. My dad cried when the guilty verdict was read, but I didn't. I refused to shed one more tear over it. Especially not when I was in a courtroom with the guy who had tried to destroy me. I wouldn't give him the satisfaction. I would, however, give him a piece of my mind.

Both of the victims were given an opportunity to speak at the sentencing. The other girl didn't want to. She's local and knew she would be recognized. I get it. This is a very personal crime. It's not something you want following you for the rest of your life.

But I wanted to. I put in a lot of thought about what I wanted to say. Nothing I say will sway the judge. His mind is already made up. But what I say will influence me. It will influence other people. It might influence that Ron guy. Doubtful, but you never know.

So now we sit and wait on these hard benches in the courtroom, waiting for my chance to speak.

"You okay, babe?" Jaxon whispers in my ear, squeezing the back of my neck. I lean into him, inhaling his scent. It calms me.

"Just ready to do this and move on."

"Did I ever tell you how proud I am of you?"

I giggle. "Only every day since this stupid trial started."

He kisses me on the top of the head. "Well, I am. So proud of you."

"I know."

Before we can say anything else, the bailiff yells, "All rise," before the judge enters the courtroom.

We all stand and wait while the judge gets settled and tells us to sit. Finally, he seems ready to go.

"We're at the sentencing hearing of Jonathan Ronald Campone. Mr. Campone, you realize you've been convicted on two counts of aggravated sexual assault of an unconscious person."

"Yes sir. I understand." I refuse to look at him when he speaks, instead staring straight at the judge.

"You also understand this is your sentencing hearing,

and once I give my judgment, it is final, and you will immediately return to your cell while you await further instructions."

"Yes, your Honor."

"And you realize if you don't agree, you have the right to appeal."

I squeeze Jaxon's knee, knowing he's rolling his eyes. From a judicial stand point, we understand the appeals process and why it's necessary. But knowing beyond a shadow of a doubt we've got the right guy, it feels more like rubbing salt into a wound.

"Yes, your Honor."

"Okay then." The judge shuffles a few more papers around. "Before we get to the sentencing, one of our victims has requested to read a statement. Mr. Campone, I highly suggest you listen closely to what she has to say."

"Yes, your Honor."

He sounds monotone, like he doesn't care. Frankly, I don't think he ever did. He's been on house arrest for the six months. His bond was set at three hundred thousand dollars and lucky us, his parents were able to come up with the thirty thousand to post his bond. It was tough knowing he was out, but a comfort knowing if he left his home, they'd snatch him up, and it would be all over.

"Victim number two. I'll have you speak first. If you'll please come stand next to the district attorney. You're welcome to begin."

I take a deep breath as Jaxon squeezes my hand in support, my dad patting me on the back. Making my way up to the front, climbing over Jaxon and his dad, who is way bigger in person than I originally anticipated, I know all eyes are on me. But it's not all those eyes I'm nervous about. It's just one pair. The pair of the man I love, who has gotten me through so much in the last year.

I stand next to the district attorney, who quietly says, "Are you ready?"

I nod.

"Victim number two, the floor is yours," the judge says kindly.

I take another deep breath and look at my paper and begin reading the notes I had carefully put together.

"You all know me as victim number two. A nineteen-year-old woman who was drugged at a bar, taken out to a back alley behind a dumpster, and violently raped. But let me tell you who I really am. My name is Annika Leander. I'm a sophomore at Southeast Texas University. I turned twenty a few months ago. I am not victim number three. I'm a survivor of an infinite number, because there are hundreds of thousands of women out there like me. They may not have been a part of this trial, but they have a stake in the outcome.

"You see, Mr. Campone, you're not special. You're not original. You didn't do anything that thousands of other men haven't done before you.

"I remember you talking to me at that club. I remember you pretending to be kind when I needed help. That's all I remember of you. That's all I'll ever remember of you.

"That night, when you chose to take my body, you thought you were taking much more. Because rape is not about sex; it's about control. The entire time you were hurting me, I'm sure you felt powerful. *Justified.*

"But the thing is, you may have taken my body, but that's all you took. You didn't take my dignity. You didn't take my pride. You didn't take my intellect or my drive or my motivation. Hell, you didn't even take away the ability for me to have a satisfying sex life with my boyfriend."

I hear Jaxon groan in the background.

"And you didn't take away the ability for me to laugh

at the fact that I just embarrassed my boyfriend in the middle of a courtroom while he sits next to his dad. And mine. Because the night you decided to rape me violently behind a dumpster is the night your life ended. But it's the night mine really began. I am much stronger than I was before then. I am much more resilient. And from what will easily be known as the worst time of my life, I ended up finding the love of my life.

"Now, while you are about to rot in prison, while you are going to have to look over your shoulder for the next however many years, while you are stuck in limbo, not able to move forward, but not able to go back, while you're stuck waiting for your life to continue, mine has already moved on.

"By the time you get out of prison, I'll have a degree. I'll have a career. I'll probably be married. I might have some children. I'll have a house. I'll be on my third new car. Because my options are endless. Where will you be? Nowhere. Your life will still be stuck.

"You'll still be looking over your shoulder. And for the rest of your life, whenever you can't do something, like get a passport so you can go on a cruise, you'll be reminded of why. You'll be reminded your life is on hold because you took from Annika Leander."

"And for the remainder of my life, you'll never even cross my mind. Because I don't have to look over my shoulder anymore. I don't have to sleep with one eye open. You took my body, but I took it back. And my future is looking bright. The only life you obliterated was your own.

"So remember as you rot in prison, remember every time you're stuck in the middle of a gang war in the cafeteria, remember every time you're sleeping with one eye open, you did this. And every time you wonder what I'm doing, rest assured, I'm not at all thinking about you.

"I would like to thank the jury. Thank you for recognizing the truth of this situation. Thank you for taking a stand to say 'enough.' Thank you, Your Honor, for allowing me the chance to stand here and show every woman out there they're stronger than the coward who attacked them."

With that, I lay my paper on the district attorney's table, I turn around, and I walk out the door to my future, not looking back.

TWENTY-NINE
Jaxon

"**F**uuuuuuuuck," I groan my release, continuing to move my hips as much as I can while Annika rides out her orgasm. Her head is thrown back, her eyes rolled to the back of her head, and she's moaning as loud as I've ever heard her. It's a beautiful sight.

Finally, she stills and collapse on top of my chest, panting.

"Holy shit that was good," she blurts out making me laugh.

I keep rubbing my fingertips up and down her naked back in our post-coital bliss.

Being in an apartment together for the summer has been awesome. I really don't want to move back into the dorms. An apartment means as much sex as we want, when we want, wherever we want, without fear of anyone walking in on us. I'm going to really miss that when the semester starts up again.

But try as I might, Annika was adamant that we have

not been dating long enough to share residency permanently. The only reason we did it temporarily was because of the trial.

With all the delays and hearing dates changing, we were never quite sure when the trial would begin. We knew it was going to be hard on both of us, and not knowing what would happen with the media, we decided it was best to prepare for the worse. We each reduced our course load, only taking one class a semester, and moved out of the dorms. If we had to drop our one class, we'd have to move off-campus anyway so it was better to be safe than homeless. Plus, the lack of privacy to process everything happening in the trial was a major concern for Annika's well-being. When my dad offered to rent us each an apartment, we refused. If we were doing this, we were doing it together.

Annika's dad wasn't thrilled about it, but when he realized the alternative was her living on her own, he changed his mind. As much as he likes me, he still gave me a stern warning of "Just don't make her a Chaps fan."

That man cracks me up.

But now that the piece of shit is away for a long, long time, possibly less if he has good behavior, our life is going back to normal. And by normal, I mean me living with Germaine in a small dorm room; Annika living with Lauren in a bigger dorm room; and us having to get creative with intimacy.

I guess it could be worse.

"Are you looking forward to moving back in with Lauren next week?" I ask, still holding my girlfriend tightly to me.

She hums her agreement, still spent from our lovemaking. *Well done, Jaxon.* I give myself a mental high five.

"Yeah," she finally says but doesn't sound convincing. "I miss her. I'm looking forward to having more girl time with her, but I've enjoyed playing house with you this summer. I don't like *why* we played house, but it was fun."

"And by fun, do you mean because of all the sexy times?"

She giggles into my chest. "Ohmygod, you're such a dork. No, I mean I enjoy being with you. Even when you have your clothes on. I know. It's hard to believe there's more to you than just your body."

I pinch her butt, making her squeal. "Are you sure you don't want to stay in the apartment?"

She rolls her eyes and moves off me, both of us groaning when I pull out of her. After the first time we were together, she immediately went to the clinic for birth control. We could have gone with condoms, but bareback was way too good. And once her follow-up checks-ups all came back clean, there was no reason to not enjoy ourselves.

Even though I was honest with Annika, and told her of the possible sterility I faced from chemo as a kid, we agreed it wasn't worth the risk. Not at our age. We have goals and dreams. Sure, we're going to be together forever (even if she hasn't figured it out yet), but we want to do it the right way. We both have too much to accomplish first.

Still, I keep trying to convince her to live with me. Despite the facts that our lease is up and my dad refuses to pay anymore rent, but I still like the fantasy.

"No, Jaxon," she says. "I love that you love living with me, and I had the best summer. But I'm not that girl."

"What girl? The girl who loves her boyfriend and wants to spend every waking minute with him?"

She punches me playfully in the shoulder. "No. The girl who is clingy with her boyfriend and has no life outside of him."

I scoff. "I kind of like that girl."

She rolls her eyes again. "You're full of shit." Then her eyes light up. "Oh! I forgot to tell you. I have news." She sits up excitedly, the sheet dropping off her chest, her gorgeous tits bouncing right in my face.

I can't help it when I lean over and take one of her nipples in my mouth and gently bite. She squeaks and then groans.

"That feels so good. Don't start something you can't finish."

"Who says I can't finish?"

She groans again as I move to the other side, giving the other breast the attention it deserves. "It's been like two minutes. You can't convince me you're hard and ready to go again."

I grab her hand and put it between my legs.

"Oh!" she says in disbelief. "I guess you can be ready to go again."

"I don't know what happened, baby. You seem to have unbroken me."

She laughs and pushes me away. "No listen, Jaxon. Listen."

Sitting crisscross while naked on the bed, gets me excited all over again. I make a show of perusing her body, my gaze ending on her sweet, sweet pussy that's right there in front of me. As I reach my hand over to play with my favorite kitty, she snatches the sheet up and covers herself.

"That's no fair. I was going to play with that," I grumble.

"I know. But listen. It's important. I got an email today."

Lying back, I tuck my arm under my head and go into serious mode. "Fine. You got an email today. What is so special about this email?"

"Guess who got into the training program?"

My eyes widen and lift up slightly. "Wait, as in going to be a trainer on the field during the season?"

She smiles and nods, her eyes wide with delight. "Yep."

"Baby, that's awesome!" I sit straight up and hug her tight. The competition was fierce to get in, so this is amazing news. "When do you start?"

"The registrar has to change my classes to add it in, so next week when we move, I have to go get that fixed," she chatters excitedly. "The class itself is only one day a week for three hours. But I'll have to be at three practices a week. And they'll rotate us, and I'll be at all the home games. It isn't until you're a grad student that they'll let you go to away games if they need you, but I'm so excited, Jaxon. Even if I only hand you a water bottle every once in a while. I. Can't. Wait."

I smile at her rambling because this is the beginning of her dream. It's hard to be a physical therapist for a professional football team. There are a lot of people who want those jobs. But getting into this program is a step in the right direction.

What she doesn't know is I have no problem getting a letter of recommendation from the most sought out retired football player when it's time. Dad loves her. He'd do anything to help her. She hasn't seen how overbearing he can be yet, so she better be careful, or she'll end up in the Dallas Chaps locker room. And wouldn't her dad love that?

"See," she finally says as she continues to ramble, "it's all coming together."

"I'm really proud of you, Annika." And I'm serious. "You're going to look really hot in those khaki shorts they're gonna make you wear."

She punches me in the arm again and I grab her, pulling her on top of me while I laugh. When I push the hair out of her face and our eyes meet, the air crackles around us. Kissing her lightly, I wait for her to open before tangling her tongue with mine. Once we're breathless again, I can't help but tell her everything I'm feeling.

"I love you so much it hurts sometimes."

She smiles. "I love you so much too."

She doesn't know it yet, but she's it for me. It won't happen soon. We're not ready. But someday, certainly before medical school, I'm going to put a ring on her finger.

And then I'm going to hope she'll be ready to live in an apartment with me.

THIRTY

Annika

"Do you ever regret how we met?"

I stop my chewing and look up at him. "Why would I regret how we met?" I ask between bites of queso.

We're at Buck's for the first NFL game of the regular season. Germaine is on his way but was sidetracked by some girl he's been wooing in his math class. I have no idea who she is or what's so special about her that he had to miss kick off, but hey. Who am I to shit on true love?

Lauren is also coming as soon as she gets out of practice, but I'm not holding my breath. Ever since a new guy joined their team, she seems to be more flaky than normal. At this point, he hasn't caught the hint yet, but I have never seen her giggly before. I've seen her flaunt, I've seen her be sassy, I've seen her be confident in her sexuality. But I've never seen her be a puddle of goo before. It's fun seeing her crush on this guy.

"I don't know." Jaxon picks up a fry and pops it in his

mouth. "We had to go through such terrible shit to find each other. Do you ever wish you could go back and change it?"

I have to think on that. Giving myself a few minutes to chew, I come up with the most honest answer I can. "I don't know. Would I change the part about that Ron guy? Yeah. That wasn't fun."

He nods in agreement, still devouring our cheesy fries.

"But you were at the club that night. So was I. Who's to say our paths wouldn't have crossed a different way, ya know? Do I regret going to Ambrosia? No. Do I regret that we didn't catch each other's eye before…you know? Of course. It would have been nice to have met you differently. Why? Where is this coming from?"

He wipes his greasy hands on a napkin. "Nowhere, really. I guess my philosophy class is making me think about different 'what if' scenarios."

"I thought you hated that class and cursed the day you thought it would be an easy elective." I wave my hands in the air exaggeratedly like he did after reading the synopsis on the first day. Turns out, it's not a space-filler class after all, but it wasn't "fact-based" either. All "speculation shit," is what he called it. "Wasn't it you who said speculation gets you nowhere?"

"It doesn't." He chuckles. "But fuck me if it hasn't made my head go all swirly with different possibilities."

The door swings open, and a couple about our age comes walking in. It's clear from their body language and shy looks that this is a first date. Jaxon follows my gaze. "What are you looking at?"

"Young love," I respond with a flutter of my eyelashes. "It's cute seeing new couples who still aren't very sure of themselves. Reminds me of our younger years."

He snorts a laugh. "I thought I was the one taking philosophy. You sound like my crackpot professor."

I shrug. "You've rubbed off on me. But seriously. Turn the question back around to you. Do you regret the way we met?"

"Not for a second," he immediately responds.

"Wow. You certainly knew that answer fast."

"The only thing I wish is that I'd seen it all happen sooner."

"I know, babe," I say quietly and put my hand on his arm. "But I'm fine, remember? We're fine."

He nods and looks at his fries. It's been close to two months since the trial ended and our lives returned to normal. Well, with a little extra unwanted notoriety.

We don't talk about it much. We're ready to put it behind us. But it does come up. Regardless of the closure, that doesn't mean the issues aren't still there. Every day we're a little stronger. Sometimes we just have to take a minute to regroup.

Just as the DA had anticipated and warned us, that Ron guy and his defense team filed an appeal. It doesn't mean we have to do anything, but it put Jaxon on edge. I know he's worried, but appeals can go on for years. It's nothing we'll necessarily have to deal with, just continue to stay informed.

I glance over at the television, waiting for the commercial break to be over. Why does it always seem like halftime takes forever?

I catch myself watching the couple that came in. They're cute together. She looks like she is a social butterfly, big smile, bright eyes. He looks like the quiet guy, shy smile, thinks she hung the moon.

As she turns around to put her purse on the back of her chair, it happens in just a second. I blink in disbelief.

"Jax," I say quickly and smack his arm multiple times, demanding he pay attention.

"What? What's wrong?"

"Ohmygod, Jax, that guy. The new couple…"

"Uh huh."

"He put something in her drink."

My heart is racing. I don't know what to do.

Jaxon looks at them then leans over the table, speaking quietly. "Are you sure?"

"Yes. Why are you asking me? Do you not believe me?"

He grabs my hand to calm me. "Stop. You're right. It was a reactionary response. What do you want to do?"

"I want to run screaming over there and dump the drink out."

He chuckles. "Let's be realistic. We don't want to scare her. We've got to handle this delicat—"

"Shit, Jax, she just took a drink."

He tosses his napkin on the table. "Fuuuck. Okay, keep an eye on her. I'm going to tell the manager."

I nod but don't take my eyes off that table. I watch as she talks and jokes with this guy, not knowing what's happening and what's at risk. Every time she takes a sip, I cringe, but I have to wait for Jaxon. Getting the police is the number one priority. I don't want to scare this guy off before they get here.

What pisses me off is how he sits there smiling at her like nothing is wrong. Like he hasn't done anything illegal. And then I see it when it happens. She puts a hand on her forehead, and I know what she's feeling. That the drug is already taking effect.

Jaxon slides back into the booth. "The manager has called the cops. We just have to play it cool."

I shake my head vehemently. "We can't play it cool, babe."

"How come?"

"She's already starting to black out. I have to go help her."

He looks at me for a second, making sure I'm emotionally ready for this then gestures with his head. "Go. I'm right behind you."

Without looking back, I walk straight up to their table and lie through my teeth. "Hi! Don't I know you from campus?"

The girl looks up at me with a bright smile and crinkled eyebrows. Her cheeks are flushed and she's clearly feeling confused. "Uh, I don't know. Do we have a class together?"

"Maybe. I'm Annika. Annika Leander."

"Hi, I'm Paige and this is my friend, Trevor."

"What's up?" Trevor asks, popping his head up the way guys do to say hi.

"Hm. Well, maybe not." I'm running out of time, so I give up the act. "Listen, Paige. I have bad news for you."

"Uh huh." I can tell by the look in her eyes she's getting drowsy.

"Trevor here put something in your drink."

"What the fuck?" Trevor yells as Paige says, "What?"

"You're feeling kind of nauseous and your head is spinning, like it's about to float away?" She nods at me. "Yeah, someone did that to me too. That's the date rape drug hitting your system."

"I…what?" I can hear the panic in her voice, so I rush to reassure her.

"Listen to me, Paige. Since I saw him do it—"

"You fucking bitch!" He slams his fist on the table and stands up. "You're lying!"

I say sweetly, "I wouldn't go anywhere Trevor. My boyfriend, Jaxon, is right behind you." Jaxon gives a menacing wave when Trevor looks over his shoulder, surprised to see someone standing behind him. "And he doesn't take too kindly to men who roofie women. You might want to turn around."

Returning my attention back to the victim, I kneel down in front of her, take her hands in mine and say, "Paige, we've already called the cops and an ambulance is on the way. You're going to feel really groggy, but I don't want you to be scared. I'm not going to leave your side. Is there someone I can call?"

Her eyes get heavy, and I know she's close to passing out. "Bethany. Call Bethany."

"Okay. I'll call Bethany and go with you to the hospital."

"Okay," she says and collapses in my arms, out like a light. I look up and Trevor is staring at me, daggers in his eyes.

"I didn't do anything, you stupid bitch."

Jaxon drops his hand on Trevor's shoulder and forces his back into the chair. Hard. "I'd think twice about calling my girlfriend a bitch. Especially when the cops are here."

A couple of police officers walk into the restaurant and the manager immediately greets them, leading them over to the table.

The next few minutes are a whirlwind of activity as police officers, detectives, and paramedics infiltrate Buck's. As Trevor is hauled away in handcuffs, the glasses are carefully collected as evidence.

When the paramedics load Paige up on the gurney, I see the concern in Jaxon's eyes. He walks up to me. "Are you sure you want to go to the hospital? Are you okay?"

"I'm good, baby, I promise." Reaching up, I rub my hands across his cheeks. "I'm just glad we were here at the right time, ya know?"

"I know." And there's no doubt in my mind he knows

exactly what I'm feeling and why this feels vindicating.

"Which hospital are we going to?" I ask the paramedic.

"Just right here to Memorial."

Turning back to Jaxon I say, "Meet me at the hospital? I'm gonna need a ride after her friend Bethany gets there."

He laughs even though the situation isn't funny at all. "Do you feel the same weird déjà vu I'm feeling?"

I kiss him lightly on the lips as the gurney is pulled away. "It's not déjà vu, but it's definitely full circle. See you there."

He nods once and turns back to the police, who begin questioning him about what he saw.

There's no doubt in my mind that we're going to end up back in the news. But this time, I don't mind. If the last year has taught me anything, it's to keep my wits about me, but also to never assume that anyone has your back. And that translates to never assuming anyone else's back is covered either.

I will live with the fact that I am victim number two for the rest of my life. What I do with that is up to me.

And Jaxon coming along with me for that journey— that's just a matter of the Hart.

The End

BONUS EPILOGUE
Heath

I really didn't want to come out tonight. It's not that I'm a homebody or anything. I enjoy a good kegger as much as the next guy. Clubs just aren't my thing. They're loud. They're crowded. And people act like idiots. It all feels very meat market to me.

Sometimes I wish I could enjoy the occasional hookup with a stranger. I am in college and the best athlete here. Hell, I'm probably the best athlete in the state if you take out the pro teams. Even then, I'm probably better than half those guys. That's not arrogance. It's what I'm banking on to relieve some of the financial stress off my parents in the future. That goal always leads back to football, which is why I'm very, very careful with anything that remotely comes to sex.

I always have been, but last year, that point was driven home when one of our star linebackers found out shortly before he was drafted that a failing condom meant his life was about to change in more ways than one. The ink was barely dry on his new contract, and he was already saddled with a fiancée and baby on the way. He remained tight-lipped about his new family, but we all knew he didn't have a girlfriend. And he still ended up with a wife.

That's not going to happen to me. Yes, I could easily take advantage of my super athletic status and how it just happens to come with a few perks of the female variety. Yes, it would be nice to have the stress relief that goes with meaningless sex with someone who could care less about anything more than bragging rights for banging a football star. But not at the expense of my current sanity, and certainly not at the expense of my future. Next time I'm with someone it's going to be because we're going to build a future together. Clubs like this are not the place to pick up women like that, even if I was looking.

A hot piece of ass ogling me from the dance floor is a prime example of someone I try to avoid. She's been watching me for a while now. Her skintight tank top shows off a very voluptuous chest. Just a small tug and a couple of inches separate my eyes from her peaked nipples. That part I can already see. Gyrating to the music, she makes no secret that she's dancing just for me. The intense stare in my direction isn't hard to read. What is hard to read, however, is if she's the kind of girl who wants to trap me or the kind of girl who wants to get to know me. And that's why I haven't reciprocated.

So, I'm sitting alone at a table off to the side of the bar. Being here is giving me a headache already. The beat is thrumming so loud, you can't hear anything unless you yell. Thank God my friends are on the dance floor so I'm not having to strain to hear them talk.

This is where Annika wanted to come, though, for reasons I can't figure out. She's been avoiding loud, crowded businesses like this since last year. Maybe coming here is part of her healing or something. Maybe her therapist suggested she take this last step. Who knows? I won't ask because it's not my business. We all have our demons, so it doesn't matter anyway. She's my friend. If this is where she wants to be, I'm here.

It's odd, I know. For as irritated as I am about being here, there is no way I wouldn't join my friends. Not because it's fun. It's much more calculated than that. We've fallen into this weird "safety in numbers" thing and now, it feels like the norm to tag along wherever the girls want to go. Lauren and Annika don't go out to bars or clubs without us guys anymore. Ever. Even if they're having a girls' night with ten other people, we're on the other side of the room, doing our own thing but always on watch. Ridiculous, maybe, but you can't unlearn the kind of lesson we all learned last year. And frankly, we care about our friends too much to not keep an eye on each other.

Yes, even Lauren.

I look over at the dance floor again to check on her. She's moving to the music like she owns the place. Her small hips sway seductively as the tiny skirt she's wearing rides up even higher. Any more movement and she'll be flashing the room. Fingers crossed she's not going commando. Not that I would mind getting a sneak peek.

Lauren thinks I don't like her, but that's not it at all. I just don't… well, gravitate toward her. I tolerate her flirty and inappropriate comments. I appreciate her love for Annika. And I have mad respect for her sport and the work she does to compete. She's just not someone I enjoy shooting the shit with. I've tried many times to figure out if it's just a personality conflict or if it's because I always feel like she's hiding something. Or because she comes across as exactly the kind of girl I try to avoid. I just can't figure out which one of those possibilities is the truth.

Shaking my head, I sip my water and continue watching her move. If nothing else, she is a hot little number. Her body is totally cut. Every time she raises her arms, her shirt rides up and I get a glimpse of her abs. I'd be lying if I said the six-pack she's sporting wasn't a total turn-on. Not at all like the other girl who is making her sexual prowess obvious. No, Lauren is more subtle. She cares less about other patrons noticing her and more about finding a good beat. Interesting. I would have thought she'd be more responsive to having an audience.

As I watch her dance, Lauren is approached by some guy. He's short, barely taller than her. I snicker to myself. We've never been at a club together, but Lauren is usually pretty picky about who she flirts with. This poor sucker is about to make a fool of himself.

Without bothering to turn around and get a good look at who she's gyrating against, she smiles and backs up into him, trying to find their groove. Hmm. It seems her standards may have changed. She raises her arms, exposing that tight stomach again. I watch as she practically melts into him and he leans down to say something in her ear.

That's when her demeanor does a complete one-eighty. She stiffens and her face takes on a pained look. I immediately sit up straight, paying closer attention.

Lauren shrugs the guy off her, face scrunching up like she's disgusted, or distressed. I can't put my finger on it, because it changes so fast into a look of anger. Still on alert, I scrutinize the scene as it unfolds. I want to race out there and squash whoever the asshole is like a bug, but I know Lauren won't appreciate it. She likes being invincible to people. That much, I've figured out on my own. So, I'll let her fight her own battle. But if it looks like she's about to lose, she won't be able to stop me from getting involved.

She pushes the guy away, then storms off the dance

floor and heads straight to the bar. The stiffness of her body tells me she's still agitated, but in true Lauren fashion, she's holding her head high.

As she waits for the bartender to notice her, she glances around the room, her eye catching something, and that's when I see the look on her face again. I don't see any tears from here, but she looks dejected. And she keeps trying to ignore whatever has her attention but can't seem to stop from taking quick looks to the same side of the room.

Turning my head to try and figure out what's going on, it suddenly all makes sense. At a different table is a group of guys. All of them are what I would consider to be pint-sized. All of them are laughing. And all of them are looking right at Lauren as they do it.

My heart pounds as I start to put two and two together. Picking her up on the side of the road this morning, her crying in my car, pushing the guy that's now laughing with his friends. It all makes sense.

"Son of a bitch," I huff.

Annika didn't want to come out tonight for fun. She wanted to help Lauren feel better because some douchebag screwed her over. Unfortunately, I think the douchebag showed up to ruin the good time.

Scanning the room, I see Jaxon and Annika getting way too close on the dance floor for my viewing pleasure. Which also means Annika doesn't realize her best friend is being harassed by what is probably the entire male gymnastics team. That's a reasonable assumption to make about a group of unusually short guys all hanging out together. Regardless, I'm not going to sit here and watch this shit go down.

Decision made, I down the rest of my drink, stand up, and walk straight to Lauren. Her expression changes as I approach, probably trying to put a strong front on. It quickly changes to one of confusion when I keep walking, backing her into the bar as I put my arms around her and rest my hands on the smooth wood, caging her in.

It's quieter over here so there's no reason to yell in her ear. Still, I want to make a statement to the assholes across the room, so I lean down anyway.

"Is that the dickwad that fucked you over this morning and made you walk home in the cold?" My big body covers hers from their view like I want.

"What?" I hear the confusion in her voice. I've never gotten this close to her before, so I know it's going to take a second for her to catch on to my game.

"The guy you pushed away on the dance floor."

"You saw that?"

"I did," I admit. "And it pissed me off. So, tell me, is that the guy?"

She shakes her head, her blonde hair brushing up against my cheek. I think I've just found something to put on my very short "like" list—her hair smells like some kind of tea tree oil. The minty kind. I like it.

"But it's one of the guys over there?"

Lauren stiffens, and I know I've assessed this situation out correctly. She doesn't even have to answer me. Her body language confirms it all.

"Which one?" I growl, halfway hoping she doesn't tell me. I'm fired up enough, I'm liable to get myself in trouble.

Lauren pushes me back so I can look down on her face. She's got long lashes. Much longer than I remember. And her blue eyes are looking up at me through them.

Huh. That's thing number three for my list. If she didn't have such a hard personality to deal with, I might be able to go for a girl like Lauren. I might even break my one-night rule.

But now isn't the time to worry about this weird turn of

events. She had a rough last night, an even rougher morning, and now those idiots are trying to make her tonight even worse. I'm not having it.

"What are you doing?" she questions softly, the most demure look I've ever seen on her face.

"I'm helping you take your power back."

Matters to Me, now available everywhere.

Want to keep up with all things M.E. Carter? Sign up for her newsletter and read Juked for free! (https://www.authormecarter.com/newsletter)

Other books written by M.E. Carter can be found here. (https://www.authormecarter.com/reading-order)

OTHER BOOKS BY M.E. CARTER

Hart Series
Change of Heart
Hart to Heart
Matters of the Hart
Matters to Me
Matters to You
Matter of Time

Texas Mutiny Series
Juked
Groupie
Goalie
Megged
Deflected

#MyNewLife Series
Getting a Grip
Balance Check
Pride & Joie
Amazing Grayson

Charitable Endeavors
(Collaborations with Andrea Johnston)
Switch Stance
Ear Candy
Model Behavior
Better than the Book

Smartypants Romance
Weight Expectations
Cutie and the Beast
Weights of Wrath

Collaborations with Sara Ney
Friend Trip
Kissmas Eve
New Years Steve

9 781948 852012